NOTORIOUS

A Nate Richards Mystery
Book One

RAY ELLIS

Notorious

By Ray Ellis

Previously Released as "N.H.I. (No Humans Involved)"
First Edition eBook: 2012
First Edition Paperback: 2013
ISBN (Kindle): 978-1-938596-05-6
ISBN (Paperback): 978-1-938596-06-3

Cover concept by Debra Burroughs
Cover design and imaging by Michael Sloane

Published in the United States of America
NCC Publishing
Meridian, Idaho, 83642, USA
www.nccpublishing.com

NCC170120130310

"And as it is appointed unto men once to die, but after this the judgment."
Heb. 9:27 KJV

NOTORIOUS

CHAPTER ONE

THE BODY OF THE TEENAGE BOY lay face down in the gutter, his bandana, his colors, still clenched in his fist, floated in the water beside him. Blood mixed with rain raced in a gurgling stream down the drain, splashing noisily as it made its way to the river.

What had it gained him? What had he proved? These were a few of the questions that flashed through Detective Nate Richards' mind as he studied the crime scene. Summer rain washed over Richards' lean frame, soaking his loose brown curls to the scalp. Flexing a muscle in his jaw, he lifted a hand to wipe water from his face. The streetlight reflected off of his cocoa-colored skin, twinkling in the early morning darkness. "Who's calling the scene?" Nate asked the group of four uniformed officers standing near a row of patrol cars, their overhead lights casting a rainbow effect on the wet pavement.

Three of the four uniformed men walked toward Nate. He looked between the men, and finding the corporal stripes, directed his comments to them. "What d'ya' got, Benson?" he asked, reading the nametag that went along with them.

"Another one down; one less to worry about shooting me in the back," Corporal Chad Benson muttered under his breath while using his hand to squeegee rainwater from his short blond hair. He chuckled to himself as he walked past the body headed for his patrol unit. He glanced at Nate as he passed.

"Does the phrase *crime scene integrity* mean anything to you, Benson?" Nate said.

"What's your problem?" Benson said in a harsh whisper. "It's not like it means anything. They breed like rats down here. Who cares if they kill each other off? We'll have two more by week's end. Mark my word. And it won't even make a difference."

The two uniformed officers, with Benson, smiled at their team commander's remarks. One of the men stared at Nate, holding his gaze for an extra heart beat longer than necessary before turning away. Nate made a mental note to remember the men's names.

"Stow it. Now!" Nate cut his gaze to a woman sitting on the curb rocking and hugging herself. The dead teen's mother. Grabbing Benson by the shoulder, Nate pulled him off to the side. "You can't see?"

Benson snatched his arm from Nate. "What?"

"You okay, Bens?" one of the other officers called and stepped toward Nate.

"Johnson, right?" Nate asked, making sure he had the man's name correct. "Is this the way you run a crime scene?" Nate had directed the question to Benson.

Looking down the desolate street, Nate pointed to the nearest intersection. "Block that off and get some cones out in the street to keep paramedics and everyone else from driving through my crime scene."

Johnson looked at Nate, but didn't move.

"You got a problem with that, patrolman?" Nate asked.

"Go 'head," Benson said, stepping between the two men. "Look, detective, we do just fine. You take care of your stuff, and I'll take care of mine."

Without responding, Nate turned away from the officer and approached the woman, hoping she hadn't overheard Benson's comments or noticed the patrolmen's cavalier attitudes.

Shielding his notepad from the rain with his arm, he checked the comments he'd recorded there. He cleared his throat. "Mrs.

Fuentes? I'm Detective Nate Richards from Treasure Valley Metro Police Department. I need to ask you a few questions."

The woman raised her dark eyes like dead pools, lifeless and cold, to meet Nate's expectant gaze. "What does it matter? We breed like rats anyway, right?" She pulled her jacket collar tight around her neck and turned away from him.

So much for her not having heard, Nate thought. He stooped to meet the woman's gaze. "Mrs. Fuentes…"

"Miss. I'm not married. But I guess that's okay when you're only a *Cricetomys emini*, huh?"

Struck by the woman's beauty, Nate thought she didn't look much older than a teen herself. "Miss Fuentes," he began again, "A what?"

"A pregnant rat," she said, anger coloring her voice.

Nate broke eye contact for the briefest of moments but watched her, *gauging* her movements. "I apologize for the officer's crudeness. There's no excuse for his behavior. I also assure you that his is not the general attitude of the police department." Nate was sincere in his response but knew avoiding an officer complaint was a good idea as well.

The woman stood abruptly. She looked again at her son lying dead in the street, took a breath, and seemed to gather herself. "Can I take him now?"

"I'm sorry Mrs.—Miss Fuentes, but the body can't be released until the coroner has been called and finishes his examination."

"You gonna cut up my baby? You gonna cut him open and play around inside him? For what? We know what killed him. The bullets killed him. Just let me take him and put him to rest."

Nate looked over the woman's shoulder at Officer Benson sitting in his patrol unit— out of the weather—and wished that it was Benson standing in the rain having to explain the bad behavior instead of him. Benson sat leaning back in the passenger's seat stuffing the last of something into his mouth.

"Miss Fuentes, I'm sorry but certain things have to be done and then—"

"I don't care. You want to assure me you don't see my son as some kind of second class citizen? You find the man who killed him, and you make him pay." She walked away, her shoulders heaving as she struggled against the sobs shaking her entire body. Stopping a short distance away, she leaned against the wall and stood there absorbed by the shadows.

Nate stormed over to the patrol car and pulled open the door. "Benson, you're a pig."

Benson looked up, a smear of mayonnaise stuck in the corner of his mouth. "What? What'd I do?"

Nate looked in the direction where the woman had disappeared. "You couldn't see the mother sitting not fifteen feet from you? What were you thinking?"

"NHI, man. Why should I get all bothered over nothing?"

Nate clenched and then relaxed his fist. He inhaled and blew out his breath in one explosive sigh, water vapor springing from around his lips. Without speaking, he turned and walked away. Kneeling beside the body, he began his investigation while fighting to control his anger at Benson's callous behavior.

CHAPTER TWO

LIEUTENANT LARRY BROWN, the dayshift Criminal Investigation Division (CID) watch commander, sat at his desk at the Meridian station reviewing the reports from the night before. A cup of bitter, hot coffee sat on the corner of his desk, wafts of steam floating lazily toward the too bright fluorescent lights overhead. The coffee matched him in both manner and mood. The small office faced the CID pod overlooking the rows of desks and cubicles, its fabricated walls vibrating with the opening and closing of each slammed door.

"Richards! Get in here," he yelled. He stood up behind his desk as soon as he saw Nate enter the CID section.

"Yeah, what's up L.T.?" Nate asked, kicking the door closed behind him. He knew from long experience that nothing good would come from this meeting and didn't care to have it broadcast.

"Just what were you thinking out there last night?" Brown began without preamble. "I come in first thing this morning and find an officer complaint on my desk with your name on it. You care to explain that?"

Deciding not to sit down, which would surrender the high ground to the lieutenant, Nate crossed his arms and leaned back against the door frame. "Good morning to you too, sir, but I have no idea what you're talking about."

"I'm talking about you botching up the investigation of the Fuentes shooting last night. Not to mention the hot water you're in for insulting Professor Fuentes."

The dawn of recognition rose across Nate's face. He had wondered where he'd seen the woman before. She was Serena Fuentes, professor at Boise State University and board member of the Mayor's Cross Cultural Outreach Program. "Oh," he said, rubbing tired eyes. "But I still don't know what this has to do with me."

"Do the letters N.H.I. mean anything to you?" Lieutenant Brown asked, walking around his desk and stopping within an arm's reach of Nate. "I can't believe you could be that stupid."

Moving forward, Nate closed the distance between them. "Sir, I think you might want to change your tone, sir."

Taking an involuntary step backward and bumping against the corner of his desk, Brown jumped as his coffee spilled. He tried, with quick hands, to stop the hot liquid's dash across his desk. Flustered, he made a poor attempt at maintaining his former rant. "Richards, you, you—get your—get out of my office!" He pointed a trembling finger at Nate. "This is not over. I will have your butt this time. I am tired of you and your self-righteous attitude...always looking down your self-righteous nose."

"As I recall, sir, it was you who called me in to your office. Now, as for *your* officer complaint, I suggest you talk to the boys in your beloved patrol unit. Benson's team handled that call. Talk to them about their conduct in public. Leave me out of it."

"Out!" Brown forced the words through clenched teeth while kissing coffee-burned fingers. "You're the worst excuse for a homicide detective I've ever seen. If I had my way, you'd be pushing a black and white on the midnight shift."

"Sir, I'm not sure how to take that. I don't work homicide. I was doing you a favor and covering for Gram last night, remember? I work sex crimes." Seeing Brown's anger, Nate fought hard to resist the smile attempting to sneak across his face. He knew, though, that it was easily visible in his eyes. Nate raised his hands, palms facing forward. He inhaled, and preparing to speak, he opened his mouth.

"Out!" Brown cut him off.

Nate pulled the door open, shaking the flimsy wall as the door stuck briefly against the jamb. Resisting the urge to slam it behind him, he pulled it shut and let out his breath in one long slow stream.

***

"That was good," Amber Coles said sarcastically. "Oh yeah, and very Christian."

Nate stopped. His smile evaporated and the smug feeling he briefly enjoyed disappeared. He rubbed his hand across his chin and smirked, feeling the fatigue he'd been ignoring. "I forgot I'd left that pass for you at the front desk. I should have known you'd choose now to walk in."

Amber smiled at him from across the small space between the desks that made up the central corridor of CID. "Really, Nate?" She smiled and it warmed him in ways that embarrassed him.

He loved looking at her. Although he typically liked long hair on women, Amber's shorter cut suited her. Rich brunette hair framed her heart-shaped face, causing her chocolate-brown eyes to play exotically against her olive complexion that danced with soft lights. But if he had to choose, he would say it was her smile and Nicole Kidman type nose that were his favorites. The twin dimples set deep in her cheeks didn't hurt either.

"Mmmh," he stammered, "I, uh…yeah."

"That's what I thought. How in the world are you going to be able to share the gospel with that guy if you keep antagonizing him? Really?" She grinned and took his arm, locking hers through his.

"You forgot you promised to buy me breakfast this morning." She smiled up at him. It had not been a question.

"No. I just got a little sidetracked with the lieutenant." He frowned when he saw her expression. "Come on, you don't like him either."

"I heard you in there. You're just trying to cover up the fact that you forgot our date. Either way, you're still buying. Let's go."

"You heard all that, huh?" he asked, indicating Brown's office with a tilt of his head. "I got called out again last night...another gang shooting. I've got to get on this." He rubbed his face again, trying to erase the effect of another night with too little sleep.

"What time you get called out?" she asked, leading him away from his desk.

"0330."

"What time you get in?" She grabbed his jacket off the back of his chair as they passed it.

"I just left the morgue, haven't been home yet."

"Figured as much," she said as she pulled him into the elevator.

"That was sneaky." He said, leaning exhausted against the far wall.

"It worked. Besides, you're worn out. You're no good like this. You need to go home and get some sleep."

Nate stood up straight and stretched his back. Exhaling roughly, he closed his eyes and leaned back again. "You know, Brown is serious, don't you? He really is going to try and slam me for this. If there's any way he can keep the blame off his beloved patrol, he will. I have no idea why the man ever accepted the promotion to CID. He hates it up here."

Amber smiled as the elevator doors opened leading to the main lobby and its yellowed tile floor. Grabbing Nate by his arm again, she led him out through the double glass doors marked Treasure Valley CID. She looked up at him and her eyes twinkled. "First, breakfast for us, and then bed for you."

CHAPTER THREE

AMBER TORE OPEN her fourth packet of Splenda sweetener and poured it into her coffee. Adding cream, she stirred gently with her spoon until a small wave of tan liquid spilled over the brim and onto the table. All the time she was speaking, her eyes never leaving Nate's.

"You know, you really do need to give Brown a break. He's not so bad."

"Leave any room for your coffee?" Nate said, changing the topic.

"What? Oh, I don't really like the taste of coffee."

"So why not order something else?"

Amber turned her attention fully to the cup, finally noticing the spill and with a soft bird like chirp, smiled, and wiped it up with her napkin.

Nate leaned back, allowing the floral patterned bench to absorb his weight. He thought again how much he loved looking at her. She smiled and he focused on her lips. *I wonder what it would be like to kiss....* He forced his thoughts back under control. *She's your friend—your best friend. Don't mess it up.*

She looked up. "What?" she asked, around a fork full of eggs.

"Oh, nothing...just tired, I guess." As if it had been an omen, Nate suddenly felt very weary, as if his shoulders had gradually turned to lead. He rubbed his eyes, grinding his palms into his eye sockets. He exhaled forcefully, and poured himself another cup of the rich, dark coffee.

Amber continued talking, telling Nate about her date from the previous evening. The latest guy had been one of her customers at the bookstore where she worked. "It had begun promisingly," she said, "but a girl could only take so much computer programming chatter."

Nate smiled and swallowed deeply, grimacing against the heat of the liquid. He hoped she hadn't noticed his reaction, and if she had, that she attributed it to the coffee.

Nate kicked himself mentally for not paying attention to what Amber had been saying. He replayed her last words just in case she asked him a question.

"...so what do you think I should do?" she finished and looked up at him.

"Well," he began slowly, "the way I see it, if the guy didn't have enough sense to focus on you, I say you're better off without him." He tried to read her eyes, to see if he had guessed correctly.

"You know, Nate, that's what I love about you. You always seem to know exactly what to say." Reaching across the table, she grabbed his hands and squeezed them.

"Well, what can I say…"

Nate's cell phone rang, and he sighed as he first patted it and then pulled it out of his chest pocket. "Richards," he said in a flat, tired voice.

Nate's face suddenly darkened, his brows knitting together.

"When? How's he doing?" He sighed, lowered his face into the palm of his left hand, and rubbed his eyes again. He pressed the phone tightly against his head, his elbows resting on the table. "I'll be right there."

Nate closed the phone and stood.

"Leaving me?"

"There's been a shooting. Franks has been shot. He's dead."

"Dan? Oh, no. What happened? I'm coming with you." She pushed her seat back and stood quickly. "Oh God, his poor mother."

"No." Nate looked past her, unfocused. "Not this time, Amber." He pulled out a ten-dollar bill and dropped it on the table.

"Why not?" She demanded, beginning to pout.

"Just trust me. Not this time. Not now." Nate tried not to show her the horror of what he was feeling. "Not now, Amber, just trust me." He turned and walked away without saying another word.

***

Amber sat back down in the now empty booth and exhaled deeply, her earlier happy countenance now crestfallen for more than one reason. She looked longingly after Nate as he hurried from the restaurant. She loved his passion, his commitment to service and wondered what it would feel like to have him be that passionate—that committed to her. Rebuffing herself for letting her thoughts travel in that direction, she said to no one in particular, "That's all you need, girl, mess up the one true friendship you do have by trying to make more out of it than you should."

She sighed again and turned her heart to prayer. Somebody, she reasoned, should be praying for poor Mrs. Franks. *Her only son killed. How would the old lady take the news?*

Amber began, "Dear Father, please send your precious Spirit to comfort Mrs. Franks. Lord, does she even know yet? She's going to need You like she never has before. Please be with her. In Jesus' name. Amen."

Amber stood and headed for the door. She still had two hours left before her shift at the bookstore began. She hadn't known Dan's mother well, had only met her on a few occasions.

But as she reasoned, there was no time like the present to fix that.

CHAPTER FOUR

NATE DROVE BENEATH THE OVERPASS. Even from a distance of a few hundred yards, he could tell that the crime scene would be bad. He was wrong. It was worse.

Parking at the mouth of the alley, Nate decided to walk into the crime scene instead of driving, a habit he picked up from his partner, Sabrina Jackson. Jackson, a 27-year veteran, one of only three black officers on the force, and the sole female detective, had been Nate's partner for the past three years.

The narrow alley opened into an abandoned parking lot. Weeds and sun-browned grasses broke through cracks in the thinning asphalt. Windowless walls rose on three sides, forming the urban box canyon that had been transformed into a killing field. Studying the debris field, Nate reasoned from the pattern and variety of shell casings, that Franks had been ambushed, or at least there had been multiple shooters.

Walking around the dead officer's patrol unit, Nate mentally catalogued the various casings: 9-millimeter, .40-caliber, and 5.56-millimeter shot casings that appeared to be twelve-gauge rifle slugs. Military issue.

The inside of the patrol vehicle had been burned; the dashboard twisted into a charred and blackened shell. The glass from the windows splintered and melted from the heat, pooled in congealed clumps as they dripped to the ground. Nate judged from the damage that the tires had been shot flat before the fire had been set. The nude body of Officer Dan Franks was stretched spread eagle across the hood of the car. An encircled sideways **A**, the anarchy symbol, had been carved into his chest.

Joining him, Sabrina Jackson interrupted his thoughts. "Ever see anything like this before?" he asked her.

"Not if I don't count the Klan killings from the South or maybe the religious killings in Iraq."

She harrumphed and walked past him. "I don't like this; I don't like this at all. What is Franks' body doing in the middle of what looks like a gang war zone?"

Shielding her eyes against the sun, she scanned the perimeter of the crime scene, looking for anyone who might be watching them.

Nate nudged her in the side with his elbow. "Here comes the press. How'd they get inside the tape?"

"I don't know, but they're 'bout to get up out of here." She turned to meet the camera crew and reporter that were setting up for a direct feed.

"Excuse me, but didn't y'all see the yellow tape stretched out across the roadway back there?"

"Yes…no…I did…yes, but I thought that was for the general public. Hi, I'm Butch—

"I know who you are, and I know where you better be in about five seconds if you don't want to be filming your report from a jail cell downtown."

"What's your name, ma'am? You obviously don't know who I am."

"Like I said, Butch, I know who you are, and the name is detective. Now get out of my crime scene." She turned and signaled to a uniformed officer. "Escort Mr. Butch here out of my crime scene, but make sure you log him in as a witness just in case we need to subpoena him later." She turned and headed back toward Nate.

The officer smiled as he took out his pen and began writing the reporter's name on his crime scene log. He pointed toward the mouth of the alley. "This way, sir."

"And they call me pushy," Nate teased as Sabrina turned back to join him.

"Well, son, when you've been here almost thirty years and you're looking forward to retirement, you finally get to say some of those things that pups like yourself only wish they could say now." She flashed a saucy smile and looked up as the rumble of an approaching fire engine filled the air and vibrated the ground.

"You going up this time?" Nate asked.

"Nope. That's for you young kids. Have at it. I'll get the camera for ya'."

A few minutes later, Nate found himself about forty feet above the crime scene looking down from the fire engine's ladder bucket. Nate smiled to himself. Riding in one of these buckets had been a dream of his ever since seeing one demonstrated as an elementary age student. He was amazed how different the alley looked from the higher vantage point.

Using one hand to steady the swinging Nikon D300 digital camera hanging from his neck, he held the handrail with his other. With a jerking motion, the bucket rose as it started panning over the burned-out patrol car, and Nate prepared himself to begin snapping photos.

Two hundred and eighty pictures and a 360-degree ride later, Nate was slowly lowered back to the ground. Even from the lofty position above the car, Nate could still see Franks' eyes frozen open in death. The deep groove in his chest, and the cake of baked-on blood beneath him, fanning out from the body, were in vivid contrast against the white hood of the patrol car.

It was starting to get warm. In this heat the stench would soon rise to engulf the man-made canyon and spread out to announce the death to any unfortunates near the expanding radius. As he stepped out of the bucket and climbed down the short metal ladder from the fire engine, the coroner's wagon pulled into the crime scene and stopped.

Mary, a rather plain woman with uninspired sandy blond hair, climbed out of the driver's seat of the coroner's van and walked directly to Nate. "We've got to stop meeting like this or people will start talking." She gave him a friendly pat on the shoulder. "One of us this time, huh?"

Nate didn't respond. It wasn't necessary. He knew she understood. She was young, but she was good. He knew she would handle Franks correctly.

***

Amber stopped her car in front of the small cottage-like home on the east side of the city. White clouds floated in deep blue skies as birdsong came to her on the wind, mingled with the laughter of playing children. Closing the car door behind her, she was disappointed that the sound of traffic from nearby Eagle Road, the Walmart shopping center and outdoor mall, disturbed the otherwise quiet neighborhood.

Mrs. Franks knelt in the dirt of the large flowerbed in front of her single story home. Black-eyed Susans, marigolds, petunias, pansies, and sunflowers made up the eclectic garden as they waved in the gentle breeze that did little to ease the oppressive heat. Pushing her sunbonnet back, the small woman stood massaging her lower back. She squinted into the bright sun, gazing at Amber, as if trying to place the face of the younger woman walking toward her.

Amber prayed for strength and wisdom as she continued up the short walk. *Help me, Lord, to know what to say.* "Mrs. Franks," she began, but her voice failed. She coughed and began again. "Mrs. Franks, I'm Amber Coles, Nate's—"

"Oh yes, you're Nate's lady friend." The older lady said, her smile stretching across her wrinkled face, causing it to glow.

Amber started at her reference of "Nate's lady friend," but she forced the thought from her mind as a thing to be dealt with later.

"Come on. Let's get out of this sun and get us something cool to drink," Mrs. Franks said, extending her hand in greeting.

Amber could feel her stomach roiling into knots as each step brought her closer to the older woman. "Mrs. Franks, there's something I need to tell you."

Mrs. Franks stopped and, focusing on Amber's face, took notice of the heaviness she saw in the younger lady's face. "What's the matter, dear? Come on inside where we can talk; I'm sure it's nothing the Lord can't handle."

Tears in her eyes, Amber looked into the older woman's face. "Mother Franks...I—"

"What's this?" Mrs. Franks said, looking past Amber as a dark-colored sedan stopped in front of the house. Two men, one in full dress uniform and the other wearing a gray single-breasted suit, got out and made their way toward the two women.

Mrs. Franks looked from Amber to the two men approaching her. "Amber?" she managed in a soft whisper. "Amber...what is this all about?" Then looking into the younger woman's eyes, she knew. "Oh God, no..." the older woman cried out and collapsed.

Amber caught the small woman and stumbled backwards beneath the sudden added weight. In the next moment, strong arms caught them, lifting them both, and they were escorted into the house.

As the door closed behind them, the air conditioning cooling them from the oppressive heat, Amber made her way to the older woman and knelt on the floor beside her. "Mother Franks, I need to make a phone call first, but I'll stay with you. I'll be right here as long as you need me."

The two men looked from one to the other with obvious relief. The older of the two men cleared his throat. "Mrs. Franks, I'm Chief Reese, and I am so sorry for your loss. I want you to know we counted Dan as one of our best men, a part of our family. We think of you as part of this family too. I want you to know we will always be here for you. You won't have to do this alone."

Amber closed her cell phone and came back to sit beside the older woman. Taking the wrinkled hand in hers, she draped her free arm around the older woman's bowed shoulders.

Mrs. Franks lifted her face, tears streaking her cheeks, and after whispering a silent prayer, she looked at the men. "Tell me what happened to my son."

***

Nate knocked on the jamb of the opened door of Lieutenant Brown's office. "Sir?"

Brown continued reading his report as if he had not heard him.

Nate knocked again, walked in, and sat in the empty chair in front of Brown's desk. "Sir, I'm sure you've heard about Franks by now. I want to be assigned to this case."

Brown raised his head slowly, a derisive smile playing at the corners of his mouth. He sat back and intertwined his fingers across the paunch overlapping his belt. "So, you want to get back into homicide? Well, Richards, I thought you were a sex-crimes-only kind of guy." The smile blossomed.

Nate tried to remain calm. "Sir, one of our own has been killed. Can't we put aside our differences for now?" Nate was leaning forward, speaking softly.

"Well, you see, that's the advantage of being me, Richards. I get to make the decisions, and you get to do what you're told." Brown rose and sauntered to the front of his desk.

"You thought you were so funny this morning, didn't you? Just couldn't wait to remind me that you were not a homicide detective. Well I agree...you're not. I don't want you anywhere near this case, and if I find out you're poking your nose where it doesn't belong, I'll roll you out to patrol so quick—"

"I get it." Nate stood, cutting Brown off mid-sentence. "The answer is no. Thank you for your time, sir." He turned and left the office, slapping the wall as he passed, causing it to shake, loosening one of Brown's framed certifications.

***

Following him to the door Brown slammed it behind him and turned with a satisfied smile as he made his way back to his seat behind the desk. Picking up the papers he tried to resume reading, gave up, and with a harrumph, flung them across the room.

A knock at the door ended his tirade, but before he could respond, the door swung open. Donald Haynes, the second-shift lieutenant, poked his head through the opening. "Why you wanna let that guy get under your skin like that, Larry? Getting all mad the way you do, you're gonna stroke out, and I don't do mouth-to-mouth. He ain't so bad. Why do you hate him so?"

"I don't hate him. He just gets on my nerves. He's always talking about God..." He pushed at the papers with the toe of his boot, "like he was best friends with Him or something stupid." Brown stooped and began collecting his papers.

Haynes came fully into the office, closing the door behind him. He sat in the seat recently vacated by Nate and smiled playfully at his counterpart. Lifting his legs, Haynes crossed his feet on the edge of the desk and rocked back in the chair. "You really gotta get over this, Larry. It's gonna give you a heart attack," he chuckled.

Indicating the splayed papers, Brown said, "You're gonna help me or what?"

"Oh, I don't know." Haynes grinned. "You worked so hard on getting those papers spread out just so. Maybe you don't want my help; maybe I'd just be in your way." The chair landed with a soft thud as Haynes hefted himself out of the seat and knelt on the floor. Grabbing the first sheet, laughing, he offered it to Brown. He shook his head as Brown continued to fume.

After the papers were collected, and the men were seated in their respective chairs, Brown poured them each a cup of coffee. "Don't mind if I do," Haynes said, accepting the proffered cup. "I like my coffee like my wife likes her man, black and strong."

"I guess she settled for just black, huh?" Brown grinned impishly. "That guy didn't spend any time on the streets." He pointed toward the wall with his cup. "Come up here straight from California thinking he knows everything." Seemingly changing gears, Brown spoke as if the words tasted bad in his mouth.

Haynes smiled as if he did not need to ask what *guy* Brown was referring to. "Yeah, but he came with experience. Besides, he spent three years here on the streets before transferring to CID."

"Three years! Three years…that's nothing. I've got boots with more time on the streets than that."

"Let it go, old man, and get out of here; it's your forty-two time. Go home." He laughed.

Brown stood again, moaning as if he were worn out from sitting behind the desk all day. "You got the briefing on Franks?"

"Yeah," Haynes replied, sobering. "He was a good kid."

"He'd been on the streets a little over a year…still wet behind the ears." He sighed, "Too bad." Brown dragged his briefcase off the desk, allowing it to drop with a thud against his thigh. He headed for the locker room. Stopping at the door, he looked toward the desks where the various detectives sat. Shaking his head, he turned toward the exit.

***

The last thing Haynes heard before the door closed behind Brown was the man mumbling under his breath, "…holy roller…" and then the door clicked shut.

Haynes laughed softly and shook his head as well. Then turning his attention to the briefing pack on the shooting, he groaned. He dropped himself in the seat behind the desk with sudden weariness. Punching the intercom on the corner of his desk, he called, "Richards, get your butt in here!"

A few minutes later, Nate walked into the lieutenant's office for the third time that day. *I've got to stop coming in here.* "You wanted me, sir?"

"Drop the old innocent-me-act, Richards. I ought to kick your butt myself. What? Are you trying to get written up?"

Nate rubbed his eyes and sat in the familiar seat again.

"You had better stop irritating that man or he's going to take a chunk out of your butt, and there won't be a darn thing either you or I will be able to do about it."

"I know. I know...it's just that he gets on my nerves."

"Funny, he said the same thing about you."

Nate raised an eyebrow.

Haynes continued, "The man gets on everybody's nerves. The chief doesn't even like him."

Nate laughed and slouched in his seat. "You seem to get along with him pretty well."

"Yeah, you laugh now, but you won't be laughing if he rolls you back into a uniform."

Nate stopped laughing and sat up. "He didn't say that, did he?"

"No, but he could have. For right now, we need you on the Fuentes case." He shuffled the papers and flipped through the two files on his desk.

He looked up at Nate, a teasing glint in his eye.

"What would your dad say if I told the good reverend that his boy had his thumb screwed tight into the old lieutenant's eye socket, huh?" He tilted his head forward before finally resting his chin on the backs of his hands, elbows on the desk.

"Well…"

"Don't that Bible you're always reading say something about respecting those in authority over you?"

"Ah…"

"Yep, in Romans chapter 13 or 14—"

"Well—"

"—but I think it's thirteen."

"Don, I—"

"You're supposed to respect those in charge of you because God put them there in the first place."

"You know, L.T., for someone who doesn't believe in God, you sure know a lot about what His book has to say."

"Well, figured I'd better know what the parameters are, just in case. But that's beside the point. You need to watch yourself with Brown; you know he doesn't like you."

"Yeah, Amber tried to tell me the same thing this morning."

"You've been here since this morning?" Haynes said, grabbing the duty roster and reading it over. "You been on for eighteen hours. Go home. Now. You're trying to get me sued."

"Copy that. But about the Franks' case, do you think you can get me assigned?"

"Get out of here, and I don't want to see you until second shift tomorrow. Why don't you get some sleep?" He smiled roguishly. "Go find that pretty little Amber, and make an honest woman of her. I think your Bible says something about that too."

"I told you there's nothing going on between Amber and me. We're just friends."

"Then you're a bigger fool than I thought you were. Now get out of here."

CHAPTER FIVE

NATE PARKED HIS DARK-GREEN 2000 JEEP Grand Cherokee on the street in front of his small, second-floor apartment. Turning the engine off, he reminded himself again that he needed to get that CD player fixed. Due to an undiagnosed problem, the system automatically kicked out any CD left in the play mode, sending it flying to the floorboard between the seats. No way, he thought to himself, would the department swing the repair bill for that. No, he'd just have to cover it out of pocket. Leaning back against the leather seats, he enjoyed the last of the coolness before opening the door against the oppressive August heat and humidity.

The humidity was what had made this summer so strange. High temperatures were not an oddity in the Treasure Valley, but the high humidity, that was something different. It reminded Nate of his youth, growing up in Alabama before his escape to Southern California with the military. Now that was humidity, he thought to himself, real southern humidity. It's the *Why did I bother to dry off after a shower* kind of humidity. Ah, the South. "Someday I'll have to move back there," he said again for the hundredth time, "but not today."

He pulled the chrome-colored handle, opening the car door. Immediately, the wet heat rushed in, surrounding him like a clinging, wet blanket. He could feel small rivulets of sweat starting at the base of his skull and running down the valley of his back. By the time he opened the door to his apartment, he had puddles of sweat gathering in his armpits.

He walked into the cool semi-darkness of his apartment; his unfinished dinner still on the table from before last night's callout. "I'll clean it later," he said, heading for the shower.

Twenty minutes later, Nate showered, shaved, and sprawled across his bed, the cool air from the small apartment-sized air conditioner tickling the hairs on his bare chest. With the slow dawning of recognition, he realized he had duplicated the pose of Franks' body, arms, and legs spread, eyes open into space. With a sigh, he rolled onto his side to disrupt the image.

Pulling the short chain on the bedside lamp, Nate flicked on the light. He grabbed the worn leather-backed book he kept beside the lamp. Opening the Bible, Nate stared unseeing at the marked and highlighted pages.

The image of Franks' body returned unbidden and unwanted. Mentally, he walked through the crime scene, reviewing the details. Something, some small detail, pulled at the edge of his mind, but he couldn't grasp it, couldn't bring it into focus. Looking down at the Bible in his hands, he saw that it had opened to the book of Psalms. He read aloud, "'Thy word is a lamp unto my feet and a light unto my path.'" Standing, he closed the Bible with a snap of his wrist.

Walking around the bedroom, Nate spoke aloud into the small circle of light generated by the bedside lamp. "If only…" he said sarcastically. "You know, Lord, I could really use Your help on this. A little light would go a long way."

He paced in silence for a while, and then lay down across his bed again. Holding the Bible against his chest, he visualized the carved body of Franks; the way the light contrasted against the dark furrows in his chest.

There was something about the light. *Thy word*, he thought to himself. Then it hit him. The symbol carved in Franks' chest. The anarchist symbol had been the same symbol on the scarf found clutched in the dead teen's hand. Jonathan Fuentes

CHAPTER SIX

FIFTEEN MINUTES UNTIL CLOSING. It was the only thought on Amber's mind. She smiled at the last of the customers as they dallied in the bookstore. Normally, she relished this time of night, using it to make contact with many of her favorite customers or to recommend one of her favorite authors. But tonight all she wanted to do was leave.

Flipping open her cell phone, she dialed Nate's desk. The recorded voice answered on the fifth ring, "Hi, this is the voicemail of Treasure Valley Police Detective Nate Richards. I'm away from my desk now, but if you will leave your name, number, and case number, I will return your call at my earliest opportunity. If this is an emergency, please hang up and dial 911. Thank you."

Beep.

"Nate, this is Amber…oh never mind, I'll call your cell." Quickly, she hung up and dialed his cell phone. Again, all she connected with was his voicemail.

She called the office again, this time using the main number. "Lieutenant Haynes, please." She waited impatiently while closing her register and waving goodnight to the last of the customers. She had met the lieutenant on only a few occasions, and hoped that he remembered her and would put her in touch with Nate.

"Haynes," came a very comfortable sounding tenor voice.

"Hi. Lieutenant Haynes, my name is Amber Coles. I'm—"

"Nate's friend. How can I help you?"

She paused, happy that he remembered her. "Yes. I was wondering if you could put me in contact with Nate. I've called both his desk and his cell, and I got no answer."

"Well that's easy enough, I sent him home. Now don't you go bothering him, little lady; he needs to get some rest before shift tomorrow." He finished with a smile in his voice.

"Bother him?"

"Well, whatever you young people are calling it these days. The man worked a double shift; he needs to get some sleep."

"I don't know what you think Nate and my relationship is, but—"

"I know, I know, Nate told me all about it. You guys are just friends." Again, his voice had that knowing tone like he was aware of a secret that he wasn't supposed to know.

Amber couldn't believe she hadn't been able to finish a sentence with him. She had chided Nate when he told her about Haynes' habit of cutting people off in conversation, but it was even worse than Nate had claimed. "Okay, well thank—"

"Yeah, I figured you'd be in a hurry to get over there," he said, interrupting her again and chuckling.

She sighed, hung up, and looked at the phone in her hand as if she couldn't believe she had just had that particular conversation. The man was impossible, she thought to herself. *Who knows what rumors he'll be starting around the station tonight.* This was yet another thing she would have to talk to Nate about.

CHAPTER SEVEN

NATE WAS JUST SLIPPING INTO A DEEP SLEEP when a loud knocking jolted him from his bed. He looked around the bedroom, darkness having laid claim to the small space, struggling to force his mind to focus. The knocking sounded again. Nate swung his legs off the bed, grabbing a pair of jeans as he did, and headed for the door.

Stumbling and jumping, trying not to fall as he forced the jeans over his still-sluggish legs, Nate banged his knee against the corner of the book table. He fell headlong onto the sofa before rolling into a comfortable slouch near the floor. Fighting the urge to swear, he sat up and yelled into the darkness. "Wait…hold your horses…I'll be right there!"

Finally getting his pants on and zipped, Nate exhaled and stomped his way to the door. He reached toward the doorknob just as the doorbell sounded. Gripping the cool metal, he snatched it open. "What!?"

Two lattés in a paper carrier held protectively between herself and the door. Amber stood startled in the doorway, her eyes stretched open in surprise, lips frozen in a small circle as if she were going to whistle or blow out a candle on a birthday cake. Her finger poised over the doorbell.

Nate was surprised to see that it was Amber at his door, but his anger at having been awakened from a much-needed sleep and having banged his knee, had him still too hot to think straight.

"Well, that's not quite the greeting I'd hoped for," she quipped. "Were you still asleep?"

Nate didn't smile, but silently turned and allowed her to follow him into the dark apartment.

"You got a package," she said, nudging a small cardboard box with the toe of her Sketchers.

Nate made a quarter turn and dropped onto the sofa rubbing his knee. Turning on the lamp, he said, "What are you talking about? That hurt!" he muttered to himself, pulling up his pant leg to inspect the damage to his shin and knee.

Amber picked up the small box, walked over to Nate, and sat beside him. She put the box on the coffee table in front of them.

"Why were you banging on the door like that? You scared me to death. I do answer the doorbell, you know." Nate said, examining his leg again.

"What? I—"

"Gee…if you're gonna knock on the door, why ring the bell?"

"But I didn't—"

"You know, it's kind of rude to wake a fella by banging on his door this time of night. What time is it, anyway?"

Amber turned toward him and grabbed his face by the chin. "Look at my mouth. I did not bang on your door. I rang the bell—once. You opened the door…and you were very rude too." She released his face, jerking her hand away and opening her latté. After she took a drink, she sat back stiffly against the sofa.

She sighed in exasperation and stared at the floor just beyond the edge of the table.

Nate looked at her for the first time since he had opened the door. His eyes shifted from her face to the second cup of coffee, hazelnut and caramel, decaf skinny, on the table and the small box sitting beside it. He knew he shouldn't, but he thought she was so cute when she pouted just so. He smiled.

He watched as her lips caressed the curve of the cup and the tan-colored liquid perched on the tip of her tongue before it darted back into her mouth.

She caught his eye and he looked away.

"Hey, look, I'm sorry, but you woke me just as I was falling asleep. You still haven't explained why you were banging on my door. What time is it?" he asked, looking toward the wall clock in the kitchen. He was fighting an urge to smile, again, so he lifted the latté from the table. He sipped it. "Mmmm, hazelnut and caramel, my favorite," he announced, savoring the flavored coffee.

She finally smiled. He leaned forward and kissed her cheek. "Thanks."

"I should have gotten you blueberry," she said, scrunching her nose and smiling. She leaned her cheek into his kiss before sitting up again.

"Like I said, I didn't bang on your door. I rang the bell once. I was about to ring it again, but you snatched the door open. I guess whoever banged on your door left this box at the door as well." She put down her cup.

Picking up the box, she shook it and listened to the package like a child sneaking under the Christmas tree. "I can't hear anything."

Nate pushed his pant leg back into place and took another drink from his coffee. The fragrance of the beverage wafted up his nose, stimulating his senses and fully awakening him. "Let me see that."

A puzzled look clouding her face, Amber handed the box to Nate and leaned forward to watch him open it. "What do you think it is? Who is it from?" She was getting excited.

"I don't know. Did you see anyone out there?"

"Nuh-uh." She folded her leg closest to Nate beneath her and sat on it. Grabbing Nate at the bend of his arm, she looked into the opening flaps of the box.

Nate reached in and removed a folded piece of cloth, about four inches square, with dark lines across its surface. He looked at Amber, their quizzical expressions, matched pairs, bookends.

Careful to not spill, just in case there had been something folded away in its creases, Nate pressed the material flat on the surface of the table. It was empty.

Lifting it to the light, Nate asked, "Why would anyone put a folded blank piece of cloth in a box and leave it at my door?"

"Nate, there's something on the back. Maybe that's what whoever left it for you wanted you to see."

Nate turned the material over and there in bold broad lines was the anarchist symbol; the same symbol carved into Franks' chest; the same symbol on the scarf in the hand of the dead teen lying face down in the rain-filled gutter.

CHAPTER EIGHT

ISRAEL VEGA SAT ON THE SOFA watching the women moving rhythmically with the music. The heavy bass and the guttural lyrics, unintelligible to the untrained ear, rapped about life on the streets and the rule and value of violence. The women's long, dark hair flashed over their shoulders as they turned and jerked in counter swing to the bass with the flow of their full, rounded hips. Like a king surveying his court, Israel ruled over his family—his gang, with absolute authority. All his ladies had to have long hair; it was the trademark of the women belonging to the Abyss.

His was a new gang, but he wasn't new to the streets. At 25, he was an O.G.—an old gangster having already outlived most of his contemporaries.

One of the women broke away from the larger group dancing toward the raised seat, her eyes locked with Israel's. She sat near his feet. Looking up at him lustily, she leaned forward, ran her hand up his thigh, and kissed his knee. He rewarded her by brushing his hand through her hair; she would be his for the day.

A large black man walked into the gang's squat; the abandoned building they claimed as their headquarters. Lorenzo James, known as "Lo" on the streets, was Israel's *first*, his lieutenant and longtime friend. He crossed quickly to where

Israel sat and whispered in his ear. Israel closed his eyes and groaned within himself. He slumped back against the cushions then stood in a quick fluid movement without speaking.

The music stopped.

Turning to Lo, he lifted his chin with a jerk toward the door at the rear of the large room, and the two men left together.

Once in the smaller room with the door sealed behind them, Israel stopped and spoke over his shoulder. "What you saying, man?" he demanded without preamble.

"Half the shipment straight off the top. We gotta put a stop to this, Israel. These fools gotta know they don't mess with Abyss." He smacked his fist into his large hand.

Israel turned and looked at his friend. He knew the fire that burned behind those dark eyes. He had felt it on many occasions himself. He smiled. "Yes-s-s," he said, drawing the word out. He walked over to his friend and placed his brown hand on the darker man's shoulder. "Yes, we need to make another hit. This time make sure we leave our tag so everyone can see it. By the time we're done here, Treasure Valley will know that Abyss has arrived. That we own the streets."

The men laughed together, and after several more minutes in private conversation, they returned to the main hall. The women swarmed them like bees drawn to the nectar of a flower.

The music rose in both decibel and intensity. The bass vibrated the walls, lyrics no longer discernible. The dancers worked themselves into a frenzy, writhing in a passion-driven craze.

The woman who had singled herself out earlier, danced sensuously as she approached Israel, her eyes hungry, and began to wrap herself around him seductively.

Grabbing the woman around her waist, Israel jerked her to him and kissed her roughly. Throwing back his head, he screamed. "ABYSS!"

The crowd of about forty souls answered as in echo.

"ABYSS!"

"ABYSS!"

"ABYSS!"

The chant traveled back and forth between the king and his court. Like a wave, the cry rose between the warlord and his army. Between the man and his family, the feeling deepened until all thought of anything else was erased. The cry continued, drowning out the music and escalating into a blood-curdling yell, issuing deep from the soul of the man.

Israel stood alone in the middle of the hall; his disciples had dropped to their knees as he yelled above their heads. "**ABYSS!**"

Framed behind him hung the symbol of Abyss, a huge circled "A" with a slash running the length of it.

***

The white 2006 Honda Civic cruised slowly past the simple row house situated in the center of the block. The vehicle's spinners caught the sun's light and reflected it back across the cracked and pitted asphalt. The heavily tinted windows effectively concealed the driver and passenger inside. In the front yard of the house, several men in their early twenties and late teens sat or stood talking and laughing as they passed numerous bottles of beer and other alcoholic beverages around their circle.

The Honda stopped, and the driver's window slowly descended. Laughing, one of the men left the group and sidled up to the car, grabbing his crotch and dragging one foot behind him. "I got this one," he called over his shoulder.

He leaned into the window. "Yo, what you want, fool?" He reached into his pants pocket, retrieving several small plastic baggies containing yellowish white powder and off-white colored crystals. "You want rocks or powder?"

"I want respect."

Startled, he cursed, jumped back, and attempted to turn and run, but the shotgun blast caught him full in the chest, sending him sprawling across what passed for a lawn. Before the men in the front yard could react, several other white Hondas sped around the corner, and the occupants began pouring out and firing into the confused and panicked cluster.

Like thunder, shot after shot exploded. Round after round tore through lumber and flesh. And just as suddenly as it began, the metallic thunderstorm ceased.

Israel Vega emerged from the first car still holding the sawed-off twelve-gauge shotgun by his side, scanning the now quiet neighborhood through the acrid blue-gray smoke leaking from the mouth of the barrel. Strutting boldly up to the front door, he went in as if he owned the house.

Lo stepped from the second vehicle into the middle of the group of men, now sprawled on the ground. One of the downed men reached for a handgun lying on the ground just out of his reach, and Lo stomped on his wrist, grinding it into the earth beneath him. The already wounded man screamed in pain.

Several others joined Lo in the yard and began to immobilize those still alive and conscious. Like a well-planned military operation, the men of Abyss had assaulted and neutralized their target and now their commander was taking the enemy's flag.

As if on cue, Israel came back onto the front porch dragging a bloodied and scared man with him. Forcing the man to his knees, Israel placed the barrel of the shotgun between the man's lips.

Israel paused and gazed out over the scene. He knew he appeared reckless to some of his underlings, and that he appeared not to care whether he lived or died. He liked it that way. Fear was his power and power was his drug.

Making sure the rival gang members could see him, Israel rammed the barrel deeper into the man's mouth, causing him to gag. Looking to Lo, he jerked his head back toward the door he'd just come through. Two members ran quickly past him through the opened passage.

A few minutes later, the men returned carrying two large duffle bags. They stopped in front of Israel and showed him the contents. Releasing the man's head with his left hand, Israel reached inside the nearest bag and hefted a large size sandwich bag packed tight with more of the yellowish-white powder.

Israel dropped the baggie back into the duffel bag, and the two men raced down the steps, jumped into their vehicle, and left the area with a squeal of tires and haze of acrid smoke. Turning his attention back to the kneeling man before him, the now defunct leader of this rival gang, Israel smirked. The thought of this self-imagined leader kneeling before him made Israel laugh; the man would have to be an equal truly to be a rival.

Israel screamed, "Abyss!"

The echo greeted him immediately. "Abyss!"

Smiling, Israel looked down at the kneeling man. He was crying. Tears streamed down his face, forming rivers running steady around his mouth as his lips kissed the warm steel of the shortened barrel.

Israel despised weakness, and this man was weak. He turned his attention to his defeated enemies. "No one steals from Abyss. No one takes what's mine and lives."

The condemned man began to sob.

Israel's voice grew in tenacity and fervor. He screamed again, "Abyss!" The resounding echo filled the street. "Abyss!"

In the distance, sirens shrieked in increasing decibels. Israel laughed again and then nodded at his *first*.

Taking the signal, Lo grinded one last time on the man's wrist and gave the command to the gang. "Back!"

Again, like a well-trained unit, the gang retreated in leapfrog fashion until only Israel remained outside his vehicle. He surveyed the scene again, looking down into the crying man's face, his smile transformed into placid contempt as he, without emotion, pulled the trigger.

One last explosion rocked the quiet neighborhood.

Israel walked calmly to his vehicle, stepping over the dead and dying. Catching the lustful gaze of his female passenger, Israel leaned over and kissed her deeply. He then drove casually away as the rest of his gang exited; all leaving in separate directions; all driving within the posted speed limit; all calmly, as if nothing had happened.

CHAPTER NINE

PATROL UNITS CAME TO A SCREECHING HALT in front of the gang flophouse. Men groaned in the yard, calling for help. Many didn't call at all. The yard looked more like a frame from a war film reel than the front yard of a suburban neighborhood in the middle of the state's largest city.

Officer Johnson exited his unit, his gun in hand, unwilling to be caught off guard, unwilling to become the victim of a gang war. "TC 916," he said into his shoulder-mounted microphone. "It's clear. Send five-one to my location. Multiple gunshot victims. Several bodies down." He turned to his partner, Officer Conley, standing beside him and said under his breath, "It's not like they have to hurry." Both men smiled.

Moments later, the first of many paramedic units rolled onto the scene. Medical personnel immediately began setting up triage stations, tending to the most critically injured and stabilizing the others for transport.

"Looks like this one won't be needing your help," Johnson called out as he approached the porch.

"Nope," the medic answered, following Johnson's gaze. "Any idea what happened here?"

"That's the easy part," Johnson said. "Hey, Conley," he called to his partner, "tell the man what happened here."

Ricky Conley turned and walked back to where the paramedic had just finished binding a stomach wound and securing an IV in an unconscious man's arm. Leaning down to speak into his ear, he said, "Gang fight. They kill their set first, and then they come over and kill 'em back. It's the law of the jungle."

The paramedic looked up, casting a shallow smile. "NHI, huh?"

"NHI, pure and simple. I just hate to see them kill off the few good people still in this old neighborhood," Johnson said.

Conley walked up. "Good people in this neighborhood? Johnson, you're a dreamer."

All around the yard, medics and officers worked to save the lives and treat the wounds of the injured. After a few minutes, all those going to the hospital were already on their way. All those left behind waited only to be bagged by the coroner.

***

Nate stopped his Jeep near the curb on the far side of the street. Getting out, he walked back a few paces and looked over the scene. He turned and noted which houses faced the street and which appeared lived in or abandoned. Pulling out his note pad, he made a simple sketch of the street and a general layout of the scene.

"Hey, Richards." Johnson yelled from across the street and waved him over.

Nate swallowed and waved back. Johnson gave him the creeps.

Nate crossed the street with slow, careful steps, studying the tire prints and deep ruts cut into the front yard. "Johnson. Hey, Conley," he greeted the two men. "This your crime scene?"

"We're just babysitting until the big boys get here," Conley said.

Johnson chuckled. "Looks like you're here so now we don't have to be." He laughed at his own joke.

Nate smirked, but it never reached his eyes. "Another case of NHI, huh?" He asked sarcastically.

"Sure looks that way," Conley answered. "Gang on gang."

"Who's that on the porch?"

Johnson checked his notes, flipping through the pages and said, "That, my friend, was Big Dawg, aka Douglas Anthony Gawns. Up until a few hours ago, he ruled the west side from here on Washington and Southwest Seventh all the way past Black Cat. He ran drugs, women, men, and anything else that was bad. If it was illegal, old Big Dawg there had a hand in it. He even had girls running for him in the middle schools."

"Treasure Valley or one of the newer ones?"

"T.V. and the rest as well, if it was on the west side, Big Dawg ran it. Period."

"Looks like old Dawg here must have sprayed on the wrong bush. Somebody didn't like him in a bad way."

"Got what he deserved, if you ask me. I just hate it when their violence spills over on the few innocent people still stuck in this part of town." Johnson glanced past Nate to the street. "Looks like your crime scene crew finally made it."

Nate considered Johnson's words, and then turned and saw the large white-and-blue CSI van park behind his car across the street. The three techs got out already wearing protective gear, only their heads were uncovered.

Nate tapped Johnson on the shoulder and shrugged toward the newly arrived CSI team. "Looks like I'd better go brief these guys and let them know what I need them to look for," he said, dismissing Johnson.

Johnson smiled and turned back to face Conley, who had been standing by quietly.

Nate looked at Johnson's back and shook his head, a puzzled look on his face, before turning to explain to the team what Johnson had relayed to him. Nate directed the team to look specifically for any identifiers that did not belong to the West-Side Razors, the name of the defeated gang.

After taking a walk through the crime scene with the evidence techs, Nate stood over the remains of Big Dawg Gawns. Looking down at what was left of him, Nate tried to imagine what it must have been like for him in the moments leading up to his death. What thoughts, what regrets must have played through his mind? Shaking his head, thoughts of eternity played at Nate's mind. Sighing, he turned and walked away.

CHAPTER TEN

"BOUT TIME YOU GOT HERE," Sabrina said, sliding over and making room for Nate to join her in the back row of seats in the police department's main briefing room.

"Got tied up at the crime scene. What a mess." Nate leaned back in his chair and flipped open the file folder on the table in front of him. "Anybody got an idea who this mystery gang is? How can we have a turf war going on and nobody know who the players are?"

Sabrina raised an eyebrow at him as if to say, "Who you asking?" She inhaled and squared her shoulders to face him, preparing to answer. Nate interrupted and raised his hands, palms facing toward her, "I know, I know, you don't do gangs." He smiled.

"I thought so," she said, sounding satisfied. She leaned back and opened her own folder. "Looks like things are about to get started."

"Looks like."

Lieutenants Brown and Haynes walked up to the front of the rectangular-shaped room. The overhead fluorescent lights emitted a yellow-gray hue and caused faint shadows to crawl across the floor. Maps and aerial photographs of the three recent crime scenes decorated the beige walls. Diagrams and handwritten notes were attached to the various scenes with different colors of yarn, creating lines connecting the various points which seemed related to each other—The war room.

"Ladies and gentlemen, we have a problem, and the chief is drooling over my butt like a dog with a bone." Lieutenant Brown gripped the edge of the pinewood lectern and scanned the room. Snickers rolled across the space in a wave.

Brown shuffled his papers and glanced over at Haynes before continuing. "Now, as you know, whatever comes down on me, rolls down on you and—"

"Like he has ever needed a reason to dump on any of us," Nate leaned over and whispered behind his hand to Sabrina. They laughed and then coughed to cover the laughter when Brown gazed in their direction.

"You better square up before he rolls you back to patrol for real," Sabrina stated, turning a suddenly sober face toward the front of the room.

Nate didn't answer but kept his face turned down, laughing behind the paperwork in his hands. After a while, he looked up to see that Brown was relinquishing the lectern to Haynes.

Haynes walked to the front of the room and focused on the stack of papers before him. He stood frozen in place for a time then slowly lifted his face. "Who's lead on the Fuentes shooting?"

Nate raised his hand and looked up. "That'd be me, sir."

"What about Franks?"

"Me too," Nate answered.

"And the gang shootout?"

Nate was standing now. "Well, that one's not mine, but I was helping out on it. I think that one's assigned to—"

"Then maybe you ought to get your behind down here and do the briefing. I get paid to sit on my butt in that office all night; you're the one on the street."

A spattering of applause greeted Nate as he walked to the front of the room.

"You go boy!" One voice called out.

"You da man!" Another encouraged.

"Stow it," Haynes spoke over the voices. "Lieutenant Brown was right. The chief's wanting someone's feet to dump this problem at, and it ain't gonna be mine. Like I said, I sit in an office all night."

Nate began debriefing the crew. "I was on call the night of the Fuentes shooting and got the call from the patrol sergeant. Rather than me telling you what they told me, I'll let patrol speak for itself. Sergeant Haywood?"

Sergeant Haywood stood almost six feet, six inches and had the broad shoulders and muscular build he earned playing tight end for the local university. Ten years after he had played his last Division 1 collegiate game, he retained his physical conditioning and his sideline view of every home game. "My boys arrived on scene at approximately 0100 hours," he began, "after receiving a 'shots fired' call in the area…"

Three and a half hours later, the last of the various team members having spoken, the war room was quiet and almost empty. Only a few small groups remained, telling war stories and finishing lukewarm coffee. Nate rubbed tired eyes and then attempted to massage away the tension building at the base of his neck and shoulders. Dropping his papers into an empty chair and slouching in a second seat, hanging his head off the backrest, Nate closed his eyes and tried to think of nothing.

After a few minutes of quiet, he opened his eyes to see Lieutenant Brown staring down at him, a scowl gouged into his face. "What, we paying you to sleep now?"

Pushing himself up to a sitting position, Nate rubbed at his eyes again. "No sir, just thinking."

"So why didn't you book that little note you got at your house last night into evidence? You planning on keeping it as a token for your efforts?"

"Not at all, sir. Just didn't know if or how it was connected to anything yet. Still don't." Nate stood and began gathering his papers, not quite turning his back to Brown.

Brown stepped back, but did not walk away. "You think you're slick, don't you, going behind my back to get that case assigned to you?"

"No, sir. I—"

Brown spoke in soft tones, ensuring Nate was the only one to hear him. "Don't worry. I won't blame Haynes for this. I know you're his favorite. I blame you. And I'm going to nail your butt to the wall, Richards. When you fail and this comes down around your head—and it will, because you're not that good of an investigator. And Richards, when it does, all the praying in the world won't save you. You understand me?"

"Perfectly."

Lieutenant Brown stared at Nate as if he wanted to ask him something or, more true to his nature, make another statement.

Nate stared at Brown. "Was there something else, sir?"

"No, nothing else, Richards, nothing else; just get out there and do the job we're paying you to do."

"My pleasure, sir." Nate watched as Brown turned and exited the briefing room. Catching Haynes' eye from across the room, Nate waved. Haynes waved back and walked out the door leaving Nate and Sabrina alone in the war room.

"It's a tale of two lovers," Sabrina said, sidling up to Nate. "Brown hates your guts, and Haynes loves the ground you walk on."

They laughed and together headed for the door. "Better turn the lights off or Brown will take it out of your paycheck," Sabrina said, slapping Nate's shoulder.

"Don't you mean our paycheck? We are a team after all."

"Brown's no fool. There are still a few things he has enough sense to leave alone, and I'm one of them."

"Why is that? No matter what you do, he never says anything to you." He turned to look at her, and saw that she was smiling. "There you go again. You're not telling me something."

"Let's just say when Brown was my trainee after he first rotated out of the jail to patrol. There were a few things that happened."

"Come on, you got to tell me. What happened? What did he do? How bad did he screw up?"

She turned to him, her cheeks swollen in a smile. "You know the rule, what happens in the car, stays in the car."

He stopped, forcing her to stop as well. "What did he do? He peed his pants, didn't he?"

She didn't answer.

"He threw up on himself?" He walked toward her, closing the short distance that separated them.

"Come on, what did he do?"

She patted the side of his face, and without uttering a word, walked away.

"You're not going to tell me, are you? But I'm your partner!" he called after her.

She swung the door open, and without looking back, stepped through. Just as the door began to close, she flicked off the lights.

Darkness engulfed the room as the door swung closed. A thin sliver of light played across Nate's face and then vanished.

CHAPTER ELEVEN

HAVING BEGUN IN THE GYMNASIUM at the university due to the number of people who attended Franks' funeral, the procession now wound its way through downtown Treasure Valley. The cavalcade of cars passed the capitol building and proceeded through tunnels of tree-covered lanes. Citizens stood for miles along the posted route with handheld flags and saluted the slowly moving hearse.

Nate stood in the cemetery at a distance from the opened grave, dressed in civilian clothes as he watched the events unfold. Leaning against his shoulder, Amber jumped as the officers in dress uniform executed the 21-gun salute, an honor performed for an officer killed in the line of duty.

Set apart from the rest of the funeral party, a lone musician played "Taps" on a set of bagpipes. As the forlorn refrain drifted across the cemetery, people slowly began to turn and walk away.

As the last of the notes died on the breeze, the resonant thumping of a pulsating bass could be heard nearby. Nate turned in search of the offending noise. About two hundred yards away sat a row of eight to ten cars, all white with deeply tinted windows.

The bass thumped across to the group of mourners over the graveyard, stunning funeral attendees into silence and freezing them where they stood. Rap lyrics could be heard, if not understood, as the line of vehicles turned and drove off in the direction they had come. Only one vehicle remained. The driver got out and leaned leisurely in the fork of the door, his elbow dangling over the doorframe and stared at Nate, or at least Nate believed he was staring at him. After a few minutes, and long before any of the uniformed patrolmen could respond to his location, the man got back into his vehicle and slowly drove away.

"What was that all about?" Amber asked, dabbing at tears on her cheeks.

"I don't know, but I intend to find out," Nate answered as he shifted his grip on Amber's arm, leading her back to his car across the uneven ground. Clicking the auto start, Nate turned on the car's engine, allowing the air conditioning to cool off the vehicle's interior before they reached it. He walked around to the passenger side to open the door for Amber.

"I've told you," she began, drawing the words out, "you don't have to do that."

"And have my mother slap me? No, thank you." He smiled, and after opening the door and seating her, he traipsed around to get in himself. Looking back to where the white vehicle had been parked, Nate lowered himself into the Jeep's interior.

A warped CD being held up for his inspection by Amber greeted him. "Ah, yeah," he said, taking the ruined disc from her hand. He looked accusingly at the CD player and arched a brow as if it had been the culprit.

"Nate, that was my favorite CD. That was the new Hillsong's CD. You're going to have to replace it." She smiled smugly.

"Oh, I'm sorry, that CD player spits them out if I forget to turn it off before I get out."

"I know, you told me. I can't believe you haven't gotten that thing fixed yet. Either way, you owe me a new CD." She smiled again. "Now do we get to find out who those white cars belong to?"

"What?"

"I know you don't think that was normal. Those guys…those cars just showing up at the cemetery right in the middle of Franks' funeral. That was obvious even to me, but obvious of what, I can't guess."

"Amber, I've told you to leave the police work to me." He smiled and slid the warped disc beneath his seat. "But what makes you think that was anything more than a bunch of punks just being silly, anyway?"

"I don't believe in coincidence, and that was just too…perfect. The timing was just too right. It doesn't feel right."

He smiled. "'Doesn't feel right', huh? Anything else not feel right?" He shifted the car into drive and pulled out into traffic, merging as the line of vehicles exited the drive.

"Yep, I feel like lunch, and it feels like it's your turn to buy. I'm starved."

Nate looked at Amber out of the corner of his eye. "Well, you're gonna have to wait for me to buy. Mom and Dad are expecting us for lunch."

"Us?" She crossed her arms and leaned back against the door smiling.

"Well, she knew we were going to the funeral together and you know how my mom is. Besides, Dad has been asking about you."

"Okay, your mom's house for lunch, but don't think you're getting off the hook. You still owe me. And you're still paying for my CD too." She leaned forward, kissed his cheek, and smiled. "You can pull it from beneath the seat now."

Getting off the freeway at the Garrity Road exit, Nate downshifted before driving up the hill leading past Ridgecrest Golf Course and Resort. Bright sunlight reflected off the deep emeralds and jades of the fairways like the swelling surf of a gently rolling sea breaking against the beach-like sand traps. Well-placed water hazards made the back nine seem to disappear into the horizon or simply melt away as tee after tee overlooked cliffs of forty feet or more above their narrow fairways.

"What?" Nate asked, dragging his gaze from the swiftly fleeing golf course and back to Amber.

"You know what?" she said. "The last time you brought me over on a Saturday, you and your dad wound up going out to play nine holes, leaving me at home with your mom to bake cookies."

"Yeah, but that was his birthday, and you volunteered to bake his favorite cookies. What was I supposed to do, sit around and watch you bake?"

They laughed at the memory, but sobered as they left the golf resort and entered the nearby subdivision. Sherwood Forest was a relatively new development, only five years old. Nate had been one of its first lot owners.

Noticing the shadow creep across Nate's face and then quickly fade, Amber studied him. "Does it still bother you?" Amber asked.

Nate tensed. Little creases folded the skin adjacent to his eyes and the set of his shoulders grew rigid as his grip suddenly tightened on the steering wheel.

"You know, since Patty and all?" She let the silence hang between them.

He exhaled slowly.

Coming around the bend, they saw the mint-green, two-story Victorian with cream-colored trim at the top of the cul-de-sac, basking in the late afternoon sun. The light of a cloudless sky lit the face of the structure making it shine. Driving slowly up the road, they both watched as the house grew closer as they made their approach.

"Nahh," he said finally. "I may have built it for me and Patty, but that didn't work out. At least it didn't go to waste, huh? Besides, Mom and Dad love living here."

Nate pulled into the driveway and eyed his dad's golf bag leaning against the far wall just inside the garage. He smiled. Facing Amber, he said, "Me and Patty not working out…that was a good thing."

"I know. I was the one who told you she wasn't good for you, remember?"

"Yeah," he opened his car door, "but that was because you were madly in love with me and afraid of losing me forever." He jumped out before she could hit him.

This time she did not wait for him to open her door but leaped out chasing him. "You wish," she called toward his fleeing back.

Laughing, Nate ran in through the opened garage, headed for the door leading into the laundry room, and stopped abruptly, barely avoiding running into his mother.

"Nathaniel Richards, I did not raise you to be a thug. I saw you make that young lady open her own door."

Just then Amber caught up to him and punched him in the shoulder.

"You see why I was running," Nate said, rubbing his shoulder.

Sherri Richards pushed her silver-streaked blond hair back from her youthful face, reached around Nate, and pulled Amber into a hug. After releasing her, she playfully slapped Nate's cheek. "I don't know what you did to this child, but I'm sure you deserved it." The petite woman hugged Amber again and led her back into the house, hands clasped like schoolgirls.

Following Sherri into the house, Amber looked back and poked her tongue at Nate, scrunching her nose as she did so.

Nate pointed his finger at her and mouthed, "You'll get yours." He smiled.

"And don't be talking behind my back either," Sherri said as the door closed.

A look of shock on his face, Nate turned as his father came into the garage from the back of the house. "How does she do that?"

"I've been married to the woman for thirty-seven years, and I still haven't figured it out," Reverend Richards answered his son, pulling him into a tight embrace.

"Women." Nate sighed and returned the hug. Nate's skin contrasted creamy-brown against the darker hue of his father's as the two men stepped apart, locked wrists, and pulled against each other in a mock test of strength. A game they'd played since Nate was a child.

"You mean, woman. Who could handle more than one?"

The men laughed and followed the ladies into the kitchen.

"Did you bring your clubs?" Reverend Richards asked in a soft voice.

"Yeah, but Amber doesn't know it yet." They both smiled as the spring-loaded door swung shut behind them.

As Nate and his father made their way into the kitchen, they found the two women already seated in two of the four chairs around the table. The natural wood floors caught the sun coming through the Prado door, giving a warm country feel to the room.

Pigs in every imaginable pose and color combination decorated the kitchen. Wallpaper prints, statuettes, and framed artwork all reflected Sherri's love of the barnyard animal. A smiling piglet served as the sugar dish in the center of the table and was complemented by several coffee mugs, which also bore images of the swine's relations.

Amber tossed her hair from her face with a shake of her head and turned slightly, acknowledging the men as they entered. Leaning across the table, she whispered something to Sherri that Nate couldn't hear.

"Hey, gossip is still a sin, you know."

"What do you think, Amber? Sounds like a guilty conscience to me," Sherri said.

"Mmmm-hmm," Amber agreed and leaned back, stretching her arm across the back of the chair.

Nate pulled the chair to the right of Amber away from the table, turned it, and straddled it rocking forward, balancing on the two rear legs.

"Boy, stop rocking in my chair," Sherri said and slapped his arm. "Twenty-eight years old and still a big kid." She stood and retrieved the coffeepot from the island counter and began pouring coffee, first for her husband and then Nate.

Nate smiled at his mother and then turned his attention to the several empty yellow sweetener packages on the table. Amber kicked his shin beneath the table, but smiled at Sherri as she refilled her mug.

"Thank you," Amber said.

After all the cups were filled, Reverend Richards turned toward his son. "Now, Son, tell us about this mess you're into this time."

Nate looked at Amber and then at both his parents. Inhaling, he said, "Okay, but it's ugly."

CHAPTER TWELVE

"SHOULD WE PRAY FIRST?" his mother asked.

"You know, that might not be a bad idea," Nate answered. From long habit, he reached for his parents' hands and Amber grasped Nate's left hand with her right and Sherri's hand with her left. Together they bowed their heads and waited for the senior Richards to begin.

For a short time, a comfortable silence filled the small kitchen as dust motes swam in shafts of sunlight playing through the slatted blinds. With a small intake of breath, Sherri began to pray first. "Father, I don't know what this darkness is that my son is having to deal with, but You know, and I know You will be with him. Give him the strength and the wisdom he will need to get through this and to glorify You in it."

"And Lord," Reverend Richards added, "we know that You have all wisdom and even the darkest secret of man is laid bare before You. In that knowledge we come. Father, we ask You to bind the spirits of darkness that are fighting for control of this valley, and I thank You for making my son one of your chosen vessels to lead in this battle."

"Yes, Father," Amber added. "And give Nate the wisdom to deal with Lieutenant Brown. Jesus, remind Nate that it is his position to love this man and to reveal Your love to him."

"Amen," Nate said and the word echoed from around the table.

"So, Son, why don't you tell us what's happening in this city?" his father said, releasing Nate's hand but holding on to his wife's.

Nate cleared his throat and began to recount what he had seen at the Fuentes crime scene, describing the waste he'd sensed looking at the dead teen. Then he spoke of finding the same symbol on Franks' body and knew somehow that the two were tied together. The main thread still evaded him. He skipped the more gruesome details, catching his father's eye when his mother was not looking. They would talk later.

For the next thirty minutes, Nate recounted the events to his family, careful not to say anything they hadn't already read in the papers.

After a while, Sherri stood up looking at the clock. "Honey, don't you have tee time for the wee nine?"

Amber cut her eyes at Nate and swatted him again.

"Don't tell me he didn't tell you his father had invited him to play a round of golf," Sherri said.

Nate scooted back out of reach just as his mother swiped at him with a dishtowel. "Nathaniel Richards!" she said.

"Wait, I didn't say I'd play. Besides, Amber is welcome to play with us if she wants," Nate said in his own defense.

"No thank you," Amber said. "I think I'll just hang out here with your mom and talk about you behind your back. Maybe she'll break out your baby book and tell me all kinds of embarrassing things about you as a child."

Nate frowned but stood to follow his father into the garage anyway. "It's probably best that I'm not here for that conversation," he said and touched Amber's cheek before turning to leave.

CHAPTER THIRTEEN

"FORE!"

Nate jumped as the errant shot landed with a dull thud beside him, accidentally kicking his ball off the tee set near his feet. He bent down, intending to pick up the ball and throw it back in the direction it had come, but thought better and stood again, leaving the ball where it lay.

"That guy's slice is as bad as yours," Reverend Richards laughed, drawing a sour look from Nate.

"Yeah, real funny," Nate said and reset his ball. Eyeing down the green, taking into account the crosswind and the lake to the right, Nate took a settling breath. Relaxing his grip on the driver, he prepared to swing.

"Sorry 'bout that, sir," an acne-faced teen said, sliding his golf cart to a stop alongside the tee. "That slice…it still gets away from me, but I'm getting better."

"Whoa! What the—" Nate said, stopping mid-swing.

"Oops. Sorry, again. I'll just get my ball and drop it over there," the boy said, pointing back to the adjacent fairway. He grabbed his ball, wiped it, and threw it back the way he'd come.

Nate stared at the teen as the boy drove off, a befuddled expression on his face.

Reverend Richards laughed. "By the way, that's a stroke."

"What? How—"

"You moved your ball. Of course, you could take it as your mulligan."

Nate laughed, dropped his three-wood at the top of his backswing, and stepped off the shot. "Whoa! Wait. Dad, come on. That kid hit me with his shot."

"Almost hit you. Almost don't count, Son." He smiled again and began swinging his own driver, loosening up.

"Come on, you're not going to make me use a mulligan on that, are you? That kid messed me up."

"Nahh, I'm just funning you. Go ahead and take your shot." He turned to face Nate and swung the head of his driver softly into the turf. "So, Son, how are you going to handle this new investigation? This whole thing feels different than the ones you've dealt with in the past. You're being careful, right?" He walked around in front of his son and rapped him on his shoulder with his knuckles, "I appreciate what you told your mother and me, but Son, you need to be praying other than just when you're sitting at my table."

"Don't I know it? This thing has had a darkness to it almost from the beginning." Nate checked his ball on the tee and adjusted his hands on the grip of the driver. "Beginning with that Fuentes kid—even his death doesn't fit the regular gang shooting scenario. There seems to be more to it." He looked at his dad, and when the silence stretched on, he sighed and turned away.

Nate lowered his head, turning his concentration to the newly teed ball and began his backswing. After a quick twist of his waist and a grunt, he sent his ball flying down the right side of the fairway.

"Not bad, Son, but that rough over there is going to cause you some trouble on your approach." The elder Richards took his shot and watched as his ball rolled and settled at about two hundred seventy yards down the middle of the fairway. "Now, that's what I call getting it done, Son." He turned and smiled at Nate.

For a short while, the two men walked in companionable silence until Nate began speaking. "Someone woke me from a sound sleep the other night pounding on my door. I banged my leg something fierce trying to get my pants on and jump walking through the house in the dark. I almost took off Amber's head when I found her standing at the door after I yanked it open."

Reverend Richards eyed his son.

"No, Dad," Nate said catching the expression on his father's face. "She had just arrived. She was bringing me coffee. She had been with me earlier when I got the call about Franks."

"I never said a word," Reverend Richards said.

"You didn't have to. If I was going to do something stupid like that, you think I would be so dumb as to mess with Amber? Be real, Dad."

"Why not Amber?"

"What?" Nate stopped and stared at his father, his eyes wide in amazement. He shook his head from side to side and opened and closed his mouth several times before actually speaking. "What are you saying?" He finally managed, his brows climbing toward his hairline.

Reverend Richards stopped, pulled out his five-iron, and began addressing his shot as if not a word had been uttered. He looked at Nate. "I mean, why haven't you asked that girl to marry you yet, Son?" He set his feet, took his shot and watched as the ball landed softly, settling easily onto the green. "On in two," he smiled. "It's looking like a birdie for your old man." He finished with a chuckle.

"You had me there for a minute. I thought you were asking why I had Amber over for the night." Nate said and exhaled.

"Like you would do something like that to that child. Your mother would skin you alive."

"Not to mention what her mom would do." Nate reached the area where his ball lay nestled in the three-inch grass of the short rough.

"So what was all the knocking on your door about?"

"Somebody dropped off a small box with a note in it. The odd thing was that the note, if you could call it that, only had an anarchy symbol on it. No message. No name. No nothing. It was the same symbol we found on the rag recovered in the hand of the Fuentes kid and at the Franks' scene.

"I thought it was the Fuentes kid's gang colors at first, but we don't have anything on record of a gang using the anarchy symbol as their icon on file. It doesn't seem to fit, but the question is, why would somebody deliver that package to my house?"

Taking out a utility-iron, Nate twisted his feet until they settled in the thick grass. Choking down on the grip of his club and careful to keep his head down through the shot, Nate swung. Hard.

Watching his ball land, Nate looked up at his father. "Looks like you're out, old man," he said as his ball landed and rolled within six feet of the cup.

"Both of them with the same symbol?" Reverend Richards asked rhetorically. "What about the ink; was it the same on both rags?"

"What?" Nate asked, looking up.

"I mean, was it the same? Was it handwritten, computer generated, marker, or what? Maybe the person—"

"The same paint. Permanent marker, I think," Nate finished for him. "I've got to call Sabrina."

After the game, the men found Amber and Sherri laughing and enjoying coffee and cookies on the covered patio. An almost-empty plate of chocolate chip cookies between them on the low table, the ladies smiled as the men came into the backyard.

Nate sat beside Amber and, with his thumb, brushed away a smear of chocolate near the corner of her mouth. She looked over at him and smiled as their eyes met.

"Enjoy your game?" she asked with an "I-told-you-so" smile.

***

The next morning Nate settled behind his desk and looked up into the knowing eyes of his partner.

"Did you enjoy your game with your dad?" Sabrina asked, taking a sip from her mug of coffee.

"How did you hear about that? He called you, didn't he?" Nate asked, leaning back from his desk, which butted up to and faced Sabrina's. "If he wasn't a preacher, I'd swear he was cheating."

"That hasn't stopped some of the preachers I know," Sabrina said. "Besides, I've seen you play." She sat a mug of coffee on the desk beside Nate. "Bon appétit. Don't ever say I never gave you nothing." She smiled before turning and walking away.

Nate rolled his eyes and began checking his e-mail and voicemail from the weekend. After twenty minutes, fifty-three emails, and seventeen voicemails, Nate finally reached for his coffee, now cold.

As Nate activated the last message, a gravelly voice, obviously distorted, filled the air. "I see you got the package I left for you. Now the question is, are you smart enough to see the connection? I suppose I'll need to give you a hint. His name is the Holy Land. Better figure it out before he starts killing taxpayers."

The recording ended and the prerecorded voice began its message. "You have no more calls. To save this call, press pound. To delete this call, press seven—"

Nate quickly pressed the pound sign and retrieved his digital recorder before pressing the replay button. After making a copy of the message, Nate played it for Sabrina.

Sabrina pressed her almond shaped eyes, closed in concentration, willing herself to hear the details of the recording. "Well," she said, looking up, "it's definitely a mechanical voice, but what does he mean by, 'His name is the Holy Land' and 'taxpayers'? Makes absolutely no sense to me. If I had to guess, I'd say it was a jokester; maybe one of those Aryan gangsters sounding off. But then you'd have to ask why he would give you, an *almost*-black man, the clue. That would be like sleeping with the enemy." She laughed at her own joke.

"The phrase," Nate began, taking on the air and manner of a social elite, "the name we Halflings have chosen for ourselves is Hapa. We prefer not to think of ourselves as being almost anything, but rather the ultimate completion of both. The best of both worlds, you see, darling." He rolled the last phrase as it were made of rubber.

"I'll tell you what I'd like to see," Lieutenant Haynes' voice broke into their revelry, "is the two of you doing some work for a change. Sitting in here all day drinking my coffee is not getting my caseload cleared."

"Your coffee?" Sabrina turned to face him, still laughing. "When was the last time you chipped in the coffee fund or anything else around here?"

"No lie, L.T.," Nate said, wiping tears from his eyes from laughing. "You're so tight, your pennies got bruises on them."

"Be that as it may," Haynes said, sitting on the corner of Nate's desk, "a man in my position has to take responsibility for his team. So you guys, my team, bring in the coffee, and I take responsibility for it." He smiled, obviously thinking he was funny.

After a while the laughter died away and the conversation turned back to the investigation.

Haynes asked, "What have you guys come up with so far?"

"That's just it," Nate began, "we're not hearing anything. There's no talk on the streets about the Fuentes shooting and nothing about the Franks hit. The only noise we're hearing anything about is the hit on Big Dawg and his boys over in Old Town."

Sabrina nodded her head and added, "As much as these bangers love to brag, you'd think if it was a gang hit, somebody would be taking credit for it by now. Somebody would be talking."

"What do you mean, 'if,'" Haynes said, turning his attention to her. He stood and walked a few paces from where the two desks sat. Rubbing his hand over his face, Haynes turned back to face the two detectives. "What are you two suggesting? We got some kind of serial killer in the city?"

"No, sir," Nate cut in, "we're just looking at all the possibilities. There's just too many things that don't make sense."

"Like?" Haynes said, drawing the word out.

"Fuentes being killed in a gang hit and no chatter on the street," Nate said.

"Franks shot, carved, and burned with some new symbol and no new gang bragging about taking out a cop," Sabrina said, her voice sounding suddenly tired and flat.

"And then," Nate added, shifting in his seat, his voice sounding tired and strained, "somebody dropping off that mystery box at my house and making sure I found it. That doesn't sound like a gang hit to me, but at the same time—"

"At the same time, nothing else comes to the surface or fits the facts as we know them," Sabrina said matter-of-factly.

Haynes leaned against the wall behind him, taking a deep breath. "Wow." Standing again and taking his coffee cup from the desk where he'd put it, he began walking back toward his office. He stopped and looked back at Nate and Sabrina who were staring at him. "And no chatter on the streets? At all?"

Haynes paused and looked away, shaking his head. "It's moments like these that make retirement look better and better." He tipped his hand as if saluting, turned, and walked back to his office, closing the door behind him.

"You know," Nate said, "he's strange, but I like him."

"We could always get Brown on the nightshift—just for you." Sabrina said, standing. "Let's go. This case isn't going to solve itself."

Nate closed the file on his desk and turned off the playback on the digital recorder. Taking a sip from the mug, he frowned and fought to keep from spitting the cold coffee out of his mouth. He forced a swallow.

"Let's get some real coffee, I'll buy."

"Library Coffeehouse here we come," Sabrina said.

"What makes you think I want to go to the Library?"

"Why else do you think I put that cup of cold Joe on your desk? It's your turn to buy, sweetie." She laughed and ducked out the door.

Nate looked at the cup of coffee sitting on his desk, swirls of cold creamer floating on its surface, shook his head, and followed her out the door.

CHAPTER FOURTEEN

BUTCH JENSEN, STAR FIELD REPORTER for Treasure Valley's Channel Six News, waited in his car, hoping that Richards and Jackson would follow their regular Monday morning ritual. He had been sitting in front of the Library Coffeehouse for over an hour and finally his patience was being rewarded.

In his rearview mirror, he watched as Nate parked his forest-green Jeep along the curb in front of the coffeehouse.

Getting out of the car, Sabrina spotted Butch first and rolled her eyes.

"Richards, Jackson, how about a second?" Jensen called after them.

"You talk to him, I'm going in to get coffee," Sabrina said, walking away. "You're still paying."

"Don't worry, I got ya'. Tell Jackie to put it on my tab." Nate smiled at Sabrina's retreating back, exhaled, composed himself, and turned a stoic face to the reporter.

"What do you want, Jensen?"

"Come on, Nate, throw me a bone. Give me something."

"We have a PIO for that purpose." Nate crossed his arms and leaned back against the grill of his Jeep.

"That Lieutenant Saul you guys have working as the public information officer is a waste. He won't say anything we don't already know."

Nate noted that Jensen's voice had taken on a pleading tone. "Okay, what do you want?"

"Anything. All I know is that there have been two murders and one gang hit and somehow, it seems to me, they are all connected."

"Well, that's an interesting theory, but what makes you say that?" Nate uncrossed his arms, lifting himself onto the hood of the Jeep.

"Come on, Richards. At least tell me about this new gang showing up on the streets, Abyss."

Nate slid off the hood. "Abyss…maybe there's something you can tell me instead."

Jensen closed the distance between himself and Nate. "Don't play me, Richards. There's no way this much activity is going on without the police knowing about it."

Nate smiled and held up both hands, his palms facing toward the reporter. "You gotta know that there are things I can't tell you, Jensen," Nate hedged. "Besides, you seem to be on the right track with this, but I can't confirm that officially." Nate hoped the newsman would take the bait and start talking.

Jensen smiled and pulled out his notepad. He began scribbling notes as soon as Nate began talking.

Nate lowered his voice and spoke directly to Jensen. "All right, there's a new threat in the valley, some group using the anarchy symbol as their tag. That's all we know so far."

"What about the rag the Fuentes kid had in his hand? Or the carving found in Franks' chest?"

Nate started to play dumb, thought better of it, and redirected his response. "You've done your homework, I see. Okay, that's the common denominator so far." Nate lowered his voice again and waved as two middle-aged women walked by. "But that's all we know. We don't know anything about the gang or its beliefs, philosophy…code. It's still too early in the game."

"Tell you what, Richards, you play straight with me, and I'll give you first review before I run anything to the station. Tit for tat. Deal?"

Nate looked at the man's outstretched hand, smirked and harrumphed and shook it firmly. "You cross me on this and I'll cut you out of the loop, and do my best to bring you up on obstruction charges. I don't have to remind you that one of us got killed in this thing, and everybody is going to be watching what you guys do." Nate's finger was in Jensen's face, and his own face had grown stern.

***

Sabrina watched the exchange between the two men from inside the coffeehouse. Shaking her head before taking another drink from her mug, she waved at the waitress as she walked by. "Bring me a large cinnamon roll, please."

"Yes, ma'am. Do you want that heated or cold? You want extra caramel for seventy-five cents more?"

"Oh, absolutely, hot. As a matter-of-fact, make it two and put caramel on both." She smiled and sat back in her seat.

Nate came in shortly after Sabrina ordered and joined her in the booth.

"So what did Butchy boy have to say?" she asked as Nate slid into the booth, facing her from the opposite side.

"He knew about the symbol," Nate said, taking a swallow of his coffee, lifting the cup and smiling at it appreciatively. "He knew about the rag and Franks' body too."

"And you wonder why I hate that guy. If he ruins my investigation, I'm going to kill him myself. He won't have to worry about *the new gang*."

They turned back to their coffee. "Oh, cinnamon rolls…thanks."

"Don't thank me, you're paying for it."

"Hey, the deal was for coffee. How did it turn into cinnamon rolls?"

"Since you started playing patty-cake with that news scrub out there," she said, scowling.

Nate laughed softly. "I had to do something; he had information we didn't have."

"Like?"

"Like Abyss."

"Don't make me slap you, Nate. What is "Abyss" besides a deep hole?"

Nate smiled at her. "The name of our mystery gang."

Sabrina leaned forward. "What…where'd he get that?"

Nate sat forward as well, his forehead wrinkled in thought. "I really don't know. I didn't want to come across like he knew stuff we didn't."

"But he does."

"He didn't know that."

They both leaned back as a comfortable silence settled between them. The soft, jazzy trumpet refrains of Chris Botti's "No Ordinary Love" flowed from the hidden speakers.

***

From outside, Jensen watched Nate and Sabrina through the opened window, engrossed in a quiet but intense conversation. As he sat in his car enjoying the air conditioning, a reprieve from the already hot day, a puzzled look crawled across his face. *I don't know what you're up to, Nate Richards*, he thought. *But I'm making it my job to find out.*

CHAPTER FIFTEEN

NATE PATTED AT HIS CHEST POCKET; his cell phone was ringing again. He rolled his eyes. "This is not going to be good." Taking another drink of his coffee before opening the phone, he answered, "Richards."

The female voice on the other end was familiar and not entirely unwelcome. "Nate," she began, drawing out the name in a pleasant greeting.

"Elva, why're you calling me this early in the morning? Can't a guy finish his coffee in peace?" he said, taking on a playful tone.

Across the booth, Sabrina, having heard Elva's name, quickly finished the cinnamon roll on her plate.

Nate frowned at her and tried snatching a piece of the roll from her hand.

She smiled and leaned away, waving the sweet roll in his face in a lazy arch.

The voice from the phone continued. "I've got a priority-one call at T.V. Middle School. An eleven-year-old girl disclosed that her stepdad's been molesting her. How soon can you meet me over there?" Elva asked in her usual casual fashion.

Unconsciously, Nate looked down at his watch, "Where are you now?"

"At the office, but I can leave right now and be at the school in twenty minutes, depending on traffic."

"Twenty minutes, huh? Okay, meet you there."

"Good. Tell Sabrina I said hi. See you guys there."

Nate closed his phone, and looking at the now empty plate, scraped his finger over it, collecting the last of the melted frosting and caramel. "Let's go, partner. We got us a molester over at the middle school."

Sabrina stood and pushed his hand away from the plate. "That's mine. Is he still on scene?"

"Nah, just his victim."

Just then his phone rang again. Nate flipped it open. "Richards." He frowned and mouthed to Sabrina, "It's Brown."

"Yes, sir." Nate carried on the one-sided conversation.

"Just got the call from CPS."

"I know, sir."

"Yes, sir, it's—yes, sir. It's my butt if I don't get it done." He held the phone away from his ear as they walked out of the coffee shop. Lieutenant Brown was still talking. After leaving a tip at the counter and waving good-bye, he spoke again into the receiver, "Yes, sir, I will give you my report before I secure for the day."

Seating himself behind the steering wheel of his Jeep, Nate turned to look at Sabrina. "I swear that man hates me." He smiled, starting the car. "He must sit by the fax machine all day waiting for a child protection referral to come across just so he'll have a reason to get on my leg."

Sabrina reached across and pinched his cheek. "Oooh, a lover's quarrel."

"Come on, Jackson, tell me what it was he did that you're holding over his head. I've got to get this man off my back."

Looking toward the stereo, she picked up a CD, Michael W. Smith. Turning on the system as if she hadn't heard him, she said, "Don't you have some real gospel music in here?"

Nate laughed and pulled away from the curb. "Center console…. Okay, keep your secrets to yourself, partner."

They laughed.

Twenty minutes later, they parked in front of the middle school to find Elva waiting for them. At four feet, eleven inches, the middle-aged Hispanic woman wasn't much taller than many of the children she dedicated her life to helping.

"That bag is as big as you, lady," Nate said, drawing her into a hug.

"Well, I never know what I'll need, so I just bring it all." She giggled. "Shall we? Hi, Sabrina." She turned and began walking toward the front door without waiting for a response; the click-click-click of her heels receding as she paced away.

"Shall we?" Nate asked, sweeping his arm across his body and bowing at the waist.

"I guess we shall," Sabrina answered, holding her chin up and strutting toward the door.

Eleven-year-old Jessica Simms came into the school resource officer's office with a smile on her face, lifting everyone's disposition. Her long blond hair lay in platted coils over her shoulders. Pushing up her glasses, she smiled at the adults in the room.

Sitting across from the little girl, Elva began the interview. "Hi, sweetie, I'm Elva and these are my friends, Detectives Richards and Jackson." The officers smiled as they were introduced.

Elva scooted her chair around the corner of the desk so that she was sitting face to face with the little girl. "My job is to talk to kids, and I talk to them about all kinds of things."

Jessica looked up at the adult faces, her smile starting to fade. Tears began to well in her eyes, and she dropped her forehead against her folded arms, hiding her face. Her shoulders began to shake with silent sobs.

Thirty minutes later, Nate helped the little girl settle herself into the backseat of Elva's car. He looked down at the child and then back up to Elva. "I'll meet you down at FACES." Then turning his back to the opened window and lowering his voice, he said, "Have Doc Sanchez get started on the physical, and set up an emergency interview with the ladies in the front office. I want to get this jerk while the getting's good."

When he finished, he leaned forward and looked into the backseat of the car again. "Okay, sweetie, I'll see you down at the doctor's office just like we talked about, okay?"

She smiled shyly and looked down; the light in her eyes not so bright anymore.

Sabrina waved at Nate from the Jeep, calling him over. "Patrol has eyes on the stepdad at his place of work; a used car lot on the corner of Fairview and Five Mile."

"Good. Have patrol stay back, but don't lose sight of him. After we finish down at CARES, I want to go pick this guy up and have him explain to me why he's messing with his little girl."

"I thought we were going to FACES," Sabrina said, nodding at Nate and relaying instructions to the patrol officers via the cell phone.

"Oh, the CARES office is in the FACES building. I forgot to tell you."

"What does all that stand for anyway, CARES and FACES? Sounds like an ad for make-up. In the old days we just took them to the ER and the duty nurse did the deed."

"Well, CARES stands for Children at Risk Evaluation Services and FACES stands for Family Advocacy Center and Education Service," Nate said, taking a breath. "I see you didn't bother to read the memos."

She arched her eyebrows and smiled as if to say, "Who, me?" She chuckled to herself. "Right, FACES. Or rather, CARES it is."

CHAPTER SIXTEEN

NATE AND SABRINA SAT IN SEMI-DARKNESS watching over the closed circuit monitor as Jessica spoke in halting sentences, disclosing her horrors to the forensic interviewer. Minute by minute the little girl revealed months of abuse at the hands of the man who should have been her guardian.

Later, meeting in the conference room, elbows on the table and brows creased, they debriefed the interview and set the investigative strategy. Child protection would arrange for safe housing while the prosecutor would begin warming up a judge just in case an arrest warrant was needed. Nate and Sabrina would head back to prepare for the suspect interview.

Slapping the tabletop and pushing back from the circle, Sabrina stood up. "I'm getting too old for this stuff."

"Yeah, we all are," Dr. Sanchez answered, looking over the top of his wire-rimmed glasses, bushy graying brows like fuzzy caterpillars knotted together in the center of his forehead.

Nate leaned back in his chair and looked again at the notes the forensic interviewer had given him. Sighing, he closed the folder in front of him. "Let's go get this jerk."

"What do you want to do? You think we've got enough for PC?" Sabrina asked successive questions, catching Nate's eye.

"If this guy is as bad as Jessica says he is, yeah, I think probable cause will hold. I don't want to take a chance on him getting to the mother and muddying up the testimony. Besides, if Jessica's mom is going to have any hope of getting her little girl back, this will be her last chance to cooperate with the investigation. She needs to decide which of these two deserves her protection."

"And…" Sabrina prompted when Nate fell silent.

"I say we bring them both in—separately. And then we question them both."

"I say we book the mother on failure to protect, for letting this monster get to her daughter," Sabrina said, a look of disgust coloring her face.

The medical staff sat back, watched the exchange between the detectives, knowing that their part, the forensic interview and medical care, was finished until, and unless, they were needed in court.

Finally, Dr. Sanchez stood. "I have a two o'clock coming in, and I need to prep for it, so if you will excuse me." He turned and left the room, followed closely by the remaining medical staff.

Nate shifted his eyes and followed the tick-tock movement of the second hand as it bumped its way around the face of the simple round black-framed wall clock. Shifting his eyes again, he saw Jessica through the one-way glass, every bit the little girl, now sitting and playing in the waiting room with two other children who were waiting their turn to go in. *They must be Doc's two o'clock appointment.* Nate looked at the children and shook his head.

"Let's go get this fool," Sabrina said and walked out the back door.

Nate turned his attention to Elva, who had been sitting quietly. "You get our girl somewhere safe for tonight, and I'll let you know how things turn out with the mommy."

"You do that, big fella," Elva said, hefting her bag onto her shoulder. "Let me know when the shelter care hearing is set and when you book this guy."

Nate smiled at the sylphlike woman as she joined Jessica in the waiting room. Standing nearly the same height, the two could have been mistaken as being merely playmates if seen from behind. After a few minutes, the two joined hands and left the building together.

***

Three hours later, Nate walked out of the interview and interrogation room and found Sabrina waiting for him. "What you get; did she talk?"

"She gave him up. The perv's been beating her and forcing her to help him take pictures of Jessica. This guy's a freak. She gave us permission to search the residence, but I've got Mac working on a search warrant. I don't want to lose anything on a stupid technicality."

"Good," Nate said brightening, "this guy's playing it close. He hasn't lawyered up yet. That's the good news. He thinks his wife is still in his corner. He's counting on her not talking; he's gonna pee his pants when he finds out she rolled on him."

They gave each other high-fives and headed back to their assignments, Nate to the interview room and Sabrina to finish the search warrant with Mac.

Back in the interview room, Nate said nothing, just stared at Christopher Simms, the stepfather of Jessica. Nate studied the man, observing as his throat worked, and a single rivulet of sweat made its way past his ear and ran down the side of his neck.

Finally, Nate opened his file but closed it again, checking the name on the accounts he'd gotten from Sabrina. With deliberate purpose, Nate looked up at Christopher again.

"Christopher," he began, his voice soft, non-threatening, "can you explain this to me?" Nate laid a copy of an ER report before Christopher.

Nate watched Christopher's face as a slow dawning began.

"Well, um, as I," he stammered.

Nate pulled another sheet of paper from the folder and laid it in front of the man. This statement came from the neighboring county; a second ER report revealing a broken arm and several fractured ribs belonging to his wife.

"Where did you get these?" Christopher asked.

"You know, Chris," Nate began, his voice still non-threatening, "you beat a woman and still expect her to keep your secrets. That's not smart."

Christopher stood abruptly. Standing with him, Nate spoke sternly for the first time. "Sit down."

Christopher sat.

"You make me nervous when you do that, Chris," Nate said, softening his voice again.

Outside the interview room, watching over closed-circuit TV, several officers relaxed when they saw Christopher sit down again.

Back in the interview room, Nate slid another sheet of paper across the table in front of Christopher. Keeping his hand on the sheet of folded paper, Nate looked hard into Christopher's face. Without moving his eyes, Nate leaned forward in his seat and lowered his voice. "Chris, this is your last chance for me to help you. Your wife gave us a written statement." He tapped the sheet of paper lying closed between the two of them.

Christopher's eyes darted between Nate and the paper.

"Chris, I know what you did to Jessica, but what I don't know is why, Chris. Chris, look at me for a minute." Nate pulled the paper back from in front of Christopher and put it inside his folder.

Sweat dripped from Christopher's temples as he sat staring at the spot where the papers had been.

"Chris. Chris." Nate waited until Christopher looked up at him. "Chris, I know about the pictures. I know about the touching. Tell me, Chris, did you do this because you love Jessica or because you were trying to hurt her?"

Christopher slumped forward and hid his face in his hands, speaking to Nate between his fingers, "I would never hurt Jessica. I love her. I'm sorry. I'm sorry."

Nate rolled his chair closer to where the man sat crying. Placing his hand on his shoulder, Nate said, "I know, I know you didn't mean to hurt Jessica, but you did. Now we can make this right, Chris. We can make this right by you taking ownership of what you did. Tell me about it, okay?"

"Okay," he croaked.

***

A half-hour later, Nate walked out of the interview room. A uniformed officer was waiting just outside the door. Nate looked at the officer and back in the room at Christopher, still sitting at the table.

"You ready, Chris?" Nate asked.

Christopher nodded and stood on weak legs, steadying himself with an outstretched hand against the wall. The uniformed officer stepped past Nate and placed his hand on Christopher's shoulder. "Turn around, sir. Put your hands on top of your head, palms facing up. Hold that position and don't move. Do you understand?"

Nate closed the door, walking out of the interview room. He passed by Lieutenant Brown as he entered the CID work pod. He dipped his chin at the lieutenant as he passed him.

"What was on the paper you slid in front of him?" Brown asked, interested in spite of himself.

Nate opened the file and gave Brown the paper, now folded in half and walked away without answering. "Blank. I should have known you had nothing. This is police work, not a poker game, Richards," Brown called after Nate.

"I don't play poker, sir. I'll put my report on your desk," Nate said, continuing to walk away.

Sabrina met him at the desk. "Get him?"

"Got him." They smiled and slapped hands again. "Now the real work begins; time to type, type, type."

"Not yet, you've got a search warrant to serve. Let's do this," Sabrina said.

With a grunt, Nate lifted himself from his desk and followed Sabrina into the elevator.

As they entered the elevator, Officer Johnson was just stepping out. "Heard you guys got another perv," Johnson said, slapping Nate on the shoulder. He looked at Sabrina, who just looked past him.

Nate shrugged and smiled. "Sick....Yeah, we got him. Now we try and fix a little girl, but at least for now this man will be where he belongs." Nate nodded his head toward the interview room where the uniformed officer was just escorting Christopher Simms to the rear of the building.

"We're headed out to execute a search warrant, want to come?" Nate asked.

Behind Johnson, Sabrina rolled her eyes and pantomimed a begging dog.

"Sure," Johnson said excitedly, "that's why I came. I wanted to go along."

"Well, close the door, Sherlock," Sabrina said, indicating the elevator door. "None of us are going anywhere as long as you stand there running your lips."

Johnson laughed and stepped inside the elevator. The doors slid shut behind them.

They rode in silence for a moment before Johnson turned to face Nate. "Any movement on the Franks shooting?" he asked.

Nate sighed, thinking of the new sexual assault case; the time, mandates, and the other half-finished investigations still on his desk. He looked from Johnson to Sabrina, "Nahh, no movement yet, but it's coming along."

Sabrina rolled her eyes again, staring at the back of Johnson's head. "So, how well did you know Franks?" she asked Johnson.

"Huh...I only worked with him on shift a few times, but he was one of us, you know?"

"Yeah, I know." She looked at Johnson this time and then looked away. "I know. We're gonna get this guy. Nobody kills a cop in my town and just walks away from it."

"Freaking yeah!" Johnson practically screeched while pumping his fist.

The elevator doors opened, and they walked out into an almost empty lobby. "The house is vacant, dad's on his way to County and mom's upstairs," Nate said, directing the conversation back to the present case. "We'll see you on site."

"Gotcha," Johnson said, turning and jogging toward his patrol unit, which sat idling about thirty feet outside the front doors.

Hearing Sabrina laughing under her breath, Nate turned toward her. "I don't like that guy," she said.

"Mmmm-hmm," Nate mumbled.

"He may be a good cop," she said, pursing her lips and shaking her head from side to side, "but I just don't like him."

"No? Really? He's not so bad, just young. He does remind me of a guy I knew in boot camp though...always on the D.I.'s leg about something or another."

They got into Nate's Jeep and followed Johnson to the Simms' residence.

CHAPTER SEVENTEEN

LO PARKED THE STOLEN MOVING TRUCK down the street from where the officer sat in his patrol vehicle, apparently doing reports. "Probably just goofing off," Lo said to himself. Checking his watch again, he sent the one-word prepared text message. "GO."

Lo leaned over and kissed the lone female as he exited the cab of the truck. "We'll be back for you."

Wrapping her hand behind his powerful neck, she pulled him to her and returned the kiss with ardent passion. "Today. Tomorrow. I'll be waiting." She pulled herself upright behind the steering wheel and checked her hair and make-up before blowing him a kiss. She looked down at him with pride and determination and shifted the transmission into drive.

"ABYSS," Lo whispered.

"ABYSS," she answered, admiring his broad shoulders and thick neck as he turned and walked away. Lifting her foot from the brake pedal, she eased the truck into traffic.

Just over a block from where the moving truck had sat idling, several white Hondas rounded the corner of South Gull Cove and backed into the cul-de-sac while others blocked entry into the road, parking horizontally across Christopher Street.

With casual grace, belying his underlying excitement, Israel strode from his car to the oversized garage at the point of the cul-de-sac. His two lieutenants trailed, each off to his sides and two steps behind him. A party of three, similarly arranged, emerged from the shadow of the door and met them on the concrete slab driveway.

Jayce Macario, the twenty-something leader of the Southside Locos, himself a veteran of the streets, sauntered out of the garage, stopping just shy of Israel's position. "So," he began, looking down his aquiline nose at the three men in his driveway, "you suggesting we make some kind of deal…. That we come to an understanding 'bout who's running the valley, huh?"

"No." Israel stared, unblinking, with cold eyes into Jayce's face.

"What? Then why you call this meeting for, fool? You crazy or something?"

With blinding speed and no telegraphing of movement, Israel backhanded the taller man across the face, dropping him to one knee. Before Jayce's cohorts could react, Israel's lieutenants pulled sawed-off shotguns from beneath their jackets, chambered a round, and aimed the weapons point blank into their faces, causing them to freeze with their hands near their waists.

Without taking his eyes from Jayce, Israel spoke to the two men who had followed him from the garage. "Unless you all want to end up like Big Dawg, you'd better pull your hands out slow and empty."

"You're crazy, man," Jayce said, looking up at Israel while wiping a rivulet of blood at the corner of his mouth with his knuckle.

Stepping forward, Israel dropped a crushing backhand across his upturned face. "You're not bright, are you?" he asked, stooping over Jayce, who was now flat on his back. "The first time you suggested I might be crazy you got slapped. One might conclude that calling me crazy was not the smart thing to do. You gett'n me?"

Jayce opened his mouth as if to speak, but then seemed to reconsider what he was about to say. "Yeah, I get you. What's this all about?" he asked and struggled to his feet.

Israel turned his back on Jayce, as if he were not paying attention, or at the least, did not consider him a threat.

Jayce's two men locked eyes with their leader, and they nodded almost imperceptibly. Jayce held his breath and launched himself at Israel's back.

In a blur of motion, Israel's two lieutenants stepped forward, crashing the butts of their weapons into the faces of the two men. In a separate vortex of action, Israel spun back toward Jayce and flicked his wrist, sidestepped, and watched as the man collapsed at his feet; a crimson pool spreading from the gash at his throat.

"Well," said Israel, "I wouldn't have respected him if he hadn't tried, would I?" He knelt down and cleaned the blade of his knife on Jayce's shirt. "Pick them up," he said to his lieutenants.

His *seconds* grabbed the two men, jerking them roughly to their feet. With obvious broken noses, the two defeated men held their faces and looked at Israel, unsure of what their future would be.

"Now, as I was about to say," Israel began, "there is no argument...or discussion about whose valley this is. It is mine. Now, you gentlemen can either do things my way or you can die. That is your choice."

The two men looked at each other over bloodied fingers and nodded; only this time it was in acquiescence to Israel.

In the distance, sirens began to wail with increasing intensity as they drew closer.

"Looks like you've got nosey neighbors," Israel said, looking around. "We'll have to take care of that."

Dipping the toe of his shoe into the spreading pool of blood, Israel drew a large "A" with a circle around it and then dragged a slash across it. Staring at the two men, he looked back at the symbol on the ground. They followed the movement of his eyes until their eyes fixed on the bloody symbol.

"Do we understand each other, gentleman?"

"Yes," they groaned.

Turning, Israel locked eyes with two of the drivers waiting near the mouth of the cul-de-sac. With great calm, he walked away, and in uniform fashion, the cars all drove away in separate directions, all driving within the posted speed limit.

***

A few blocks away, the neighborhood officer dropped his clipboard into the passenger seat and answered dispatch's call of a neighborhood disturbance, possible weapons involved. "TV-S1 copy and en route. Code three."

As the patrol unit's overhead lights activated and the vehicle pulled out from the curb, Sheila accelerated as well, putting the moving truck directly into the path of the oncoming patrol car.

The resulting crash was not fatal, but it served the purpose of delaying the nearest police response and snarling traffic.

Israel approached the accident as he headed north on Meridian-Kuna Road, rush-hour traffic having the exact effect he had planned. As he drove, he did not look at the woman with the long brown hair trying to explain to the uniformed officer how she had not seen him or his emergency lights.

Israel Vega passed the scene unnoticed and unconcerned.

CHAPTER EIGHTEEN

"ABYSS. EVERYWHERE WE LOOK THESE DAYS this Abyss gang is showing up, like it was the only gang in the valley," Sabrina said and cursed, betraying her frustration.

Nate looked up from the file on his desk and sighed. "You know," he began, "sometimes this job stinks."

"Yeah, like Monday through Friday and once every five weeks or so over the weekends too," she said wryly.

They both laughed at the reference to having the on-call duty, but their laughter sounded hollow.

"I still haven't found the 'why' of the connection between Franks and that Fuentes kid. The only thing that makes any kind of sense is the gang rivalry killings," Nate said.

Sighing, Sabrina turned her attention back to the file photos on her desk. "Something's got to break sooner or later. Mrs. Fuentes over at the mayor's office is stirring up a stink. She's saying there's no way her son was in a street gang—just the opposite."

"Don't they all say that as soon as somebody gets themselves killed? He was always the best dad, the best son…the ideal mom or daughter."

"Whoa there, Rambo, you're starting to sound a bit like the L.T. Besides, everything about this kid suggests she's right."

"Ouch, that's low," Nate said, throwing a wadded piece of paper at her head.

"We can't go there, Flatbush. We start thinking that some people are of lesser value than others and bad things happen."

Nate sat, looking unfocused somewhere near the far wall. "I know, but sometimes it just seems like—"

"Like what? Like Blacks are stupid or Chinese are only good for doing the wash and planting dynamite? Once you start going down that road, where do you call it good? It's better not to start. Besides, your mom would pinch your ear right off your head if I told her what you'd been thinking."

"Thanks for keeping it to yourself," he said, turning back to face her and chuckling.

"Who said I would?" she asked, smiling. Her desk phone rang, and she turned back to her desk, still laughing.

Nate returned her smile and picked up the stack of files from his own desk. Leaning back in his seat, he opened the top folder and reread the details of the reports, hoping that some new fact would stand out.

"Detective Richards, contact records desk at 4501. Detective Richards, please contact records at 4501," the voice called above the din of CID from the ceiling-mounted speakers.

Nate grabbed the receiver and dialed the numbers for the downstairs office. "Hey Clair, this is Nate," he said after one ring. "What you got?"

"There's a young lady down here. Says she has an appointment with you."

Nate checked his schedule before answering, "I don't have anything on my calendar. Get her name and number and tell her I'll call her back."

Nate could hear Clair speaking to the lady, who would have been standing outside the glass. "Yes, ma'am, Amber Coles. Your number?"

Nate jumped up and yelled into the receiver. "Clair, wait. I'll be right down."

A few minutes later, Nate and Amber were walking along Main Street, speaking in quiet voices. Brushing wisps of hair from her face, Amber smiled at the children playing in the zero-depth pool in the downtown plaza. Then turning serious eyes toward Nate, she said, "I've been worried about you."

"Worried? About me? About what?"

She stared into his face, a concerned look slightly darkening her features. "I've been praying for you, and I'm just not liking the feelings I'm getting. You haven't been coming to prayer meetings anymore, and you've missed the last two Sunday worship services."

"Hey, some of us do have real jobs, you know," he said, a tad sharper than he had intended.

She looked away, ignoring his barb, and they walked for a moment in silence. When she looked up again her eyes were moist. "Nate, you know..." She stopped, collected herself, and started again. "I know. I'm in between jobs now, but Nate, this isn't about me, is it? What's happening to you?" She stepped closer to him. "It's this case, isn't it?"

"This is not the bookstore, Amber. I just can't go to the back room if an unpleasant customer walks in. I don't have that luxury. I don't get to just drop this and pick it up again next semester. It doesn't work like that in the real world." He turned and paced a few steps away, knowing he was being unreasonably harsh, but not sure why.

Heat tendrils rose like spirits from the asphalt as a testimony to the August heat. Traffic moved in slow procession through the downtown lanes as pedestrians darted back and forth across the roadway. Above, in a brilliant blue sky, thick white clouds cast soft gray shadows along the tree-strewn street, offering the only other respite from the heat besides the water where the children played.

After a minute of uncomfortable silence, Nate looked back at Amber. He knew he had hurt her with his words, and he knew she hadn't deserved it. If her countenance had been darkened earlier, now it was clouded over and if the tears were any indication, it was storming. Nate stifled a curse.

"Look," he began and walked back to where she had settled on a bus stop bench, "I'm a jerk. There's nothing wrong with working at the bookstore. It's like I said, I'm a jerk."

She smiled through her tears. "Well, tell me something I don't already know."

He reached toward her, tucking sun-lightened strains of brunette hair behind her ear. "I'm sorry. I know you're going to finish school, and you'll be a fantastic teacher. Just ignore me, okay?"

She searched his eyes.

"You're right, it is this case. It's kicking my butt. One of our own was killed and carved up; a little boy shot down like a dog in the street, and I'm no closer to figuring it out than I was two weeks ago." He turned with vulnerable eyes to look at her. "On top of all that, Brown is riding my butt like stink on poop."

"I don't have the answers you're looking for, but—"

"That's the problem, Amber. Nobody has the answers, but I need to—"

"But," she continued as if he hadn't interrupted her, "I know who does. Have you even stopped to pray about all this, Nate? Have you asked Jesus to help you?"

He looked at her dumbfounded.

"What, you don't believe the Bible anymore?" She turned her shoulders to face him directly, locking his gaze with hers. She wasn't angry, more surprised by his expression. "You forget—oh, what verse is that about putting God first and Him leading you or directing you along the way? You're the pastor's kid, you should know this stuff."

"Proverbs. The verse you're looking for is Proverbs chapter three, verses five and six."

"Yeah, that's it," she said pumping her fist for emphasis.

Smiling at her, he knew she was right, and he would have to tell her. He laughed out loud.

"What?" she asked, the hint of a pout returning to her face.

A smile warmed his and she smiled in return. "You're right," he admitted. "'Trust in the Lord with all your heart and lean not to your own understanding and in all your ways acknowledge Him and He will direct your path.' Proverbs 3:5-6 and you're right about me too. I'd forgotten who I am supposed to be."

He grabbed her hands, pulling her to her feet, and wrapped her in a hug. "Don't give up on me, kid."

She mumbled into his shoulder.

"What?" he asked, loosening his embrace.

"You're smushing my nose," she said, rubbing the offended appendage. They laughed and embraced again, only this time no one got smushed.

"Come on, buy you a coffee," Nate said.

"Library?"

"Where else? Besides, if those girls found out I went anywhere else for coffee, they would have my hide."

"Not a great trade on their part, huh?" She laughed and danced out of his reach as he tried to grab her.

"Funny."

They laughed again and walked back toward Nate's car.

***

Stopped at the crosswalk, Israel Vega watched them as they walked together. Activating the window control, he closed the window, concealing himself behind the heavy tint. He waited at the traffic light and studied them as they crossed in front of his car.

Israel stared at the woman with an appreciation reaching toward lust. He recognized the man and knew him to be a cop. He didn't know who she was, yet. But he would. He stared at the way she moved, admiring her feminine grace, the way her curves moved beneath the soft fabric of her clothing. He liked her smile.

She didn't have long hair, but he decided he could fix that. Yes indeed, he could fix that. They reached the far curb just as the light changed. Israel smiled and drove away.

CHAPTER NINETEEN

"WHAT DO YOU KNOW, he's got all his rounds accounted for," Range Sergeant Jasper said, counting Nate's rounds. Usually it's you detective types that come up short, but it was one of my own this quarter."

Nate laughed and slapped hands with Sabrina. "Score one for the good guys. I think you owe us a six-pack."

"Yeah, yeah, don't be a sore winner," Jasper said, chuckling. "One six-pack of Diet Coke coming up."

"Only the best for the best," Sabrina said, bumping knuckles with Nate.

"So, who was short this time? It was one of those SWAT guys, I bet," Nate said, laughing.

"And you'd be wrong," Jasper said, pulling a six-pack of Diet Coke from the fridge. "It was a patrol guy, Johnson. Surprised me too, he's usually pretty sharp about round count. He's down here shooting all the time. Must have fired off one of his regulation rounds instead of the practice stuff.... It happens."

Nate laughed again. "I don't see why you think we'd lose; we're never down here practicing. Once you give us our duty count—"

"We never take them out of the box," Sabrina finished.

"You guys are all the same. They promote you to a desk, and you leave all your training on the front seat of the patrol car when you get out."

This time they all laughed as Nate and Sabrina continued packing their gear. The rangemaster disappeared inside his small hut and Sabrina turned to face Nate. "What caliber round was it that the coroner determined was the kill shot on Franks?" Sabrina asked, putting her gear into her tactical bag.

"Forty-cal, why," Nate answered, only half listening.

"And Fuentes?"

"Same. Where you going with this? You know something I don't?"

"Nahh, not yet anyway, but I'll let you know when I get it straight in my own mind."

"Come on…a hint?"

She said nothing and he knew it was worthless to continue asking. She would tell him when she was ready or not at all.

"How about some lunch?"

Sabrina didn't answer, but stared off distracted.

"Hey you, Sabrina…what do you think; feel like some lunch?" Nate asked, turning to look his partner full in the face.

"Oh, yeah," she said, focusing on him. "Negatory morning glory, I've got something I've got to check on first. Rain check?"

"Oh sure, it's your turn to pay," Nate said, laughing, but not really amused. Something was up with his partner, and he didn't know what it was. And not knowing bothered him.

He watched as Sabrina loaded her gear and drove away, a cloud of dust billowing in her wake. Wiping the dust-crusted sweat from his face, Nate turned his attention back to packing his gear. Just before getting into his own car, Nate looked up in time just as Sabrina's sedan disappeared in the red haze of sunset and heavy dust that hovered over the road.

***

Back at the station, Sabrina flicked on the light over her desk as she reviewed the lab reports on ballistics and metallurgical findings. Examining the wound signature from both Franks and Fuentes, she scratched her chin and swore under her breath.

"What's up?" Haynes said, coming out of his office. "I thought you and Nate worked the dayshift today. What are you doing here now?" He asked in his usual lazy tone.

"Oh, just checking a hunch. You remember what that was like, don't you?"

"I haven't been off the streets that long. Coffee?" he asked, reaching for a mug on the counter near the coffee pot.

"No, I'm good. How do you drink that stuff? I bet it's been sitting there since morning." She closed the folder on her desk and grabbed another from a second stack.

Haynes smiled and made a showing over pouring the heavy liquid into his coffee-stained cup.

Sabrina shook her head. "Who was the coroner on the Franks' case, you know?"

"I think it was Bossmon. Why? What're you working on?" Haynes walked up behind Sabrina and attempted to read over her shoulder. "Lab reports, coroner's report…what's on your mind girl? Don't you go trying to be no superstar now; you're too close to retirement for that kind of action."

When she didn't answer, Haynes asked, "Where's your partner? He know about this?"

"I'll call him when I know something for sure," she said, standing and closing the folders. "You know how it goes. No need to get everybody excited over nothing."

"Where you headed now?"

"Home. I'm not supposed to be here, remember? Unless you want to pay me O.T." She placed her hands on her lower back and arched backwards, stretching tired muscles.

With a loud moan, Sabrina headed toward the elevator. "See ya'," she said, turning to face Haynes as the elevator doors slid apart.

He waved a hand dismissively at her and smiled into his cup of coffee as she backed into the elevator.

As the door closed, separating her temporarily from his world, Sabrina returned the smile.

Opening the main doors into the night, the still oppressive heat rolled up like a wave to greet her, causing her to pause to enjoy the air conditioning for just a moment longer. Sweat beaded first on her forehead and then on her upper lip before pooling and running in thin streams down the sides of her face.

Crossing the empty parking lot, Sabrina walked absentmindedly, still thinking about what she had discovered in the files. Just as she reached her car, her cell phone rang. Fumbling with the keys, she answered in a still-distracted tone of voice, "Jackson."

"I hope you're on your way home. I'm missing my woman." It was Karl, her husband.

Dropping the files she was carrying onto the passenger seat, she allowed herself a smile. "You are, are you? So what's in it for me?" she responded playfully.

"Now that's the question, isn't it?" He laughed. "What do you say we meet at that Chinese place near the mall you like so much and grab some dinner."

"Dinner, huh?" Her voice carried a playful tease. "What about dessert?"

"Well, after that we can return home for dessert. What d'ya' say? Fifteen minutes?"

She was about to answer when a tone alert sounded from her unit's radio, signaling the transmission of emergency traffic.

The dispatcher's voice was calm, but carried an edge.

"Silent alarm. Two-Eleven in progress at the Reid Diamonds store; 427 South Progress Road. Units to respond?"

Several patrol units responded and advised running silent code; no lights, no sirens. Sabrina realized she was the closest officer to the scene. "Got to go, honey. I'll call you when this is over."

"You be careful, girl," Karl said, concern in his voice. "Let the young guns do the chasing. You just run on home to me."

She smiled as she closed the cell phone and then advised dispatch of her location. "Dispatch, D975. I'm 10-23 at Reid's. I'll be taking position on the south side of the building. Advise approaching units that I'm a plainclothes officer already on scene wearing jeans and a red polo shirt. I'll have my badge around my neck."

"TV 916, 10-23," a voice sounded over her radio.

"Good," Sabrina said under her breath. "Now that the cavalry's here, maybe we can catch these boys with their hands in the cookie jar." *Or in this case*, she thought, *the jewelry display case.*

She made her way around the corner of the building, approaching with slow, careful steps, being sure not to silhouette herself against the street lights. She could see uniformed officers positioning themselves around and behind her car while others made their approach to the building at tactical angles.

Just as officers were taking position on the opposite corner, the rear door burst open and three figures ran out, masks still covering their faces.

"Police! Stop!" Sabrina yelled, pointing her gun at the two subjects nearest to her. "Drop the bag and get on your face. Do it now, dirt bag!"

The first man dropped the dark colored cloth bag and put both hands on top of his head. The second dropped his bag, but as he did, he pulled a gun that was hidden in his waistband and fired two rounds at Sabrina.

Seeing the furtive action, Sabrina dove to her side and rolled, settling on her knees and returning fire. She saw the closest assailant fall as her first two rounds tore into his chest. The second man screamed a primal roar, seeing that his partner was down, and rushed pell-mell at Sabrina. Pulling up a semi-automatic mini-rifle, he began spraying the parking lot with nine-millimeter rounds as he tried to flee.

Continuing to move laterally, Sabrina fired again, this time watching as the round slammed into the man's shoulder. The bullet ripped through him at the joint, dislocating the arm and tearing the weapon from his grasp, sending him into a spin and crashing to the ground. A third assailant ran out the door of the building. The masked man stopped, seeming to study the scene as it stretched out before him. Seeing his partners fall, he dropped the bag he was carrying and disappeared into the shadows around the far side of the building.

Rising up from her crouched position, Sabrina started after the man. Turning to look over her shoulder, she shouted directions to the approaching officers. As she turned back to the direction, the man had fled. A flash of light lit up the night darkness just before her face. The last thing Sabrina saw was the blast of light coming from her right side just as a thunderous explosion rang in her ear. Then everything went black and silent.

CHAPTER TWENTY

NATE STOOD JUST OUTSIDE THE ICU cubicle and watched as tubes ran from the machines beside the bed to the woman lying unconscious in it. Karl turned, saw him, and with a trembling arm, waved him in.

"Hey, look...Karl, I'm sorry, man. I should've been with her. I should've had her back."

Karl pulled Nate into a tight embrace, wrapping his large muscular arms around his neck as he did. "It's gonna be all right. She'll be okay. It's okay," Karl said, comforting Nate in his own grief. "I called Reverend Richards. Your dad...he's on his way down. All we can do now is pray," he finished, his voice weak with fatigue and worry.

They both turned back toward the bed and looked at the swollen head and face, hardly recognizable beneath the gauze and bandages. A tube extending through swollen lips was taped to the corner of her mouth and pulled her face slightly to one side while the respirator maintained a constant flow of oxygen. Sabrina lay motionless on the bed.

They stood in relative silence; the only sounds were the electronic beep-beep-beep of the monitor and the whir of air through the ventilator as it first filled then emptied the BVM bag.

One of the ICU nurses came in. "Mr. Jackson?" she began, her accent revealing her southern roots. "I'm sorry, but y'all gonna have to wait outside. It's time for us to do our check of Mrs. Jackson's dressings, and it's best if you're not here for that." Seeing the set of Karl's jaw, she looked to Nate for support.

When Karl did not respond, she tried again, "Mr. Jackson?"

"Come on Karl, let's let the woman do her job. They're doing everything they can. Sabrina's a fighter. She'll get through this just fine." Even as he said it, Nate wondered if he believed it was true. *God, please let it be true.*

Karl allowed himself to be led back to the ICU waiting room. He looked up, his eyes unfocused. "I haven't even told the kids. I still got to call them."

Nate and Karl walked past the uniformed officer posted on duty just outside the main door leading into the ICU. The younger man, Sabrina's guard, looked at Nate first and then to Karl. With a tilt of his chin, he acknowledged their grief while simultaneously reassuring them that he was there standing by.

Nate took note of the officer's presence with a shallow dip of his chin and then turned his attention back to Karl, escorting him to the secluded waiting area. "Let me take care of telling the kids. You just sit here; I'll do it." Nate looked past Karl out the window and took note of what had to be many thousands of lights across the city. He found himself wondering in how many of those houses where the lights shone warm, were people enduring bad news tonight? How many had gotten news that a loved one had been hurt and wouldn't be coming back home?

Sobered by the darkness of his thoughts, Nate stood, turned his back to the window, leaned against the glass, and began to pray. He prayed silently at first, but as the pain grew in his chest, he reached out to Karl and they both began to pray out loud, asking God to intervene on Sabrina's behalf. They prayed for themselves as well, that they too would endure.

After a while, all Nate could say was, "Jesus." He repeated the name over and over, taking comfort in the sound of it. While sitting beside him, Karl did the same.

The waiting room door opened, and Nate's mother and father came in, Amber right behind them. Reverend Richards went straight to Karl and grabbed the big man in a bear hug. His mother stood beside them with her hand on Karl's shoulder. Amber went to Nate.

"You all right?" she asked.

"I don't know." He dropped his face and looked away, his voice barely above a whisper.

She pulled him against her and held him against her breast. They stood that way for some time before either of them spoke. Finally, Nate looked at her with tears brimming in his eyes. "It's my fault, Amber. It's my fault. I knew she was on to something; I should have gone with her." He spoke softly, guilt weakening his voice, "But I—"

"No, no. Nate, from what I heard it was a hot call. It could've been anybody. You had no idea she would be the one to take that call."

"But she's my partner," he said, slamming his palms against the wall. He turned away from Amber, not able to look at her.

Amber stepped back, but held on to his hand. "You're right," she said, "You're a lousy partner. Sabrina's in there fighting for her life, and you're out here feeling sorry for yourself instead of praying for her."

Nate looked up. "What?"

"You heard me. This is not the time for feeling bad. Your partner got shot, and the guys who did it are all dead, from what I heard. That means two...no, three souls went into judgment tonight, and one more may, unless we do what we can to keep her on this side of the grave."

"You're the strangest counselor I have ever heard of," Nate said, sobering. He looked over her shoulder and saw his parents in deep and intense prayer with Karl. "You're right, though. Come on, let's join them."

They walked together arm-in-arm and each placed one hand on Reverend Richards' shoulder and the other on Karl's. Bowing their heads, they joined them in prayer.

As they finished their prayers, the same nurse entered the waiting area and addressed Karl. "We just finished changing the dressings, but Dr. Allison is in with her right now. He'll come out and speak with you as soon as he's finished. Okay?"

Karl did not speak but nodded his head, not trusting his voice.

Joyce, a young redheaded nurse from the South walked over and laid a hand on Karl's shoulder. "I saw you folks out here praying, and I just wanted to let you know I'm a praying woman too, and I'm praying for your wife, sir. Now, Dr. Allison, he's a good Christian man as well as a good doctor, so don't you worry none. You keep praying, and I bet you in no time flat we'll begin to see a real difference in your wife's condition." She fumbled with her hands as if she thought she'd said too much, and then abruptly turned and walked back into the ICU.

About fifteen minutes later, a tall white man, about 60 years old, came into the waiting area. He wore green hospital scrubs and a white lab coat. He moved to Karl's side and extended his hand. "Mr. Jackson, I'm Dr. Allison."

Dr. Allison had gray-flecked hair and kind blue-gray eyes. Taking the seat next to Karl, he spoke softly but firmly as he looked over the top of his bifocal glasses. "I won't lie to you, Karl; we're not out of the woods yet. The bullet creased her skull but did not penetrate it. There's massive fracturing, as you might suspect, and severe swelling of the brain—and therein lies the danger. We won't know for sure if there is any permanent damage until we can get that swelling down and wake her up."

Karl cut his eyes up at the doctor as if to ask what it was he was trying to say.

Dr. Allison noticed the unasked question and headed off. "Yeah, I'm sorry, I thought they told you. She's sedated now...heavily. We didn't want her waking up and hurting herself." He shifted in his seat and allowed a moment for Karl to understand what he said.

After the pause, he continued. "Like I said, we have her heavily sedated now, but that's just to make sure she doesn't hurt herself tossing and turning. We want to keep her as still as possible until that swelling is under control."

"Our biggest fear right now is fever and infection. We need to watch her temp and make sure it doesn't rise. The nurses will be with her all night just in case it does. Do you have any questions, Karl?" he asked as he stood.

"I'm sure I do, but I can't think of one right now."

Both men chuckled. "I'll make my rounds tomorrow morning by ten, and I'll be sure to make some time to sit down and chat with you, all right?"

Karl stood and shook the doctor's hand. "Thanks, Doc, and God bless you."

"Oh, He does," Dr. Allison said, smiling.

As the doctor walked through the door, Karl called after him. "Say, Doc, for now, what do we say about her condition? I mean, what should I tell the children?"

The doctor turned and reentered the waiting room. "I'm sorry I didn't say…we've upgraded her condition from serious to stable. All we can do for now is pray and watch that fever. Goodnight." He smiled again, turned, and let the doors swing shut behind him with a soft swoosh and a click.

"Goodnight," an echo of voices answered him.

At that moment the doors leading from the main hall swung open and Officer Johnson and a new partner, Officer Fletcher, walked in. "How is she?" he asked breathlessly. His eyes were stern, as if some decision had been hard fought and well met.

Nate met him and led him away from the group. "She's, ah, she's still unconscious, but the doctor said she's stable now."

Johnson exhaled in obvious relief and sagged against the wall. "I was there…I got the fool that shot her, but it was—I was too late." Johnson said, rubbing his eyes. "I should have been quicker."

The second officer, the escort, walked up beside Johnson and tapped his wrist, looking nervous. Johnson smiled at the man. Turning his attention back to Nate he said, "Fletcher here, is my escort. I'm supposed to be on my way to the hotel for debrief, but I talked him in to stopping by first."

Nate gripped Johnson's shoulder and squeezed it. For the first time, Nate thought he saw something in the man that he could like. "It's okay," he said. "Come on, I'll introduce you to the family."

CHAPTER TWENTY- ONE

ISRAEL VEGA WALKED INTO THE BOOKSTORE and searched for the exotic beauty he'd been watching for the past two days. After pretending to struggle between two titles, he feigned a puzzled expression and turned to the sales clerk.

Amber smiled at Israel as she approached him. "Can I help you find something?" she asked.

"Ah, yeah, I was hoping to find something on Native American heritage and the Christian faith," Israel said with a shy, warm smile. "I'm trying to learn what impact the Christian faith has had on my people."

"You're native? Me too—well kind of," Amber answered, warming up to him. "My grandfather was full Paiute Northern Tribe."

"Apache."

"I thought so. I thought I saw a warrior's bearing in the way you held yourself."

Israel smiled again as she led him to the multicultural selections in the bookstore. He studied her in motion and took special note of the curve of her lip as she smiled. The only thing lacking, he thought, was the long hair.

She turned to him. "You a Believer?"

The question caught him off guard. "A what?"

"I just thought maybe you were a Christian and wanted to do some research or something on how to better minister to your people." Her expression changed, curiosity replacing familiarity.

"No. Christianity killed my people," he said curtly.

Amber took an involuntary step back.

"Sorry," he apologized.

"No, it's okay. That's why we're here...to sell books and provide information. If I can be any help, I'll be at the reception desk." She started to turn.

"I've offended you," Israel said in a soft voice.

"No, no," Amber answered hurriedly, pushing loose strands of hair from her face. "You surprised me is all."

"Really?" He stared into her eyes.

Amber could feel her neck growing warm.

He smiled. "Maybe you could explain this Christianity to me over coffee."

She glanced around.

"We wouldn't even have to leave the bookstore. You take your break, and I'll buy the coffee. We can sit right over there and talk," he finished, pointing in the direction of the coffee and baked goods island in the middle of the store.

"I don't know..."

"Who knows, maybe you'll convert me," he said, smiling disarmingly at her. He pretended to read her nametag. "Come on, Amber, what harm could it do?"

She raised an eyebrow and tilted her head, startled at hearing her name until he smiled and pointed at her nametag. She returned the smile and nodded her head. "Get a table; I'll meet you in five."

Sitting with her back to the door, Amber adjusted in her seat, warming to the conversation. Leaning forward and opening her mouth to answer a question posed to her, she stopped when Israel looked up abruptly, his attention drawn to the front of the store. "What is it?" she asked instead, seeing that he was distracted.

"I just remembered something. I have to be somewhere."

He smiled at her, and Amber could feel herself blushing again under the intensity of his gaze. He stood, suddenly serious.

Amber watched as Israel looked toward the door again, and then turned and walked away, disappearing around a bookshelf.

Amber dropped her gaze, focusing on nothing, lost in thought about the peculiar young man. She jumped when she felt a hand settle on her shoulder.

"Whoa, princess, it's just me," Nate said, taking the recently vacated seat. I thought you were waiting for me. You did remember I was dropping by, right?"

Turning and looking up, smiling, she said, "Sure, what took you so long?"

He laughed and waved the waiter over. "Don't tell the girls at the Library, but I'm gonna have coffee."

She smiled and twisted a pretend key between her lips. She stared down at her mug of coffee, but did not touch it. Five unopened Splenda packets lay on the table near the painted nails of her curled fingers.

"Hey, earth to Amber. Where are you?"

"Huh, I just had the weirdest customer. He came in here looking for books on Native American culture and how Christianity had impacted it."

Nate craned his neck, looking around the store.

She touched his hand. "He's gone. Those were his books there," she said, pointing to the two volumes on the table near Nate's elbow.

"He didn't do anything inappropriate, but it just felt kind of, you know, funny." She was twirling her finger in her hair absentmindedly. "He said he wanted me to tell him about Christianity then all of a sudden he just stood up, said he had somewhere to be, and without another word, turned and walked away." She gazed at him, puzzled. "Weird, huh?"

"Yeah, too weird, with everything else that's been going on. Did mister fantastic have a name?" Nate pulled a notepad from his chest pocket, pen in hand—full cop mode.

"Nope. Knew mine though." She finally picked up the sweeteners and began opening them. "Said he read it on my nametag, but..."

"But what?" Nate asked, watching her empty the packets into her mug.

"Like I said...weird. I kind of got the feeling that he was waiting for me."

"Well," Nate began, scanning the bookstore again, "I can understand why any man would want to get to know you."

"Nate? Are you flirting with me?" she asked, taking a sip of coffee and smiling.

"Right." Nate evaded answering her. Once again, thoughts of what could be between them raced through his mind. And once again, he forced them into retreat.

"Come on," she said, "look who's wandering now. He's gone. I'll probably never see him again."

They settled in companionable conversation about Sabrina and her condition. Amber told him about the women from church helping Karl with food and getting the children to and from their various appointments. It was stopgap at best; not a real solution and would need to be adjusted for the long term.

***

From just outside the bookstore, Israel watched Nate and Amber through the window, and with purposeful action, put his dark glasses back on. As he studied them, his demeanor changed into the more familiar persona of the alpha male. People instinctively walked around him, granting him more than the usual personal space. No one greeted him or dared make eye contact with him. As mothers passed, they held their children's hands a little tighter, and men placed protective arms around their female counterparts.

As he stared, he saw Amber touch Nate's hand, and he noted that they laughed together in easy familiarity. He watched as her face grew concerned. Nate leaned forward, spoke, and the curve of her shoulders relaxed. He noticed the way Nate gazed at her, and this made him angry.

He licked his lips. The wanting grew stronger, more insistent, and demanded to be satisfied. He inhaled knowing that to gain his prize it would require patience. Like a predator, he would wait; he would stalk her; and he would take her when he was ready—in a place he chose. *When I pounce, your police detective boyfriend will be powerless to stop me. I am Chaos. I am Abyss.*

CHAPTER TWENTY- TWO

"RICHARDS!" BROWN'S VOICE BOOMED over the CID cubicles. "Richards! Where is he?" Brown demanded of no one in particular.

The combination of men and women busy at their desks barely took note of his tirade as Brown stomped his way through the geometrically ordered workstations.

Brown rounded the corner in a huff, exhaled, and came face to face with Nate's unoccupied desk. The desktop was cluttered, buried beneath several files and papers; the phone's message light flashing red. Adjacent to Nate's desk sat Sabrina's, which was just as she'd left it the night of the shooting.

Compared to Nate's, Sabrina's desk was well ordered, although she also had left files and papers atop her workspace. Brown began moving files and perusing papers, a scowl darkening his already ruddy face.

"Can I help you?" Nate said, coming up behind him, his voice tired and edged with temper.

Snapping his head up, Brown spun to face him. "I, ah," he began stuttering. "I, ah…was looking for that report on the L&L…the little girl at the middle school." He tried to regain his bluster.

Nate brushed past him and began closing folders on his desk and checking the papers Brown had been looking at. After a moment of tension-filled silence, he turned and looked at Brown. "The report has been filed. The dad's in jail. The girl's in foster care, and the mom has entered a voluntary agreement with CPS for follow-up counseling. Charges for fail to protect on the mom have been routed to the P.A. for warrant."

Nate sat at his desk, leaving Brown standing with a self-conscious expression on his face, like a child caught sneaking a treat. Nate stacked his papers without looking up and added, "And sir, a hard copy of the report is in your inbox."

Brown rubbed his face, cupping his jaw in his palm before turning to leave. "Good. I'll review the report for errors and get it back to you."

Nate still hadn't looked at Brown, but as the lieutenant turned to leave, he called after him. "Sir?"

Brown stopped, looking back over his shoulder.

"Sabrina, she's still in a coma. Her condition is stable; the swelling on her brain is down." He paused. "I just thought you might want to know."

"Ahhh…thanks," Brown said. "Yes—yes, I did want to know." Brown turned to face Nate. His voice uncharacteristically soft, he said, "Look, Richards, it's no secret I don't like you, but hear me on this: Whether it's Franks, Sabrina, or your lousy butt laid up in a hospital bed because some punk tried to kill you, I have a problem with it. I will do everything in my power to make sure the guy who hurts one of us either goes to jail or to Hell, whichever. I don't care. You understand me?"

Nate didn't answer at first. Then he raised his head and met the lieutenant's gaze. After a moment, he stood and extended his hand. "I understand you, sir."

After a brief shake, Brown turned and left. Nate settled behind his desk while watching Brown's back recede into the space of the room.

Turning his attention back to the piles of papers and folders on his desk, Nate dropped his face into his palms. Hiding his face in his hands, Nate slumped in his seat. With a deep sigh, his shoulders drooped and his spine curved as he collapsed onto his desk in resignation.

The desk phone rang. Nate rolled his head to the side and watched as the red light blinked in chorus with the ring tone. He turned his face away, deciding to ignore the phone. After a while, the ringing ceased but the voicemail light continued on, a steady amber bubble glowing against the dark plastic surface of the phone.

Pushing the stack of papers aside, Nate stood abruptly and headed for the door. As he grabbed the door handle, a voice sounded from behind him.

"Nate, Nate, hold up," Mac called, running to catch up. Though three years his junior, Mac was graying already, which when combined with his soft hazel eyes, made him look older and more mature.

Nate turned to the younger officer chasing after him. "What? What do you want?"

Undaunted, Mac smiled and cupped him on the shoulder. "Hey, I'm sorry about Sabrina. How is she doing?"

Nate swallowed and dropped his eyes before answering. "Still in a coma."

"Yeah. Hey, the reason I stopped you, though, is I got those reports she asked me for. Thought you might want them. She acted like they might be something." He handed Nate a large manila envelope fastened at one end with a brass clasp.

Nate took the packet from Mac and looked at it in his hand. Puzzled, he glanced from the envelope to Mac and back to the envelope. "Sorry 'bout that, I didn't mean to blow up at you—"

"Forget about it. I saw Brown leaving your cubicle. That's enough to set anybody off." Mac smiled. "Going to see Sabrina?"

Nate hadn't known where he was going, but knew he had to leave. "Yeah, I just need to see her." He looked past Mac, his focus drifting.

Silence hung uncomfortably between the two men, and after a long while, Mac turned and walked away, leaving Nate standing alone; the door handle still in his hand.

Nate stared from Mac's back to the packet in his hand to the opened folders and files lying atop Sabrina's desk. He looked back at Mac and tossed the envelope unopened onto Sabrina's desk, turned, and walked out.

CHAPTER TWENTY- THREE

NATE DROVE MINDLESSLY through the eastbound traffic on Interstate 84. The twin towers of Saint Alphonsus Regional Hospital and Trauma Center crested the horizon as he maneuvered his Jeep onto the City Center connector heading toward downtown. Traffic began to thin as some of the vehicles exited at the Curtis Road off-ramp near the hospital. Nate was not one of them.

A few minutes later, fighting tears of frustration and doubt, Nate pulled into Ann Morrison Park in downtown Treasure Valley. With the air conditioning working, he sat undecided as to whether or not to get out. He sat and watched the ducks floating lazily across the sun-speckled surface of the pond.

Nate got out of his vehicle and walked along the path beside the river. Dappled shadows played across his face as sunlight broke through the tree canopy overhead. Nate sauntered the meandering path of the Greenbelt lost in his thoughts. The sounds of children playing and a diverse mix of music, from rock to rap to classic strings, floated between the trees, carried on the warm summer breeze. But all of this still did not penetrate the fog inside Nate's mind.

Propelled by the cacophony of noises in his head, Nate wandered the trail. Eventually he found himself leaning against a large boulder, a monument for slain airline attendant, Lynn

Henneman, who had been found raped and murdered on this very same Greenbelt. The stone sat like a sentinel overlooking a bend in the Boise River. The university's campus sprawled out for several hundred acres in every direction behind him.

The memory of the case still haunted Nate. The image of the young lady found slain after visiting the Treasure Valley merely as a stopover. The nonsensical reason for assault had cost him, had almost broken him. And now, the craziness, the evil, was starting all over again. Nate turned tear-filled eyes to the monument and wondered how many more people like Lynn would have to suffer before all the evil was made to end.

"Why?" Nate shouted to the azure vault above him. Lowering his eyes, he could see on the ground evidence of illegal drug activity and in the distance, a number of streetwalkers, some he had arrested for prostitution. He repeated his question, now elevated into a demand, "Why?!"

Trailing his hand along the surface of the stone, Nate stopped when his finger crossed the face carved into the monument. He knelt and read the inscription, "In Memory of Lynn Henneman. Her loving nature lives in eternal time. 'All things have a reason at a point in time we return whence we came.' Lynn."

With tears streaking his stoic features, Nate stood and pressed his back against the stone before sliding down into a sitting position. With face in hands, he dropped his head between his knees and cried angry tears.

After several minutes, Nate stood and looked again at the vaulted ceiling of the cloudless sky. *"Johnson was right,"* he said in a derisive tone. "Some people don't deserve Your love—Your protection. They're just not human." Finishing his tirade and feeling spent, he slapped his thighs, knocking dirt and grass from his pants. Sighing deeply, he started back along the trail toward the parking lot.

Again, walking in silence, Nate muttered contritely under his breath, "Okay, maybe I was wrong, but You have to admit that this doesn't make any sense. Good people dying...crooks and gangsters getting richer without anything ever happening to them." He stopped, ran his hand over his face, spun in place, and raised his face to the sky again. "I just don't get it. Okay?" He lowered his head and shook it. "I just don't get it."

"You okay, mister?" said a small child sitting on the edge of a stone picnic table. "You don't look so good."

Nate froze, turned toward the little girl, and wondered how many other people had witnessed his lapse of control and reported on the crazy man talking to himself on the Greenbelt.

"No, I mean—yeah. I was just practicing for a part in a play...sorta kinda. Know what I mean?" he stammered, wincing at the lie.

The child nodded and licked the melting ice cream as it ran from the cone clutched in her chubby fist. Fighting to catch each drip as it ran down the length of her, she lapped at her arm before it dripped from her elbow. "Yeah...I do. I do that sometimes too. My mommy says I just haveta practice learning my lines."

"Right," Nate said, turning toward his car on the far side of the park. "See ya' later. Bye now." He waved as he walked away.

"Nate." Amber called to him from the cement path. "Hey, Nate, hold up." She ran to catch up with him.

Nate turned and waved, feeling like he'd been followed.

"What are you doing on the Greenbelt in the middle of the day? Looks like somebody's playing hooky from work," she teased.

"No, I was just taking my break. I do get lunch, you know."

"Relax. I'm not going to tell the good lieutenant. Besides you're the police, remember?" She laughed again, wiping a line of sweat from her brow.

He forced a smile. "What's got you out here? Shouldn't you be at the bookstore?"

She looked at him without answering, and instead spread her arms to the side emphasizing her sweaty appearance. Taking a deep breath, she leaned forward, rested her hands on her knees, and smiled up at him.

Nate looked away.

"It's Tuesday. You know I don't have to be in until four." She wiped more sweat from her face. "Anyway, like you don't know I run the Greenbelt all the time. So you gonna tell me why you're out here?"

He looked back at her and then dropped his gaze. "Amber, there are some things that just don't—it feels like God's lost control of this whole mess." He turned his back, unwilling to see the disappointment he knew would be painted on her face.

She closed the distance between them, laying her hand on his shoulder. "You know better than that," she said softly.

"Do I?"

"Yes, you do." She leaned her head against his shoulder. "Sometimes things get dark, like now. But that doesn't mean the Lord's not still our shepherd."

"That sounds good, but at moments like these—at moments like these, it seems so...so cliché."

She pulled him around so she could face him. "Do you really believe that? Have you given up on all you once held true?" Her brown eyes locked with his, forcing him to hear her.

He dropped his gaze. "I don't—I don't know—," he began.

She grabbed his chin, forcing his eyes to meet hers. "You don't know what? You think your father has been lying to you his entire life? Or that your mother is insane, telling you to believe in and trust in a God that doesn't exist? Which is it, Nate?" She released him and brushed wet strands of hair from her face with a quick swipe of her hand.

She inhaled deeply, resting her hands on her hips. "So you don't believe that there's a real devil who's trying to destroy your soul and take you to Hell? What? What, Nate? What exactly is it that you don't believe?"

Nate stared at her slacked-jawed. "I ah, I ah...well." He paused. "I'll tell you what I do believe, that you could preach my dad right off his pulpit!" He grinned.

She smiled, losing some of her ire. "Well, anyway, what are you going to do?"

He smiled back at her and leaned his forehead against hers. "I don't know. I really don't, but I won't be giving up my faith anytime soon." He sighed. "It's just that things are different for me, now. Harder."

She nodded against him. They rubbed foreheads. "I won't give up on you, Nathan Richards."

"You'd better not. Right now you're the best thing I got going."

"Come on. Let's get something to drink. I hear the Orange Julius here is pretty good."

"I know," he said, turning and grabbing her hand. "My treat?"

"Well, I don't have any pockets," she said, gesturing to the black running shorts and pink tank top she was wearing.

He laughed and headed for his car. "Let's get that drink and then check on Sabrina. That's where I was supposed to be heading when I wound up here." He waved absently, indicating the park in general.

She squeezed his hand, smiled mischievously, and took off at a trot toward the drink cart.

He watched her run, appreciating her athletic grace; he laughed out loud and took off after her. Pulling on the wet shirt where she rested her sweaty forehead against his shoulder, he laughed again, thinking he would need to change his shirt before heading back to the office.

CHAPTER TWENTY- FOUR

NATE AND AMBER STOOD IN SILENCE, hands clasped, as the crash cart sped past them and into Sabrina's room. Alarms blared. Lights flickered and flashed. They watched as Karl was escorted past them out of the alcove. An ICU nurse snatched the curtain closed behind him.

The steady, unvarying tone sounded from the heart monitor, a clear declaration of the emergency on the other side of the drape. The uniformed officer, one of the newer officers, looked at Nate, hoping for some instruction on what to do.

From the overhead speakers, an urgent voice announced the crisis, "Code blue, bed seventeen. I repeat, code blue, bed seventeen. Dr. Allison, report to the ICU, stat." All around them, the ICU staff began shifting into emergency mode.

Nate looked at Sabrina's husband and wondered what was going through his mind. Wondered what was going on behind the curtain. Karl's face was blank, his eyes vacant.

"Karl," the young redheaded nurse prompted. "Mr. Jackson, please follow me to the waiting room. We'll call you as soon as we know something." She paused. "Mr. Jackson?"

Nate walked over to Karl and gently grasped his upper arm. "Come on, man. I got you."

Amber joined them from the opposite side and slipped her arm around Karl's waist. "Come on, Karl. Let's go."

As they walked through the door, a harried Doctor Allison burst through the double doors and slipped his glasses on his nose. "What's going on?"

Nate stopped and turned, listening to the frenzied movement of the frenetic energy that he could best describe as organized chaos.

"Status," Dr. Allison barked.

"Grand mal seizure followed by cardiac arrest—"

The double doors swung shut with a soft click just as Nate passed the threshold and the stream of information ceased. Nate turned back toward Karl and Amber, now seated by the window and speaking in soft voices.

"...I was just sitting with her, reading some scripture to her. She loves the Psalms, you know. And she began to shake, and then the alarms went off and the nurses came running in." He lowered his face into his hands as his voice faded, swallowed by sobs. His shoulders quaked.

Nate stood over them, hoping for the right words to come. Nothing did. He looked at Amber, their eyes locking.

Tears brimming in her eyes as understanding washed over her; she began to shake her head from side to side.

Nate's spine stiffened. Turning his face away, breaking the connection, he stormed out without speaking.

Amber watched in sorrow-filled silence as Nate's retreating back, stiff shoulders, and clipped stride disappeared through the doors.

Nate felt like a steel band had been strapped around his chest, his breath coming in short, harsh pulls. Unwilling to wait for the elevator, he turned to the stairs, walking the five flights instead.

Reaching the back parking lot, he leaned hard against the hot brick surface of the hospital just outside the ER. Forcing himself to slow his breathing, Nate turned his face toward the sun.

Breathe, just breathe. Just breathe, Nate. One thing at a time. He started as the electronic doors slid open behind him. He stood and tried to compose himself.

"Hey, I thought that was you," Johnson said, walking over to him. "Just brought in a DUI blood draw. Not even my collar, just transporting for Collins," he said, indicating the ER with a tilt of his head. "Right place at the wrong time, know what I mean?"

"Yeah, wrong place wrong time," Nate managed in response.

"So what brings you down? Checking on Sabrina? Anyway, got anything new on the shootings?"

Johnson continued talking, either oblivious to or choosing to ignore Nate's discomfiture, a small favor for which Nate was grateful.

Johnson continued, "I spoke with Harding in Narcotics about that new mystery gang on the streets. Looks like they go by the name Abyss."

Johnson pulled a notepad from his uniform's breast pocket. After flipping a few pages, he appeared to be reading. "All he knows so far is that their leader is new to the area, but he's well connected."

Johnson laughed. "Whew, these guys do it all: drugs, prostitution, arms dealing. There's nothing they're not into. Word is they are responsible for the hit on Big Dawg and his boys as well as the latest hit on the South-Siders."

Johnson prattled on while Nate's mind locked onto and began to run with one word, Abyss. This one word, this one concept and everything it stands for could possibly be behind all that was going wrong in his life.

Abyss. If this Abyss, he reasoned, was what was causing him so much trouble, he figured it was time to return the favor.

"Bring him in," Nate said in a neutral voice.

***

The patrol officer guided the handcuffed teen into the interview room and sat him, still cuffed, in the single hard plastic chair. Nate watched the youth through the one-way glass situated about four feet off the floor in the small six-by-six concrete room.

"What do you want me to do with him?" the younger patrolman asked, not looking much older than the young man he'd just secured in the interview/interrogation room.

"Nothing." Nate took a sip of his coffee. "Let him sit." Nate settled, backing away from the knife of light coming in through the opened door.

"Well, if you don't mind, I'm gonna grab seven; I haven't eaten since the beginning of shift."

"What time you going, forty-two? I want to be finished with him before you go off shift," Nate said with a smile in his voice.

"Thanks," the younger man said sarcastically. "Don't do me no favors. Back in about thirty."

Nate smirked and took another sip of coffee. "No worries, he'll still be here."

The patrolman tipped his fingers as if saluting and backed out into the foyer, leaving Nate sitting on the edge of an old wooden desk, which rocked back and forth beneath his shifting weight.

"Now, let's see what you're made of, Mr. Abyss," Nate said into the relative darkness of the observation room. Nate's brows creased in concentration as he leaned forward, studying the figure on the other side of the darkened glass.

Frightened eyes looked back at him—frightened, but edged with anger. Nate knew the young man's frantic searching of the room was an attempt to locate the camera.

Nate slammed his palm against the window, eliciting a startled jump from the youth, and smiled upon receiving the desired reaction. Nate left his hand there, knowing the youth could see his palm fixed in space, like the finger of God writing on the wall of King Belshazzar's banquet hall in the book of Daniel.

Slowly, Nate curled his fingers back, leaving the index finger as the lone symbol on the glass. He withdrew his hand with a jerk. The dark glass once again a mirror reflecting the image of the young man staring back at himself bound and scared.

Again, Nate sat back and drank from his mug of coffee, taking slow, measured sips and studying the young man through the glass. He opened the file he had with him and began to read the report the patrol officer had left with him. *Burglary.*

As Nate read the probable cause block, the portion of the report describing the legal reasons for arresting the youth, he had to smile. He compared it to the two other reports on the same youth, both burglaries as well. In each case, the youth had stolen high-end electronics and had been caught attempting to return the stolen property for a cash refund.

"How many times didn't you get caught you little punk?" Nate muttered to himself, savoring the feelings of power and satisfaction at having the youth at a disadvantage.

Nate slammed the folders on the desktop and stood abruptly. "Time to go in," he said to himself like a fighter waiting for the first bell, adrenaline sharpening his senses. He reached for the door and bumped into Mac who was just coming in.

"Hey, there you are. I was looking for you. I heard Stephens brought in one of those Abyss bangers. You going in? I'll observe."

Nate felt a very real sense of disappointment settle over him and wondered at it. Was he put off because Mac had broken his stream of thought or because Mac would be observing him, thus holding him accountable? It bothered him that he did not know the answer.

"Oh, good," Nate said. "The file's on the desk. I don't care about the burg, but I'm going to pump him about the gang. We need to know something about who these guys are."

"Copy that. I got your back."

Nate closed the door behind him and leaned against it, momentarily needing its support. He closed his eyes. "What am I doing, Lord?" he whispered in prayer. "I was going in there and hoping that kid would give me a reason to beat the living snot out of him. Help me. I think I'm losing it." *Help me.* He closed his eyes tight and, taking a deep breath, prepared himself to do the interview.

Nate opened the door and watched as the child recoiled from him. He looked at his watch and noted the kid had been sitting in the cuffs for over a half-hour since his arrest. He walked toward the teen and put his hand on his shoulder. "What's your name, son?"

The cockiness returned. "Yo—"

Nate walked around in front of the youth, making direct eye contact. "If the next words out of your mouth have anything to do with my mother's heritage or sexual practices, I'm going to take those cuffs off you and see if you're half the man you pretend to be."

The kid's throat bobbed as he swallowed.

Nate walked back behind the kid again and pulled him to his feet. Pulling a handcuff key from his pocket, Nate removed the cuffs and put them in his rear pants pocket.

Nate walked back around in front of the youth and pushed him down into the chair. He fell with a thump, causing the chair to slide backwards a few inches. "What's your name?"

"Yo," the teen began, but stopped when he saw Nate's brow arch. "No, no, they call me Yo-yo. Don't hit me, man."

Nate stepped backwards, giving the kid some space. "So Mr. Yo-yo, what does your momma call you?"

"Ain't got no momma. Not since she got locked up. Anyway, I ain't claiming no ho as my momma."

"Where's your daddy, locked up too?" Nate asked, not to be rude, but because it was the most probable answer.

"Yeah, he's in California, San Quentin, I think. Killed a dude. Why you asking me all this stuff anyway? What's it got to do with me ripping off Fred Meyer's? It's not like they can't afford it." Yo-yo sat up then slouched in his seat, kicking his legs straight out in front of him.

"You still haven't answered my question, have you?"

"Arthur. My momma use' ta call me Arthur, but my real family calls me Yo-yo."

Nate leaned back against the glass and crossed his arms in front of his chest. He realized that Arthur was watching him, noting his muscle tone, and undoubtedly judging the strength of his arms. *Sizing me up.* Nate smiled.

"Your real family, huh?"

"What's it to ya?" The teen said putting up a front.

"Your real family, huh? Yeah…your real family is going to let you go to prison for shooting a cop." Nate stepped forward and placed his foot on the chair between the teen's legs, stepping on the slack in the crotch of the baggy jeans.

"Hey, I ain't got nothing to do with no cop getting shot." Arthur sat up, leaning forward now; the fear returning to his eyes.

Nate shoved the chair with his foot, sending it and Arthur crashing backward into the far wall. "You know what the sad part about this is, Arthur? In the big picture, you don't even matter. That's why they let you get caught, and you're the one down here in cuffs."

"Wait—"

"Shut up! I'm doing the talking now. You should be used to this, doing what you're told. Like a zombie without a brain. Just do what you're told. Don't think. Don't ask why. Just do it. Just like the sad little puppy you are. Now you're going to prison— murder one." Nate turned to leave the room.

Arthur jumped to his feet. "No, wait, man."

Nate turned back and leveled his gaze at Arthur. "How old are you, son—fourteen? fifteen?"

He swallowed. "Fifteen."

Nate shook his head. "Fifteen years old. That's too bad, son. That's too bad." He walked out, closing the door behind him.

Arthur followed Nate to the door and tried to open it.

It was locked.

Arthur spun around like an animal suddenly trapped and studied the room, taking into account the hard plastic chair and the contrast of its drab, faded green against the dull, beige paint of the walls. Pressing his back against the door and hiding his face in his hands, Arthur slid down, wrapped his knees in the crook of his arms, and covered his face.

Nate slipped back into the observation room and sat across from Mac. "What do you think?" he asked, sinking into his seat.

"He'll break. Look at him, he's already about to pee his pants."

Again, Nate narrowed his eyes and stared at the young man on the other side of the glass. "I hope so." He inhaled deeply, rubbed his eyes, and exhaled with a grunt. He checked his watch. "What time is it anyway?"

"Almost 2100, why?" Mac said, as he stood and arched his back. "The way I see it, he'll either tell us everything we need to know and have no gang to go back to, or he's so afraid of them he won't say a word. Either way—"

They both jumped, turning their attention at the sound of a loud crash from the other room. They watched as Arthur slammed the chair against the wall several times, managing to fracture it. He then began to jump up and down on it, attempting to break a smaller piece from the whole.

"The fool," Nate muttered and ran from the room. "He's trying to build a shank; he's going to cut himself."

Nate burst into the room, Mac right on his heels, just as Arthur broke a hand-sized piece of the compressed plastic free. Nate dove.

As the youth's arm started its downward arc, Nate crashed into him, knocking the wind out of him. Nate landed on top of the teen, and Mac quickly reapplied the handcuffs.

"Not that easy, bucko. You're going to pay for this one. You're going to be tried as an adult and go to prison."

"Somebody's special little friend," Mac chimed in.

Arthur struggled against the cuffs and the weight bearing down on him. Soon he became still, giving into the fear, and began to cry.

Nate rolled him over and sat him up. "You have one chance to save yourself, kid, and I'm the only help you're gonna get."

Mac grabbed Arthur by his left arm while Nate took hold of the right. "Get up!" Mac said.

"You ready to talk?" Nate asked.

Arthur dropped his chin to his chest, exhaled, and then looked up at Nate. "Wha' do ya' wanna know?"

CHAPTER TWENTY- FIVE

"SO WHAT DID HE GIVE YOU?" Brown said as he came into the pod, talking way too loud for the early hour. Taking a sip from the cup, he blew on the coffee to cool it. "He better have been worth all the hassle you put me through, or both you and him are gonna wind up somewhere you really don't want to be."

Nate looked up at the sunrise breaking over the foothills and rubbed eyes that were red and gritty from the previous night's work. "Good morning, sir."

"Yeah, yeah," Brown said, waving the words away like a troublesome gnat. "Time's wasting, gentlemen."

Mac leaned over and whispered to Nate, "When is he ever in such a good mood?" He snickered.

"Hee, hee, hee, my butt, MacGilvery; I'll roll you back to patrol right along with your new friend here," Brown said, turning his attention to the younger detective.

"Well, sir," Nate said, drawing the lieutenant's attention back, "it is pretty early. We had a long night."

"Maybe I should play some music to go with this sob story, but right now, I want to know what I put my butt on the line for. I want to know if it was worth it. Talk," Brown said, pulling a chair over and sitting directly in front of Nate.

"Well," Nate began, pulling himself upright. "Israel Vega is our man—"

"Vega, Israel Vega. Who is Israel Vega?" Brown asked impatiently.

"—just got up here from Southern Cal. No ties to this area other than gang relations," Nate concluded.

Brown inhaled as if to speak, but Nate raised his hand, showing Brown his palm. "We have his history out of Southern California and it's deep. Prison on both the juvenile and the adult sides. This kid's done just about everything—drugs, violence. He ran his first stable of girls when he was just a tenth-grader in high school."

"Where is—" Brown began.

"Somewhere over in Old Town," Mac added.

"But how—" Brown said, turning to face Mac.

"That's what we're trying to figure out, sir," Nate said, forcing Brown to turn again in order to see him. "We know where approximately, but we don't know for how long or how deep his roots go in the city."

Brown raised his hand near his face, his index finger extended. He furrowed his brows and inhaled, preparing to speak.

"We already have patrol running with it, sir," Nate said.

Lieutenant Brown sat back and exhaled then, with exaggerated effort, rocked forward and got up from the chair. He walked toward the hall, stopped, looked back at Nate, and shook his head, smiling.

"I told you it was a long night," Nate said.

"Yeah, O.T., baby," Mac said, standing and slapping Nate's raised hand in a high-five.

Brown shook his head again, completed his turn, and walked out of the pod.

Nate leaned back, his chair creaking with the movement. "Got him."

"Got 'im," Mac agreed.

"I feel like celebrating. Let's get some coffee."

"You finally taking me to the Library?"

"Since you're buying, you get to pick the spot," Nate said, standing and grabbing his sunglasses off the desk. "It's been a few days since I've been by the Library. Come on rookie, you're buying."

***

"Ah, there you go, the best caramel and chocolate latte in the valley," Nate said and took a sip from his coffee. He tipped his cup toward the barista behind the counter as he smiled. Nate led the way to the back room where they sat in front of the darkened fireplace. "My favorite spot," he sighed.

Mac smiled and looked around at all the different knick-knacks and the multiple shelves of books from which the coffeehouse derived its name. "Are all the artists locals?" Mac asked, noting the several paintings, sculptures, and photographs adorning the walls and shelves.

"Yeah, as far as I know," Nate answered. "On the weekends they have live jazz too, and open mic on Tuesdays."

Getting to the table first, Mac grabbed the seat facing the opened doorway, leaving Nate with the less desirable seat with his back to the open door. This was why his gaze was now fixed at a spot about two feet above Nate's head.

Noticing Mac's line of sight, Nate tensed and prepared to confront whatever it was that had captured his new partner's attention.

"Hi, Nate."

At the sound of her voice Nate relaxed but then tensed again for a different reason. He did not turn to look at the speaker nor did he respond.

Mac stood, excusing himself. "Hey, I'm gonna go check on those mugs I saw near the front. I'm thinking about picking up a set for the missus." Smiling at the visitor, he quick-stepped to the front room.

Amber sat in the vacated seat and looked across the table at Nate. His gaze was downcast as if divining images cast in the swirl of foam in his latte.

When he still didn't respond, she reached over, took his mug, and drank from it. "Milky Way, I should have known," she said with a timid smile.

Nate finally looked up with his face set. Amber had a foam mustache on her top lip, which in his mind only made her cuter. "Look, Amber, I was going to call you."

"When? It's been the better part of a week, Nate." Her smile was gone.

"I, ah," Nate began.

Amber took another sip of Nate's coffee and then claimed the mug as her own. "Thanks," she said.

"Ah, yeah, 'bout me not calling, I've really been busy with this case and—"

"Nathaniel Richards, are you going to sit right across from me at this table and lie to my face? You haven't been at prayer meeting, and you didn't go to church Sunday. I checked with your parents, so don't bother lying about going to the early service. So what gives? You hiding from me or God?" Though it had been a question, it came across as a statement.

It was so like Amber, thought Nate, to go straight to the point. Although her face was serious, her eyes held only compassion. Compassion he knew he did not deserve. It made him feel even worse about how he had treated her.

"Okay, I was hiding, but I was such a jerk. I didn't even stick around to see how Sabrina came through that—that episode. Karl must think I'm such a flake."

"Well…" she said, and the smile returned.

"All right, I'll call him."

The smile disappeared.

"I'll stop by and see him." Nate said, matching the smile that suddenly reappeared on her face.

She reached across the table and touched the back of his knuckle.

Nate looked up and saw tears in her eyes. "Amber, I, ah, well..."

She brushed away the tear that dangled from her lashes and took another drink from the mug.

Nate began again. "Amber, you are such a special woman. How do I deserve our friendship?"

"You don't," she said and chuckled softly. Then sobering, she locked eyes with him. "You know, Nate, you're not supposed to do all this by yourself."

He looked askance at her.

"This investigation. This life," she finished, waving her hands for emphasis.

He smiled at her. "Is that a proposal?"

It was her turn to look puzzled. "Stop distracting me, Nate Richards. You know full well what I'm talking about. You're running around this valley and dancing around Lieutenant Brown like it's your job alone to solve the world's problems. What about Jesus and the partnership you're supposed to have with Him?"

"That's different, this is work. Police work."

"Oh, I would love to hear you explain that to your momma," she said.

"You know what I mean."

"No, not really. I have no idea how you can turn your faith on and off like that. Explain it to me." She was leaning forward, both elbows on the table, cheeks cupped in her hands, and an impish smile on her face.

"Okay," Nate said drawing the word out for several syllables, "what I really mean is that I'm wrong. It's just that I don't know what to do or how to deal with half the things I'm feeling these days."

"That's why He told us to ask Him for help, knucklehead." She sat back in her chair. "Hey," she said, looking down at the small face of her wristwatch, "I've got to go; got to be on shift. That guy is supposed to come back by today. He's been dropping by almost every day this week. He seems real interested in the Bible—asks a lot of questions. Who knows, maybe he'll become a brother in the next few days."

"Whoa, what guy?"

"Oooh, look who's jealous," she said, teasing him. "You remember that guy I told you about. He left right before you came in the bookstore last week. He seemed really weird at first, but lately he's been a real nice guy, kind of sweet in his own way."

Nate sat up. "What's this guy's name?"

"He says his name is Isaac Velasquez. He just moved here from Nevada."

Noting the worried looked on Nate's face, she said, "You don't always have to be such a cop, you know." She stood. "See you at Bible Study tonight?" Taking the last drink from his cup, she turned to leave. "I'm bringing him with me."

"Yeah, I'll see you tonight. I want to hear all about this Velasquez guy."

"See ya'," she called over her shoulder and disappeared under the archway.

Mac came back into the room just as Amber left. "Everything okay?" he asked.

"I don't know," Nate said. "I need to check on a guy. Let's head back to the office."

CHAPTER TWENTY- SIX

FROM ACROSS THE STREET, ISRAEL VEGA watched Amber enter
the bookstore. Removing his sunglasses and adopting his Isaac
persona, he hurried across the road, waving to Amber when she
saw him coming.

"Hey, Amber," he called in a cordial greeting. He smiled at
her in the shy, unimposing fashion he'd noted had the most
effect on her.

She blushed slightly and waved back. "Hi Isaac, I thought
you might come by today."

He reached toward her, touching her elbow. "What? Miss a
chance at seeing you, no way. Besides, I got some more
questions for you. I read that book of John in the Bible like you
said." He pulled out the paperback copy of the New Testament,
which she had given him a few days earlier.

Seeing the Bible, Amber's smile glowed with new intensity.
She noticed that it was now marked and underscored as if it had
been intently studied. "Come on in and when I get a break,
maybe I can answer some of your questions."

"That'd be great," Israel said.

He opened the door for her and followed her in, smiling and
talking softly as he did so. He knew, even now, that it was just a
matter of time before he had her where he wanted her; where

she would beg him for his attention, and he would lavish her with his own kind of love in return.

But he reminded himself when she turned and saw him staring at her, first things first. He flashed a shy smile and chided himself for getting too relaxed. He would have to be more careful. He had come too far, was too close to reaching his goal to mess it up now by being impatient.

Israel could not remember the last time a woman had filled him with such passion, with such a drive to conquer. When he looked at her his heart raced, his breaths became short and ragged. He knew he could not wait much longer. He would have to have her and soon. *Perhaps tonight.*

***

On her first break, Amber came over, bringing two cups of coffee with her. Setting the coffee on the table, she opened a copy of the New Testament she had with her and sat across from Israel. "So Isaac," she began, "what questions do you have?"

He accepted the proffered cup of coffee and noted how she put several packets of sweetener in her own. "Wow, a little coffee with your sugar?"

She giggled at the familiar refrain and thought briefly of Nate.

Israel noticed the look of wonder across her face and leaned forward, opening the Bible. "Yeah," he said, "this whole thing in chapter three about God sending his Son to die for us. That sounds kind of weak to me. Looks like to me if God was all powerful and all, he would be the one doing the killing, not letting his Son get killed by a bunch of fools." To his amazement, Israel noted that he had been serious about the question. Although initially he had only read the first few chapters so he would have a common ground for talking with Amber, some part of him really did want to know the answer.

She smiled again and began to explain that it was really about God's love for a fallen man....

All Israel really heard was the sound of her voice. He looked deep into her eyes and hoped she did not feel his lust burning for her. The more she talked, the more he wanted her. He smiled at something she said, and in that moment, decided that tonight would be her night. She would become his and leave her world of light and join him in the place of darkness. Tonight, she would join him and become Abyss.

***

Nate arrived at the Greater Abundant Life Christian Church a full half-hour before the seven o'clock Bible study, hoping to have some time to talk with Amber about this Isaac character. A check of the local "wants" and "warrants" had turned up nothing, not that that in itself was anything to get upset about. But when the DMV records showed no such person on file, Nate had become somewhat concerned.

At fifteen minutes to the hour, his dad arrived and, after a few minutes of small talk, went inside to set up for the worship service.

First came a few couples, then larger groups and singles along with family groups started to arrive. And before long, the fellowship hall was almost full, and still, Amber had not shown up.

Just as Nate turned to go inside, presuming Amber had entered through the east door and he had missed her, Reverend Richards touched Nate's shoulder and asked, "Amber not coming tonight?"

"I was just about to come in and see if she had come in through the east door. I was supposed to meet her here tonight. A kind of penance for me not coming last week," Nate said, forcing his voice to remain calm.

"Not to mention Sunday morning service," his father added cynically.

"Yeah, that too," Nate laughed.

Contemporary worship music began to flow out through the opened door and blended voices filled the pleasant summer night. Nate smiled to himself, thinking of his father on the pulpit with a rock band, electric guitars, and amplified bass behind him playing Amazing Grace like the Stones in concert. If only his dad had dreadlocks instead of being nearly bald, the image would have held.

"Well," the elder Richards said sighing, "I'd better get in there."

"Yeah," Nate said, distracted.

"What is it, Son?"

Nate turned and focused on his father. "It's this case. It's driving me batty and now Amber's met some guy at the bookstore and they've been hanging out."

Reverend Richards arched an eyebrow at his son.

Nate didn't notice. "She was supposed to see him today and then meet me here to discuss it—him—it."

"Is Amber in trouble, Son?"

"I don't know, Dad. I don't know. I know she's not here and she should be. I'm going to the bookstore to see if she's still there." Nate pulled out his cell phone, figuring a quick call wouldn't hurt.

Reverend Richards dropped his chin in question, paused a second, and then went inside, leaving his son standing just outside the door.

Nate forced a smile for his father then turned his back to the opened door, bringing the cell phone to his ear.

Nate dialed Amber's cell phone, and as the first ring died in the earpiece, he heard the corresponding ring around the corner of the building. Realizing he was hearing Amber's phone, he smiled in relief. He walked around the corner, preparing himself to give her a hard time for being late when he saw, lying on the sidewalk, Amber's cell phone.

The familiar ring tone sounded in Nate's ear, but its meaning eluded him. It took his mind a minute to recognize what he was actually seeing, and a minute longer to compute what this could possibly mean.

Amber was missing.

CHAPTER TWENTY-SEVEN

AMBER AWOKE IN DARKNESS. Her head throbbed in rhythm with a loud but indiscernible beat, which seemed to surround her. Pushing against the floor with trembling arms, she sat up and rubbed her eyes, trying to focus and remember what happened. Running her tongue over her lips, she frowned at the bitter chemical taste that lingered there.

The last thing she recalled was walking from her car to the church with Isaac. When she turned to explain something, to answer a question he'd asked, Isaac had grabbed her and held a foul-smelling cloth over her nose and mouth. She realized that's where the chemical taste must have come from. He had drugged her. Chloroform most likely.

She rubbed her temples. The pounding was lessening, and her eyes were starting to adjust to the low light. She could see she was in a small room, about eight by ten feet with no windows and a single door. She was laying on the edge of a mattress on a concrete floor. Her shoes had been removed.

Rolling to her knees, she could now see a pulsating red light flashing beneath the crack of the door, keeping time with the pounding. She realized the noise was music; the pounding a heavy bass line.

With an effort, Amber got to her feet but had to steady herself against the wall before trusting herself to walk. She moaned and felt her way along the wall to the door.

It was locked.

Sinking to the floor again, she rested her back against the wall and draped her wrists over her knees. Her head felt heavy, so she allowed it to fall forward and dropped her chin to her chest. She began to pray.

"Father, I need help. Help me." Tears dripped from her lowered face and fell to the floor between her bare feet.

A sudden burst of nervous laughter escaped her lips. Looking at her bare feet and seeing that, even though she made it a point to do so, she still had not remembered to paint her toenails. "What a time to remember something so stupid," she stated into the darkness and forced herself up and paced around the room.

Time dragged in the semi-darkness, but as she walked, the effects of the drug wore off. With her head a little clearer, Amber began to beat on the door, calling out as she did. "Hey, let me out of here!"

No response.

She banged harder, slamming the sides of her fist against the solid wood of the door. "Hey, who's out there? Hey! Let me out!"

Lying down on the floor, Amber squinted, looking beneath the door. She could see shadows of people moving on the other side of the door, and she knew they were close enough to hear her. Standing again, she began screaming and banging again. The thumping of the bass continued.

Amber went back, sat on the mattress cross-legged, and watched the door for movement. She began rocking, hugging herself with her arms. She was startled to hear herself singing, "Hear my cry, oh God, attend unto my prayer. From the ends of the Earth will I cry unto Thee. And when my heart is overwhelmed, lead me to that Rock that is higher than I; that is higher than I."

She was just about to start the second verse of the Psalm when the lock clicked and the door swung open. She froze.

Standing framed by the pulsating red light was a young Hispanic female, about 18 to 20 years old. She wore a white fishnet tank top, which left her stomach uncovered, and a pair of low rider jean shorts.

"Good, you're awake. Israel wants you," the girl said with a thick accent.

"Where's Isaac? Isaac brought me here; tell Isaac I want to see him...now." Amber said, fear amplifying her voice.

The girl handed Amber a black leather miniskirt and red shirt, like the one the younger girl was wearing. "Israel says for you to put these on." When Amber did not take the clothes, the girl dropped them on the floor. "Makes no never mind to me."

Amber darted toward the door, trying to get past her and out of the room. The girl blocked her.

"Look," Amber began, "I don't know who this Israel is, but I don't wear clothes like, like that—"

The girl rolled her eyes and pushed Amber in her chest causing her to stumble backwards. "You think you're better 'n me, huh? Well you ain't nothing. We'll see how high and mighty you are when Israel gets through with you."

She cursed, calling Amber by several foul names, before turning to look back into the larger room. Leaning past the doorjamb, she spoke to someone, but Amber could not hear what was said. The girl turned her attention back to Amber. "Now, miss righteous, are you going to put those clothes on, or are we going to have to dress you?"

At this, two more women came into the room, followed by a rather large black man. The man stepped forward and stooping, picked up the clothes. He sniffed them as if they were a bouquet of flowers and, looking over the bundle, smiled greedily at Amber.

Amber felt a quiver of fear run up her spine. Panicked by the dark light glowing in the man's deep-set eyes, she looked around again; searching for an avenue of escape that she knew wouldn't be there.

The three women cackled like drunken witches and fell on Amber with brutal force, grabbing and forcing her down onto the mattress. She began to fight, kicking and twisting, trying to free her legs and arms, anything to free herself.

She could feel hands slapping and hitting her, pulling at the zipper on her jeans while others tore open her blouse. All the while, the huge black man stood over her glaring, raking her with hungry, mocking eyes. She screamed.

"Stop!" A commanding voice sounded from near the door and echoed in the room.

The man snapped his attention from Amber to the figure standing in the door. The women froze with their hands still wrapped in the pulled and ripped clothing. Amber folded into a fetal position, crying and trying to cover herself.

"What are you doing?" Israel demanded.

The three women dropped the tattered rags, lowered their heads, and tried sneaking by him like dogs with their tails tucked between their legs. As the first woman neared him, Israel stepped on her splayed fingers, crushing them to the floor. He kept his eyes on the man who stood before him, now silent in the middle of the room. Not shifting his eyes, he spoke to the woman on whose fingers he was standing, "I asked you a question."

"I wa-wass g-g-getting her dr-dressed like you said, Israel. That's all."

Israel looked down at the trembling woman. "I don't remember asking you to rape her." He reached down and grabbed a handful of the woman's hair, lifting her to a standing position. He glared at her and threw her on the floor back to where Amber sat with a look of fear and confusion warring on her face.

"Apologize to the lady," he said in a pleasant voice. His soft tone seemed out of place in the setting.

Amber had been stunned by what she was seeing, but now began to rearrange her clothing. "Isaac," she said in a barely controlled voice.

He did not answer but only looked at her; this time the lust was obvious. With slow, deliberate motion, he turned his attention to the three women cowering on the floor in front of him. He narrowed his eyes. "Get out."

The women apologized quickly as they scurried past him, keeping their eyes on the floor and hurrying through the opened door.

Israel walked up to the man who was still standing statue-like in the middle of the room. He stood off to one side of the man, but leaned close to him, speaking directly in his ear. "She's beautiful, yes?"

The man nodded.

"She's like a flower whose fragrance fills the room."

In contrast to the tone and cadence of Israel's voice, which was soft and inviting, a single line of perspiration dripped from the man's temple and disappeared into his collar.

"Yes, she is special; she is unique," Israel whispered to the man, his breath tickling the man's ear.

Across the room, Amber looked on with a mixture of shock and surprise. Was this the same man she had shared Bible studies with all week; the same man that seemed so eager to go with her to mid-week prayer service at the church; *the same man that drugged me and brought me here…wherever here was?*

Israel moved around to the man's opposite shoulder. "Did you touch her?"

"No, Israel," he said, even as he shook his head side to side.

"But you wanted to, didn't you? Didn't you?"

The man did not answer, nor did he make eye contact with Israel. He jumped when he heard the spring-loaded click of a knife blade locking into place.

Israel stopped behind the man and placed the point of the knife at the base of his skull. "Good. Because…if you had touched her, you'd be dead right now. Do you understand me?" He pricked the skin, drawing a line of blood.

The man flinched but did not move otherwise. Israel walked in front of him again. "What's your name?"

"Big Jake, Israel," he answered, his voice strained by stress.

"Well, Jake," Israel said, purposefully leaving off the big. "You can thank the lady too, because I don't think she would be happy if I gutted you right here in front of her. So today's your lucky day."

Amber looked up at the man she knew as Isaac, and a new horror settled over her. "Isaac, don't," she said as she began to understand what his intentions had been.

Big Jake cut his eyes and looked at Israel for the first time, but didn't speak.

"Tell her thank you," Israel said, never taking his eyes from Jake's. As he spoke, he had drawn the blade across Jake's cheek causing a welt to rise in its wake.

"Thank you, ma'am," Big Jake said and nodded toward Amber.

"You're welcome," Amber managed through a dry throat, glad the man capitulated.

Israel lowered his knife and Big Jake turned to face him. Israel smiled. "I know what you're thinking, Jake, but it's not a good idea. Regardless of what the lady says, if you do anything other than what I tell you, I will open you up like a cheap suitcase."

Big Jake looked at Israel and weighed his options. He tilted his head in acquiescence and smiled a cheerless smile. "Maybe some other time then?"

Israel laughed out loud. "Indeed. I look forward to it. Anytime you think you want to be me…" He opened his arms and bowed with a flourish. And then the light in his eyes was replaced by a cold darkness. "You're welcome to try."

Big Jake backed out of the room, turned, and walked away.

Israel turned his attention to Amber. "I suppose you want to know why."

"For beginners," she said, starting to find her voice.

"I want you. And I always get what I want." He walked over to where she now knelt on the mattress and stood over her. "I want you, and I *will* have you." He paused and looked over her body. "And when I do, you will be mine. I will own you." He leaned over and kissed the top of her head. "Now, get up and come with me. And bring those clothes."

Amber looked at the pile of clothing left on the floor where Big Jake had dropped them. "But I—"

She never got to finish her sentence, cut off by a slap across her face. "Don't ever talk back to me…and do what you're told the first time." He turned and headed for the door. "Don't make me ask you again."

Stunned, Amber rubbed her face and picked up the pile of clothing. She used them to dry the tears that ran down her face in rivulets. With slow, heavy steps, she walked to the door, leaned against the frame, and looked out into the dusky interior of the warehouse type room.

Red lights flashed on and off and the music blared from concert-sized speakers in the far corner. All around the room couples sat and talked or danced while others made out. Small groups of men sat at various locations drinking and talking or playing various games.

Uncoupled women clustered together and looked at Amber with a combination of hatred and envy. She closed her eyes against the garish image and prayed for strength and deliverance. Opening her eyes again, she looked toward the ceiling and whispered-hummed under her breath, "Hear my cry, oh God, attend unto my prayers—"

"I'm waiting," Israel said from about twenty paces ahead of her. He held out his hand like a parent reaching for a child and smiled as he saw her take her first shuffling step in his direction.

Amber dropped her head again, this time not attempting to hide her tears.

CHAPTER TWENTY- EIGHT

NATE KICKED THE FILE CABINET CLOSED with a snap of his foot and swung his chair around to open the cabinet on the opposite side of his pod. Snatching the folder he wanted, he slammed it on top of a growing stack of files in the center of his desk.

"You finished?" Lieutenant Haynes asked in his lazy drawl, "cause if not, I can come back."

Nate stopped and looked up at the dark-skinned lieutenant. "Somebody's taken her, Don. I don't know where she is."

"Look, Nate," the older man said, grabbing a nearby chair, spinning it around, and straddling it. He leaned his chest against the backrest of the seat and rocked forward. "We'll find her. It's just a matter of time."

"The first 24, that's what we've got, Don. Twenty-four hours, that's all, and five of those are already gone." Nate said, his voice strained and irritated. "I've got to... I've got to do something," he added.

At that moment, Mac walked into the pod, looking as disheveled and tired as Nate. "Brown's looking for us," he said in a weary voice. Dropping his chin and arching an eyebrow, he leaned against the wall and sighed.

Nate met his gaze. "For what?" He snapped.

"Because the citizens of this fine city are not paying your salary to have you sit around here crying for your girlfriend," Brown said, coming around the corner.

Haynes put a hand on Nate's shoulder, aborting his attempt to stand. "I've got this, Larry," Haynes said.

Nate sat back. "Got what?" he said, looking up at Haynes.

"Oh, look who's full of questions this morning," Brown said sarcastically.

Again, Nate tried to stand, and again, Haynes held him down.

"I said, I've got this," Haynes said with a stern, chastising tone.

Mac melted back against the wall, trying not to be seen.

"No," Nate said, turning his attention to Haynes. "The man obviously has something on his mind. Let him say it."

Brown folded his arms across his chest and spread his feet apart. Inhaling and then resetting himself, he pointed his finger at Nate, taking a step forward as he did. "You mister, are a waste of time and money. First, you barge into my office begging for the Fuentes and Franks' cases. You've done nothing with either of them for the last two and a half weeks. And now you want to dump them both because your girlfriend's come up missing. Maybe she just found a better man."

This time Nate did stand and found himself nose to nose with Brown. "You can say whatever you want to say about me, sir, but if you ever so much as hint at the character of Amber Coles, I will personally whip you like your mama should have." Nate stepped closer, bumping his chest against Brown's.

"You're about two seconds from an insubordination report, detective."

"And you're about a second from a—"

Mac grabbed Nate and pulled him away from Brown while Haynes grabbed the lieutenant and did the same.

"Whoa, Rocky and Apollo Creed," Haynes interjected, "we've seen this fight; already know how it turns out. Nobody's getting whipped, and nobody's getting written up. Far as I can tell, you're both acting like pubescent teens." Haynes looked both men in their faces. "Now both of you sit down and shut up." To his surprise, they both did.

First, he turned his attention to Brown. "I told you to let me handle this. Now, head on back to the office and I'll be there in a minute."

Without waiting for an answer, Haynes turned his back to Brown and his attention to Nate.

"That man is such a—," Nate began.

"The next word out of your mouth had better be lieutenant," Haynes said, an edge to his voice. "Of all the foolish things you could have done, you go and pick a fight with a superior officer right dead smack in the middle of the office. Half the pod could hear you guys yelling."

Once it was clear that Brown was leaving the pod, Mac released Nate's arm, and then sat behind Sabrina's desk watching the events unfold.

"You saw him, Don," Nate said in complaint. "He was trying to egg me on," he finished, looking for support.

"Up until now, I never would have believed it if someone had told me that Reverend Richards' boy was a fool," Haynes said.

Nate stared at him slack-jawed.

"You pick a fight with an officer over an issue where you know you're wrong."

Nate started to speak, but Haynes waved him off with a raised hand. "You have two high priority cases on your desk. One of which involves an in-the-line-of-duty officer's death, and you want to drop them both to pursue a missing person's report?"

Haynes walked back to where he'd left his chair and once again straddled it. He pointed to the empty chair behind Nate's desk indicating that he should sit. "You seem to forget that the mayor's office is watching the Fuentes investigation, and everybody else is watching the Franks' case, and both of those are yours. You starting to see a pattern here, son?"

When Nate didn't answer, Haynes continued, "You're off the missing person. Period." Again, Nate started to speak, but Haynes cut him off. "You're too close to it, Nate. You need to trust your team. Let them do their job…you do yours. Find those killers."

Nate slapped the surface of his desk then rubbed his chin in frustration. "I knew Brown would try this. He's been wait—"

"It was my call. I informed Brown of your connection with Amber, and I pulled you off the case," Haynes said, staring at Nate's surprised face.

"What?" Nate said, looking at his friend and feeling betrayed. "But, Don, you know Amber. You know her." His voice was weak. Slumping in his chair, he stared up at his lieutenant, unable to formulate his thoughts.

Lieutenant Haynes stood and placed a hand on Nate's shoulder. "You're too close to it, Nate. You're no good to me or Amber or anyone else this way. You're not thinking clear." He swore and scratched the side of his face. "Nate, you just threatened to assault your lieutenant right in the middle of the CID pod. How's that for clear thinking?"

Haynes looked at Mac and lowered his voice. He said, not without sympathy, "Get him out of here for a few hours. Make sure he gets some sleep. You too. I don't want to see either one of you around here until you've both had a few hours sleep. Now go on, get out of here."

Haynes walked away, and Mac grabbed his sunglasses and stood. "Shall we take the man's offer?"

Nate stood, snatching his sunglasses from the desk. "Yeah," he managed through a throat that sounded as if it had been sanded raw.

"Gonna kick Brown's butt, huh? Right in front of God and everybody…wow! They told me you were an odd duck, but I have to tell you, this was way cool," Mac said and jumped back as Nate took a playful swing at him.

"Come on," Nate said, "get me out of here before I really do something stupid."

CHAPTER TWENTY- NINE

AMBER SAT ON THE FLOOR TREMBLING. She looked up at Israel seated on the elevated platform like a king enthroned. Tucking her knees beneath her, she tried to cover what the miniskirt left exposed. "So" she began, "is this what the Bible Study thing was all about, just a lie to get me to trust you?"

Israel looked down at her, admiring the way the tank top fit and then lifted his gaze back to the rest of his family around him.

"At least answer me this one question," she said, rising to her knees. "Is it Israel or Isaac?"

No answer.

"Is your last name at least Velasquez?"

Israel shifted his vision back to her, looking down from his perch.

Lo stepped closer and leaned over Israel's shoulder, speaking softly. "You want me to get her out of here?" Amber heard him whisper.

Israel waved his hand from the wrist, the elbow resting on the arm of his chair. He rested his index and middle fingers alongside his nose and stared at her contemplatively.

"What, now you won't talk to me? You can't talk?" Amber said, forcing bravado into her voice. "Why are you doing this to me? I thought we were becoming friends, Isaa—Israel."

He still didn't answer her, but stared at her with dark, brooding, lust-filled eyes.

"Please, Israel, let me go." She rested her hand on the footboard of his seat.

Dropping his hand to the armrest, Israel drummed his fingers and stared back at her. "Amber, I want you." He spoke just above a whisper, his voice a breathy declaration.

She drew her hand back, startled by his assertion. "Israel, you have to let me go. The police will be looking for me and—"

Enraged, Israel moved with panther-like grace and grabbed Amber by her hair, pulling her head back until she grimaced in pain. He leaned into her face, his lips brushing the side of her cheek. "No one tells me what I can or cannot do. I do what I want. Do you know who I am?"

"Isaac, you're hurting me. Please, Isa—please, Israel," she cried, grabbing at his hand.

Then just as suddenly as he'd grabbed her, he let her go. She collapsed to the floor at his feet. Whimpering and trying to catch her voice, she lay unmoving, catching her breath. "Oh God," she whispered softly through her tears. *How can this be happening?*

She thought of the great heroes of the Bible and wondered how they might have felt during the darkness of their trials. She remembered a study from the book of 1 Samuel about Ahinoam and Abigail, two of King David's wives, who had been kidnapped by the Amalekites. She thought of their fear of being sold as slaves, but took hope when she remembered that David came, killed the Amalekites, and brought them all home safely.

Amber looked past Israel's angry face and prayed that her David would come and rescue her. She dropped her head and, using her hands, scooted back against the nearest wall, curling her legs beneath her.

Israel rose slowly and walked across the room to where Amber sat curled in a defensive knot. He stood over her, looking down at her like she were cornered prey.

"Don't, Israel," she tried. "Please don't do this." She began to cry as he knelt down and reached out, touching the skin of her exposed thigh.

She pushed his hand away. "Israel, don't. You can't do this—"

The blow landed with a solid thud, sending her sprawling, face first across the floor. "I told you, nobody tells me what I can or can't do. I do what I want."

Amber laid face down, her tears pooling beneath her bruised cheek. She stiffened when she felt Israel's hand sliding slowly up the back of her thigh. Clenching her fist, she stifled a scream into the floor.

She could feel his weight settling onto her back and soon she could feel the heat of his breath on her neck. "Please, please, Israel...don't do this," she cried.

Israel kissed the side of her face and nibbled at her earlobe. "I want you, Amber. I want you now."

"Please, God, make him stop. Make him stop," she cried softly.

Israel grabbed Amber by her shoulder and rolled her onto her back. She lay still, unmoving; her eyes squeezed shut.

Israel leaned over her, rubbing her bare stomach and kissing the skin of her neck.

Amber trembled beneath him.

He sat back on his haunches and removed his shirt, pulling it above his head. Branded into the right side of his chest was a large circled 'A' with a slash carved through it. She stifled a scream as she remembered the description of Franks' body.

He straddled her and rested both his hands on her stomach. Amber lay still and locked eyes with him. With all the effort she could muster, she slapped him.

He smiled.

She drew back to hit him again only to find both her arms being held, trapped over her head. Lo, who had come to stand behind her, now knelt down, pressing her hands down hard against the concrete floor. Her shoulders screamed in pain.

She refused to look at either of them or give them the pleasure of seeing the fear that gripped her heart.

Israel leaned forward and began kissing her face as Lo held her wrists in his vice-like fists. Lo leered down at her.

At that moment, one of the women of Abyss burst into the room. Seeing the two men and a woman on the floor, her face filled with envy. "Israel…" She paused, looking longingly at the two men.

Israel sat up, the sweat, a fine patina, on his bare chest. "What?" he growled.

"The delivery is, ah, here," she said, her eyes glowing with jealous desire. "You told me to tell you immediately when it arrived."

With a sigh, Israel rocked back and then stood with resignation. "Later, little dove," he said to Amber, blowing her a kiss. He turned, grabbing his shirt from the girl who now held it out to him.

The two men left the room, and the crowd filed out behind them. Amber curled into the fetal position and cried. When she heard footsteps coming toward her again, she began pulling at her clothes, trying to stretch the small pieces of material to cover her exposed body. Despite herself, she screamed when she felt hands touch her.

"Hey," the young lady that had delivered the message said as she knelt down. Brushing strands of damp hair from Amber's face, she whispered in her ear, "It's not so bad here. Israel treats all his girls real good. He's an awesome lover. I wish it was me he wanted so bad," she said wistfully. "You can see his desire when he looks at you." She sighed.

Amber looked up at her, crying. "But it's wrong to take a woman against her will. It's rape!" she said, anger in her voice. Although she wasn't sure herself who she was most mad at, Israel or these people who allowed him to do his evil.

"Come on; let's get you cleaned up before Israel comes back." She reached her hand out to Amber, helping her to get up.

"Can I get some proper clothes?" Amber said, spreading her arms.

"Sure, besides, there musta' been some'n Israel saw in you in your old life. Amber noted the words "old life" but chose not to comment. The last thing she wanted to do was treat this possible ally like a fool and lose her chance of getting out of here— wherever she happened to be. "How long have you been here?" she asked instead.

"Oh, I've only lived in the crash for a few months, but I've been a Honey since I was thirteen."

So that's what they're calling them now. "Excuse me, but how old are you? You don't look much older than thirteen now."

"Thanks," she said and turned and smiled at Amber. "Looking younger has its advantages."

"Like?"

"Well, it always helps with the cops. They treat kids different, you know?"

"Oh," Amber said, hoping she sounded like she didn't know. "But you never told me…just how old are you?"

"Sixteen."

"Sixteen? But, where are your parents? Aren't they looking for you?

"Yeah, I bet they are. I don't know my real dad; my mom only spent one night with him anyway. Then came a whole series of daddies." She laughed bitterly. "But once I got old enough to fight 'em off, I figured I could hang on the streets with less trouble. At least that way if I had to give it up, I could at least make a little money for my efforts." She laughed as if her story were a common tale.

Amber's anger dissipated as she came to see the child that was leading her through this labyrinth of boxes and crates. She looked around at the various girls, many as young as her escort. Now that she was seeing her more clearly, Amber could see the marks of abuse and hard living that scarred the girl. "What's your name?" she asked, coughing to cover the sudden sadness in her voice.

"Grace Marie, but you can call me Gracie," she said, heading up a flight of rusted metal stairs attached to what Amber thought must be an exterior wall. "Up here, this is where we sleep when the guys don't need us."

"So you just hang around…waiting to be ah, needed," Amber said, trying not to be embarrassed for this girl.

"Not all day. We have jobs too. Some of us are runners, and once in a while we work the streets— just to keep in practice. We don't like doing it, but Israel insists we stay tuned up just in case sales drop off, and the gang needs some quick money."

Reaching the landing, the ladies followed the catwalk until it turned back toward the center of the building. From her new vantage point, Amber could see that the building was indeed a warehouse. She figured they must be in the business district in Old Town. "So," she said, keeping the conversation alive, "what do the guys do while you ladies are doing…" she paused, "all that it is you do?"

Gracie giggled. "For an old lady, you're kind of naïve, aren't you?" She stopped. "Here we are; the flop room."

Stepping inside, Amber was surprised. In contrast to the rusted out, used-up look of the first floor, this room was plush. The touch of a lady's hand was evident everywhere, from the cool pastel and cream painted walls to coordinating carpet and rugs. Richly colored paintings decorated the walls and tasteful statuary accented exquisite furniture. Spotlighting shone softly in cones of brilliance on various figures of art, both hanging and freestanding.

Soft jazz floated down from speakers hidden in the walls and ceiling. An almost-industrial-sized kitchen with stainless steel appliances occupied one corner, while in the opposite corner was a fully stocked and furnished family room, including what appeared to be a fifty-two-inch plasma HDTV mounted against the wall with surround sound.

A few of the Honeys, as they referred to themselves, sat lounging in pajama pants and t-shirts, watching Oprah cry with a guest as they cried along with them.

"Here's your room," Gracie said, pushing open a door into a master suite.

Surprised, Amber caught her breath. The room spread before her like a luxury hotel suite. A hardwood door stood opened and led to a private bath with a walk-in sunken tub and wall-mounted speakers. A private sitting room was situated just off the bath and adjacent to the bedroom. Here, smaller, but equally nice, HDTVs were mounted above a simulated fireplace and another hung on the wall opposite the bed.

"Wow," Amber said before she could catch herself. And again, "Wow."

"I told you Israel treats his woman nice." Gracie giggled again, obviously enjoying the impact all this had on Amber.

Then, as if sobering, Amber turned and looked at the girl standing beside her. "So all this in trade for what—sex?" She asked, trying to draw Gracie closer to her point of understanding.

"Well, it's better than selling your tail on the street or being, as you put it, raped by your stepdad a couple times a week."

"Wait, I'm sorry," Amber said, putting her hand on Gracie's shoulder as she turned to leave the room. "I didn't mean to offend you. It's just that this is so far from what I know—from what I believe to be right."

Gracie turned, looking at Amber. "I know your type. You goody-goodies thinking you're better than everybody else, always judging people."

"Whoa," Amber said, crossing her arms and leaning against the doorjamb. "Who's judging now?"

Gracie smiled, "Okay, you got me on that one, but this life, it ain't so bad."

Amber sobered again and smiled softly before she began, "Look Gracie, the life you've had, I can't imagine. My dad was great. He loved my mom, my two sisters, my brother, and me. He never beat us. Heck, I still have problems imagining him and my mom even sleeping together, let alone him trying to sleep with one of his kids. He was just a regular old boring dad. So if it takes me a minute to wrap my mind around this," she waved her hand as if taking it all in, "I'm gonna need you to try and understand that, okay?"

Gracie looked hard at Amber, as if she was trying to figure her out. "What does Israel want with you anyways? You got short hair, your boobs are small, and as far as I can tell, you don't even like sex. What gives?"

"It's not that I don't like sex. I just believe sex is a special gift from God to be enjoyed between one woman and one man over a lifetime in marriage."

Gracie nodded her head, but wore a glazed-over expression.

"What Israel and Lo were about to do to me was not good or loving," Amber said, fighting off a shiver and remembering that she was still not safe yet. "So the gang—"

"Abyss," Gracie said with pride.

"Ah, the Abyss—"

"Not 'the Abyss', just Abyss. That's who we are; that's what we call ourselves. Abyss."

"So the guys just call for one of you girls, and you have to go to him to sleep with him?"

"I know it sounds bad, but most of the guys are real cool, and there are ways to avoid the few you might not like. Besides, Israel and Lo don't tolerate nobody hurting us. So it's all good."

"What do you call what they were doing to me when you walked in? Oh yeah, thanks for your timing."

"That's different, you're new. You're Israel's Honey, off limits to everybody else. That's why you get the suite," she said, swinging her arm to indicate the large well-appointed room.

I've got to get out of here—and help this girl too, Amber thought. "Gracie, can I ask you a question?"

"Sure."

"If you could have another life, a different life, I mean not being anybody's Honey, would you want it? Would you go for it?"

Gracie didn't answer, but turned her back to Amber and walked to the other side of the room. At the far wall, she turned with sunken shoulders and a forlorn expression. "Who would want me? I've been had more times than a boy scout on a used car lot." She looked around, drawing Amber's eyes along with hers. "Do you think there's any way I could get all this working for $5.75 an hour at McDonald's? I got no education. All I got is these," she finished, spreading her arms and nodding toward her ample breasts.

Amber went to her and gathered her in her arms. "I'm going to tell you something, okay? I want you to just listen, don't try and think about it now, just listen."

Amber led her to the sitting area and sat beside her on a small sofa. Taking Gracie's hands in hers, she looked into the youthful face, hiding behind mascara and make-up. "There's a Man—"

Gracie pulled her hands away, "I thought you had somethin' different. You—"

Amber smiled, "No, the Man I'm talking about is Jesus. Jesus loves you, Gracie, and He's not trying to get anything from you. As a matter of fact, the reason for Him coming was to give you something."

Gracie raised her brow and crossed her arms, but she had given her word and she would listen.

"Jesus died on a cross over two thousand years ago because He knew you would need Him. He's not about all that stuff you see on TV and all the fussing you hear about whose church is best. The key is that He loves you, and He wants you to have His very special gift of eternal life." She smiled warmly.

Amber stood and walked over toward the sunken tub. She looked back at Gracie. "I don't need to tell you that there's sin in the world. You've seen and lived through a lot more than I hope to ever know, but the good thing is, you don't have to stay in that world—this world. When Jesus died, He made a way for you and me to be clean from all this."

She stopped when she saw the look on Gracie's face. She allowed the silence to hang between them for a few moments and then spoke softly. "I won't lie to you, Gracie. I don't like your world, and I will do everything in my power to get out of here." She walked back and sat beside the teen again, taking her hands into her own. "When I go, I want you to come with me."

This time Gracie snatched her hands away and stood up, walking very quickly toward the door. "Israel will be done soon. You'd better get bathed and dressed into something nice. He doesn't like his women dirty." She grabbed for the doorknob.

"Okay, I won't push you, but I meant what I said. All of it." Amber closed the distance between her and the teen and laid her hand on the back of the girl's, which rested on the French-styled doorknob.

Gracie looked down before making eye contact with Amber and shook her head from side to side. "Why would you give all this up? Every girl here would kill to be in your place. One man's woman. Your own room, everything you could ever want is right here for your asking," she said, tears and confusion twisting her youthful features.

"Everything but freedom and self-respect," Amber said in a soft and non-condemning voice.

Their eyes met and new tears made their way down Gracie's cheeks matching the twin rivulets on Amber's face.

"Yeah," Gracie said, turning away and walking quickly toward the family room where the girls were watching Oprah.

Amber closed the door, collapsed against it, and found there was no lock. She clenched her fist and exhaled through gritted teeth. Taking a breath, she lifted her face and voice toward heaven in silent, desperate prayer.

CHAPTER THIRTY

ISRAEL WALKED WITH QUIET STEPS coming up behind the man whose back was still turned to him. The man's attention was on the partially opened car trunk. "Not very smart leaving your back exposed," he said from near the man's shoulder.

The man laughed and turned in a casual manner, the sun reflecting off the lenses of his sunglasses. "Israel," he began, "you hurt my feelings. You'd think we'd be able to trust each other by now," he said with a wry smile, his eyes hidden behind gold-trimmed aviators' glasses.

"Yeah," Israel said sarcastically. "Lo."

At the prompting, the big man stepped forward with agile grace, pushed open the trunk of the car, and began passing handguns, rifles, and other weapons to the line of gang members forming behind him.

"He's short on count again," Lo said, his voice a low rumble issuing from deep in his throat.

"Hey," the man said hurriedly, "I get what I can, when I can. Besides, just as soon as I bring you guys the gear, you manage to leave it behind, right in the middle of one of your messes."

A cold hatred filled his heart, and Israel narrowed his eyes at the man smiling the fake smile. He knew the man hated him and his kind, but that was okay. When the man's value had exceeded his usefulness, Israel would finally allow Lo to deal with him. Israel uncrossed his arms before turning and walking away.

"Hey, what about my money?"

Israel stopped and looked over his shoulder at the two men standing behind the car. "Pay the man."

Lo approached the man and looked down his nose at him. Flexing his huge arms, he reached into an inside pocket of his leather vest and pulled out a roll of twenty-dollar bills about two inches in diameter and gave it to him.

"Thank you, Lo, you're a good man," the pale-skinned man said, his hand a stark contrast against Lo's darker skin.

Lo didn't bother to answer, but looked disdainfully at the shorter man.

Taking the money and stuffing it into his pants pocket, the man smiled up at Lo. "You know, one of these days you and I will have to finish this little dance we've been having."

Lo raised one hand and pointed his index finger to the side of the shorter man's head, dropping his thumb as if firing a handgun, and poked him in the temple.

"Ooooh, you hurt my feelings. Just like yo' massa, huh boy?" he said, matching the coldness of Lo's glare.

Lo leaned forward over the man and whispered, his voice rumbling like gravel in a metal bucket, "Soon." After this, Lo turned and walked in crisp, disciplined strides back into the building, leaving the crew to unload the rest of the weapons.

***

As the last of the weapons were offloaded, the man reentered his car and removed the sunglasses, stuffing them in the glove box. Shifting the car into gear, he eased it out of the alley and made his way back onto the main road. He checked his mirrors, making sure his exit from the alley went unnoticed.

Turning the vehicle's radio on, his attention was instantly drawn to the box near his right knee.

The dispatcher's voice came across the radio in a clipped steady cadence. "TV916 security check…TV916 no answer. Request unit to security check TV916. Last known location out on foot patrol in the 1700 block of Main Street, Old Town."

Several units responded at once, their voices blending together and overlapping, the tension of the recent officer's death making them anxious.

Patrol Officer Johnson picked up the handheld microphone, took a deep breath, and spoke crisply into the mouthpiece, "TV916 code-four. I'm back in my unit, cancel security check. My antenna worked itself loose on my handheld."

From the shadow of the bay door, Lo had watched the small, white officer trot around his patrol car and slide in behind the steering wheel. He knew that he would soon have to kill the irritating little man. Johnson was useful for now, and that bought him time, but Lo hated a traitor, and according to the code of the streets, Johnson deserved no less. He had to die. As thoughts of how Johnson would eventually get his due played across his mind, a narrow smile crept across Lo's face. Pleasure.

Israel's voice drew him out of his reverie. "Well, my friend, all in good time." He laid his hand on the large man's shoulder.

Lo turned, amazed at how Israel always seemed to know what he was thinking. "Just promise me that when the time comes, he'll be mine to do."

Israel laughed and jumped down from the crate he'd been standing on. Slapping Lo's shoulder, he said, "Just make him cry before you kill him."

The two men laughed, watching the patrol car drive out of the alley, the bright sun reflecting off the white roof. The light-bar contrasted against the black paint and city shield on the sides and rear of the police car. They turned and headed back into the warehouse still laughing.

***

Later that same afternoon, Nate walked out of Sabrina's room and bumped into Officer Johnson. "Hey, Johnson," he said, startled, "what brings you down?"

"So how's she doing, any change?" Johnson asked, looking past Nate onto Sabrina's unconscious form. "I just got off shift and volunteered to pull the duty at her room for a few hours."

Nate kept walking, drawing Johnson along with him away from the partially opened door. "Yeah, she's opening her eyes, mostly just reflexive stuff. The doc says they might soon take her off the meds and allow her to wake up naturally. The brain swelling has gone down."

"That's good news," Johnson said with a slight hesitation. "It's just that being there that night, I still feel like it's kinda my fault. Know what I mean?" Johnson turned away and faced back toward the partially opened curtain. "It was my call—"

"Nobody's blaming you, man. Stuff happens. We all know that going in, nobody better than Sabrina," Nate said to Johnson, remembering a similar conversation he'd had with Amber. The thought of her made him stiffen.

Johnson stopped, noticing Nate's reaction. When he didn't make an effort to explain, Johnson played it off by rubbing his eyes. "Yeah, you're right, I suppose. Heck, look at me, big tough street cop, huh?"

"Aren't we all?" Nate answered with a harsh chuckle. "I see Holly's on duty now. How well do you know him?" More as a means to change the subject than true interest, Nate asked about the uniformed officer sitting by the entrance to ICU.

"He's a newbie, but he's a good troop. Don't worry, he'll do right by Sabrina," Johnson said and faced Nate fully, but still looked distracted. "Any word on that missing person case? Coles…she was a friend of yours, right?"

"Yeah," Nate said feeling his throat tighten.

"Well, you know how it goes, they go missing for a few days, and then they pop up again no worse for the wear. I'm sure she'll be fine," Johnson said, looking back toward Sabrina again. "Well, I'd better go and let Holly get his break so I can head home and get some sleep myself. I go 10-41 at 0630 hours. Don't want to be late. Sergeant Haywood's a pain in the butt about being on time." Johnson seemed to force a smile, and then turned and walked toward the ICU entrance.

As he approached, the main doors swung open, and Mac walked in and greeted Johnson who passed without acknowledging him. Looking back at Johnson, Mac stopped near Nate. "There's something weird about that guy," he said with a tilt of his head. "I don't know what it is, but there's definitely something strange about him."

"Yeah," Nate said absentmindedly, watching Johnson retreat down the hall. "You know, he comes across a little too sweet sometimes."

"Like Eddie Haskell, huh? Just weird." He turned his attention back to Nate just as Johnson disappeared around the corner at the end of the hall.

Nate raised a brow, furrowing his forehead as if in thought. Something niggled at the corner of his mind, but he couldn't bring it into focus. Something about what Johnson had said.

"I got a list of the bookstore crew members who were working the night Amber went missing," Mac was saying as he flipped through his notes. "If we get going right now we can still catch 'em on duty."

Nate looked back at Sabrina before answering him. "What was it Sabrina had you checking on before she got...before all this happened?" He managed to catch himself, almost having said the word shot.

"What?" Mac said, caught off guard by the question. "Ahhh-ah, I think it was evidence disposition and some destruction reports. Why? What's that got to do with anything?"

"I don't know, but whatever it was, Sabrina sure thought it was important." Nate rubbed his chin and looked back toward the room where his partner lay unmoving.

"You ready?" Mac asked, turning toward the door.

Nate stood still, lost in thought. "There's something I'm not seeing, and it's driving me crazy," he said with growing frustration.

"The problem is," Mac began as they again started toward the door, "there's no private parts involved."

Nate turned and looked full on at his new partner as if to say, *What?*

Mac continued not noticing, or simply ignoring Nate's quizzical expression. "We sex crimes guys are at our best when there's private parts involved. This thing is just too ordinary. We can't get our minds wrapped around it." He looked at Nate deadpan.

Nate smiled and then laughed out loud. "You know, you got a point. At least with sex crimes you can follow the passion. In this mess, there doesn't seem to be any. Just randomness. That's what we've got to do, Mac," Nate said, getting animated.

"What?"

"We've got to find the passion. We've been working this thing like we're homicide guys. What do we know about that? Nothing. We're just guessing. Let's start with the people," Nate said, getting excited, his words coming quicker as he spoke. "That's what we'd do with a sex crime."

"Yeah, but with a sex crime the victim generally knows who the perp is. This thing—we got bodies. Two bodies and nobody's talking. Pardon the pun."

"But what do we know about the bodies?"

"They're both dead."

"Don't be a butt. Of course they're both dead, but what else do we know?"

"I don't know," Mac said, shaking his head. "Where are you going with this, Nate?" As they walked, the automatic doors opened with a swoosh, and then sealed behind them, securing the ICU from the rest of the hospital. Once in the hall, their voices carried along the tiled corridors and bounced back at them from odd angles.

"What we've got to do is find out what Fuentes and Franks' had in common," Nate said, lowering his voice. "We've got to find out what the real connection is beyond them being killed so close together. And that symbol," he added as an afterthought.

"And?" Mac prompted.

"What if they are totally unrelated? That is, other than by coincidence?" Nate asked.

Mac nodded again, not needing to give voice to the question. They stopped and faced each other.

"Think about it," Nate said in answer to Mac's puzzled expression.

"Now that would be weird. Totally unrelated?" Mac mumbled under his breath.

Nate grabbed Mac's shoulder and started him walking again. "Fuentes goes down before Franks by what, six hours?"

"But what if Fuentes was killed to cover up or distract from the Franks shooting? The coroner put Franks' time of death at about eight hours before actual discovery. He could have been dead a whole hour to ninety minutes before Fuentes was even shot."

They stopped outside the elevator. The bell dinged and they walked on, still lost in conversation. Nate leaned against the back wall. "So the question is: Who would benefit from Franks being dead? Let's find the passion and we'll find the shooters."

"Yeah, but it's more fun when there's private parts involved."

The elevator door slid open, and for the first time, they noticed they were not alone. A gray-haired hospital volunteer stood in the far corner wide-eyed and suspicious of the two men. She clutched her papers against her chest then adjusted her glasses, undoubtedly getting a good description of them just in case the need arose later.

Noticing the woman, Mac pulled out his ID. "We're cops, ma'am. We were just discussing a case—an investigation." The woman walked past them without speaking but kept looking over her shoulder as she made her way out of the elevator and down the hall.

Nate rubbed his face and sagged against the wall. "I just hope Brown doesn't hear about us terrorizing senior citizens in the hospital elevators." They laughed and walked quickstep into the bright sunlight, feeling better for finally having a sense of direction.

CHAPTER THIRTY- ONE

NATE PARKED HIS JEEP about half a block from the bookstore, preferring to walk in rather than driving all the way to the front door.

"Why do you always do this?" Mac asked. "You forget it's almost a hundred degrees out there?"

"It's not that bad. Just stay in the shade. Besides, you see more when you walk in. You never know what or who you might see," Nate answered with a smile.

Mac got out of the car with a moan of complaint, securing his sunglasses against the glare of the late evening sun. "All I know is come this winter, I'm driving and I'm gonna see how much you like walking in on snow and ice."

Nate laughed. It was well known that he avoided the cold like the plague. He would just have to make sure that Mac forgot his threat by the time September and October rolled around and the cold weather set in.

As if reading Nate's mind, Mac looked over, taking out his note pad and said, "Nope, I'm not gonna forget about it either." He made himself a note.

"Baby," Nate said, closing the car door, remembering to remove the CD before leaving. Then standing, he scanned the area around him.

"What you looking for anyway?" Mac asked, coming up alongside.

"Whatever, I guess. You know people. You never know who might be watching you and maybe someone around here saw something yesterday."

Together they started toward the bookstore about half a block up the road. Even though it was close to nine in the evening, the sun shone bright and dappled the sidewalk through the canopy of trees, which lined the street. Overhead, the wind rushed like surf through the leaves and sang in chorus with the voices of birds and children laughing and the sound of slow-moving traffic in the background.

"There's a lot going on out here," Nate observed as vendors and customers busied themselves at the various shops and markets.

"What time did Amber get off last night?" Mac asked.

Continuing to look around, Nate said, "About six. She was supposed to meet that Isaac character and then bring him with her to Bible study at the church. It would have taken her at least thirty-five minutes to drive to the church from here, and we know she made it."

"Yeah, her cell phone. What did forensics show; who was her last phone contact?" Mac looked around, taking note of the level of activity.

"Me," Nate said with a sigh. "Nothing there. I was hoping we'd get at least a nudge in the right direction from the phone."

Mac turned and faced Nate, walking backwards down the sidewalk. "How we gonna keep Brown from finding out we're working the missing person case?"

"About that—" Nate began.

"Don't even say it," Mac said, waving his hand back and forth, cutting him off. "We're either in this together or we both get out. Partners, right?" He stopped in front of Nate, forcing Nate to stop as well.

Nate looked down at Mac's extended hand. He reached out and took a firm hold of it, wrapping his fingers around Mac's wrist just as Mac secured his in a mirrored grip. "Yeah," he said. "Partners."

"Well, partner," Mac said, spinning around and heading off again, "let's get to work. We've got a shooter to catch and a woman to find—and a lieutenant to keep in the dark." He smiled. "But not necessarily in that order."

Nate shook his head and smiled. He was really beginning to like this new partner. He had never considered working with anyone else other than Sabrina, but since the shooting, the thought had begun to work its way into his thinking.

Reaching the store, they separated, dividing the building in half and canvassing the room, talking to both employees and customers alike.

Thirty minutes later, Nate made his way back toward the coffee island and saw Mac already sitting waiting for him. Dropping his folder on the table, Nate sat across from Mac, their dour expressions matching.

Mac sighed, raising his brows, palms up on the tabletop. "Nothing. Nada. Zilch," he said.

Nate pursed his lips and exhaled. "Coffee?" he asked.

"Long as you're buying," Mac said and leaned back against the chair's backrest.

"I got you," Nate raised his hand, getting the waitress's attention. He smiled as the lady, Jill, acknowledged him and started in his direction. He checked his pocket and looked up at Mac smiling.

"Know what? You're cheap," Mac said.

"Not cheap, just broke," Nate answered, looking up at the waitress.

Jill placed two cups of house blend on the table in front of the men. Between chewing her gum, she managed, "No charge gents, just find that girl, and get her back safe." Looking up, they noticed she'd stopped chewing her gum and was brushing away a tear with the back of her hand.

Nate stood and opened his arms, giving the older woman a hug as Mac looked on in an uncomfortable silence. After a long moment, he stepped back, releasing her, and bumped the table causing his file to fall to the floor. The papers fanned out in an arc surrounding them. Nate smiled reassuringly and looked into the woman's tear streaked face. Cupping her chin in his hand, he said purposefully, "Jill, we are going to find her."

Suddenly embarrassed she looked away. "Oh my, let me help you with these," Jill said, stooping to pick up the papers.

"Don't worry about that, Jill, I can get those. You okay?" Nate said, stooping beside her. He reached out, collecting the papers and slipping them back into the folder.

They stood together, Jill handing a small stack of papers back to him. "Are you sure you're okay?" Nate asked.

"Yeah, I'm fine. Don't mind me," she groaned. Standing to her full five feet two inches, she put both hands on her lower back and stretched. She flashed a maternal smile and turned, heading back to the cashier's counter.

Nate watched the woman walk away and shook his head. She worked at the bookstore since way before Amber was hired and had become somewhat of a mother figure to the younger woman.

"So what's next?" Mac asked, tapping the file with his knuckle.

Nate drew his attention back to Mac and began rereading the reports and narratives, hoping to see a clue or even the smallest of leads that maybe he'd missed before.

Both men were leaned over the table concentrating on their various papers, lost in individual thoughts.

"Ahem."

Both Nate and Mac looked up to see Jill standing over them, a piece of paper held in trembling hands. "I-I, I found this over there...on the floor," she said and handed the paper to Nate.

Nate looked at the photograph Jill held in her hand and tried to make sense of the woman's reaction. "You know this man?"

"That's him. That's Isaac. He's the man that was meeting with Amber all them times."

Both Nate and Mac stood up, pushing their chairs back with their knees. "Are you sure?" Nate asked, anxiousness making him sound brusque and on edge.

"This is Israel Vega. He's been in here before?" Mac asked, clarifying.

"I don't know what you call him, but he told Amber his name was Isaac, ah...Velasquez. Yep, Isaac Velasquez."

"And this is the guy that met with Amber on the day she went missing?" Nate asked, grabbing his papers and folders from the table.

"We gotta go," Mac said and gulped down his coffee. The two men rushed from the store, stuffing papers into the folder as they hurried out.

"I hope this helps," Jill called after them.

The two men ran out the door, dodging customers who were trying to get in through the suddenly-too-small opening.

"Where to first?" Mac said, breathing hard.

"Narcotics," Nate called back. "But first we'd better call Brown, and let him know the three cases are connected."

"All three?"

Rushing into the Jeep, Nate slammed the door behind him. He pressed the gas pedal a bit too hard, causing the vehicle to lurch with acceleration, squealing its wheels as it sped from the curb.

"We'll get calls about that," Mac said, laughing, as he strapped on his seatbelt.

CHAPTER THIRTY- TWO

AMBER PACED THE LARGE ROOM, exploring its luxuries. It had been hours since anyone had checked on her, and oddly enough, she was beginning to think they had forgotten about her. Opening the door, she looked out again and saw a different set of girls lounging in the TV room.

"Hey," a male voice called out.

Startled by the husky voice, Amber pulled back into the relative safety of the doorway, nearly shutting the door. Peeking through the slant of the opening, she saw one of the men of Abyss come into view.

The nondescript, average-sized man swung his long ebony braid out of his face with a jerk of his head and walked up to the group of women, laughing and teasing as he approached them. He selected two women at random, leaning over and kissing the one as he caressed the other. With slow, careful movements, he led the two women away from the TV lounge to one of the bedrooms. Amber closed the door against the scene, shivering, with a combination of revulsion and fear; and she hoped her nightmare would soon end.

Wandering around her cage, she checked again for a way out or anything that could be used as a weapon. Pulling open the nightstand, she located the paperback Bible she had given to

Israel back at the bookstore. Sitting on the edge of the bed, she opened the small book and began to read silently.

The creak of the door withdrew her attention from the book in her hands.

"So you find the bed and the room to your liking?" Israel asked, his smile back in place. He closed the door behind him.

Amber met his gaze in stoic silence. Standing, she moved with purpose away from the bed.

Circling, Israel matched her movements. "Come on, Amber, we once sat in comfortable conversation. Shall we not again?" He gestured toward the sofa with a sweep of his hand. Israel sat, leaned back, and rested his arm along the backrest as he smiled up at her.

A wave of nausea gripped Amber's stomach when she remembered how she had once enjoyed this man's smile, had allowed herself to be flattered by the intensity of his gaze. Pulling a small blanket from the back of the sofa, she wrapped it around herself.

He smiled again and allowed his eyes to rove over her, pausing at her breast line. "Do you fear me?"

She looked at him, refusing to drop her gaze.

"About before," Israel began. "That was not what I wanted for you. This," he said gesturing to the room, "has always been my plan for you—for us. You are to be my queen."

"Your queen?" Amber said in disbelief, extending her hands, palms facing outward and fingers splayed, as if to push him away. "You kidnapped me, betrayed my trust, and tried to rape me," Amber said, anger and disgust coloring her voice.

Israel leaped to his feet pointing at her. "You forced me." With quick steps, he closed the distance between them and grabbed her shoulders. "No one tells me what I can or cannot do. No one. Not even you." He exhaled alcohol-laced breath in her face. "But I will give you some time…to ah, consider the situation. When I come back, you will need to have made your choice."

Fear overcome by her anger, Amber yelled at him, "Choice? What choice have you given me?"

"You will either be my queen or be my whore; either way I will have you." Grabbing her, he kissed her roughly on her mouth and pushed her backward, causing her to fall onto the sofa. Turning, he headed toward the door, but paused when he reached it. "You have until tomorrow, Amber. I have been patient with you, but I will wait no longer," he said, pointing a condemning finger at her. He snatched the door open and started through it.

Furious, Amber jumped up from the sofa and ran at him. She slapped him soundly across the face, and then slammed the door shut.

Jumping out of the way of the closing door, Israel staggered backward as much from surprise as from being hit. He smiled an evil, dark smile, his brows knitting together and then glared at her.

Amber faced him, matching his glare. She squared her shoulders and tilted her chin upward with a small jerk. "You might as well kill me now because I will never give myself to you, and I will never let you take me," she breathed out through clenched teeth.

Israel rubbed his cheek and rushed her, grabbing her again by her shoulders.

Refusing to back down, Amber said, "You can wait 'til tomorrow or a year from now, my answer won't change. God will be my defense."

Israel drew back his arm, bent at the elbow, preparing to backhand her. She stared up at him unblinking.

He froze, his arm hovering between them.

After an intense moment of silence, Israel lowered his arm and instead pointed a shaking finger in her face. "You have until the morning but no longer. No longer," he finished, his voice trembling as he dragged out the words as if speaking them had caused him intense pain. He spun and walked away, pulling the door closed, but not locked behind him.

Alone, Amber sunk to the sofa, hiding her face in her hands and crying. Several minutes passed as the only sound in the room was that of her own sobbing.

When the door swung open, Amber jumped back to her feet, squaring her shoulders, preparing to do battle with Israel. Instead, Gracie stood in the doorway.

Seeing it was only Gracie, Amber dropped back down on the sofa and wrapped herself again in the throw. She watched as the younger girl walked over to her. Neither spoke for a protracted moment, merely observing each other in silence.

"Did you mean all that?" Gracie asked, finally, in a small, shy voice. "What you said to Israel?"

"Every word of it!"

"But he'll do it. He'll rape you, or worse," Gracie said, leaning toward Amber and whispering. "I know he can be charming, but he can be very mean when he wants to." She got up, went to the door, and after peeking out, closed it. Coming back to the sofa, she said, "I've seen him do horrible things. If you don't come to him the way he wants," she whispered through trembling fingers, "he'll make it so you come to hate yourself."

Amber cupped the girl's face. Looking into her eyes, she said, "God is my defense." Her voice was quiet but firm.

"B-b-but what if your God don't help you? What then? Is that Jesus of yours gonna drag Israel off top of you?"

"I don't know," Amber said, sobering. "But I can't go along with what he wants. It goes against everything I believe."

"But he'll hurt you bad—"

"Sh-sh-shhh, now. Come here," Amber said and opened the blanket, receiving the girl into her embrace. They sat that way for a while, rocking gently. "There's something I want you to try and understand. It's something my friend taught me," Amber whispered into the girl's hair.

"That cop boyfriend you told me about?"

Amber smiled, "Yeah, but he's not my boyfriend, exactly."

Gracie turned a confused expression up toward Amber but didn't speak when she saw the older girl's reticent smile.

"Well," Amber began clearing her throat, "Nate told me about Doctor Martin Luther King Junior—"

"I learnt about him back in school, before I quit," Gracie interrupted excitedly.

Amber continued, smiling at the girl's enthusiasm, "Dr. King said in one of his speeches—I think it was in Chicago, that 'any man who does not have something for which he is willing to die, is not fit to live.'"

Gracie sat up and looked directly into Amber's face.

"Do you understand what that means?" Amber asked.

"No, not really," Gracie said, looking again like the lost teen instead of the streetwise gang member.

"Well," Amber began, taking Gracie's hand, "it means that there has to be something that is so important to you as a person that you won't compromise…that you won't give in even to the point of giving your life for it." She sat back and looked at Gracie's face. "Understand?"

Gracie stood quickly and walked away. She looked back at Amber sitting on the sofa. Rubbing her hands together, she wondered at the tears glistening on Amber's face.

"Gracie, about Israel, it's just something that I have to do. If he tries to—If Israel tries to take me, I will fight him." She chewed her lip and lowered her face, brushing away tears.

After a minute, Gracie walked back and sat next to Amber on the sofa. "It won't matter, he'll just beat you. I've se—"

Amber took the girl's hands into her own, cutting her off and leaned close to her. "Gracie, help me get out of here and come with me. We can leave tonight. If I can get to a phone, I can get us both help."

Gracie snatched her hands away and turned away from Amber. "Go against Israel? Go against Abyss? Are you crazy?! He'll kill us both." Her voice rose in intensity with each word spoken. She looked around the room as if she expected she was being watched. "You can't get away from Abyss. He owns us."

Amber caught the girl's face in her hands, "Israel does not own you. You do not belong to Abyss. You can get out. We can help each other. We can—"

"No! No! No!" Gracie all but screamed. "You're crazy, you're crazy, you're gonna get me beat! I can't talk to you no more. I'm sorry. I can't help you." She jumped up and ran from the room.

"Gracie, Gracie," Amber called after the girl, running behind her as far as the door. By the time Amber got to the opening, she could see Gracie settling down on the far side of the loft in front of the TV.

Amber tried to get the girl's attention without drawing anyone else's. Just as she thought Gracie would turn to look back at her, a huge black man stepped in her line of sight. Amber covered her mouth, stifling a scream. It was Jake, the same man that came in to help dress her.

Big Jake turned and saw Amber, locking eyes with her. He smiled when he saw that she had been signaling to Gracie, trying to get the girl's attention. He leaned forward, and grabbing Gracie by her hair, gently pulled her head back and kissed her deep on the mouth. Looking up, he managed to keep his eyes on Amber, all the while kissing the younger girl.

When he saw Amber's revulsion, he smiled.

Taking Gracie by the hand, with casual strides, he led her away to one of the bedrooms.

Amber shut the door quietly and made her way back to the edge of the bed. Sitting, and with hesitant movements, she opened the small Bible again and tried to read. After a troubled moment, she closed it, not able to tear her mind away from the image of the lust-filled man leading the teenager away. She sank from the bed to her knees and began to pray. She prayed first for Gracie, and then she prayed for herself; finally, she prayed that Nate would find her and put an end to this nightmare.

CHAPTER THIRTY- THREE

"IT'S 1700 HOURS and you're just dragging your butt in here," Lieutenant Brown scolded. "I left you a message over three hours ago to get in here ASAP. What part of right now don't you understand, mister?" Brown stopped near the corner of his desk.

Nate opened his mouth to respond, but the lieutenant cut him off. "Secondly, I thought I told you to stay off the missing person case and to follow up on the two homicides you begged to have assigned to you."

Nate raised his hand and inhaled, again, preparing to speak.

"Where have you been, Richards?" he asked. Brown continued talking, holding up a stapled sheath of papers in Nate's face. "Do you know what these are, mister? These are disciplinary forms. I'm writing your tired butt up. And in my opinion, it's way beyond time. Maybe the captain will finally roll you back to patrol where you can learn what it means to be a real cop." Brown sat on the corner of the desk, his chest heaving from his exertion. "What do you have to say for yourself, Detective Richards?"

Nate looked to the corner where Lieutenant Haynes sat quietly with an odd expression on his face, waiting to make sure that Brown was finished.

"Darn, Larry," Lieutenant Haynes cut in, "if you'd shut up for half a minute maybe the man can account for himself."

Mac sat quietly. Being the new guy, he thought that the better tactic.

Nate looked to Lieutenant Brown who nodded at him to go ahead. "I got your message, sir, but the message said to come in ASAP, not right away. Since I was already at Narcs going through their files, I thought it could wait until I finished. I didn't plan on it taking the better part of four hours. Sorry, sir." Nate held up his hands, palms toward Brown.

The lieutenant grunted, walked around, and sat behind the desk. Kicking his feet up, he threw the sheaf of papers face up between him and Nate on the desktop. "So how do you justify your working on the missing person's case instead of following up on the homicides I assigned you?" Brown said steepling his fingers across the arc of his growing paunch.

"Well, sir—"

"Actually, sir," Mac broke in, "we were getting coffee when clumsy me dropped my file folder. It just so happened that one of the waitresses there recognized the picture of the suspect and told us that this was the same guy that patrol officers had been asking her about involving the missing person. Just dumb luck, really."

"Just dumb luck, huh?" Brown looked from Mac to Nate, who was focusing on a spot on the wall just over the lieutenant's left ear. "Figures," he said with an air of disgust. Dropping his feet from the desk with a loud thud, Brown grabbed the sheaf of papers and slid them back into his center desk drawer.

"You just gonna keep those there?" Nate asked, tilting his head toward the drawer with the papers.

"Yeah," Brown answered with a sour smile, "knowing you, I'll be needing them soon enough."

Nate exhaled and lifted his hands in surrender. "Was there something else, sir?"

Haynes rolled his eyes at Mac and tried to hide a smirk. He mouthed, "Dumb luck my butt."

Mac laughed and tried hiding it behind his hand, faking a cough.

Brown cleared his throat and shifted his gaze between the three men. "We had a command staff meeting this afternoon, and the chief wanted an update on the Fuentes shooting, not to mention the Franks' case. I needed the update on the case to give to the chief, but I couldn't do that because you didn't respond back 10-19 like you were supposed to."

"Sir, as I was trying to explain, your message said—" Nate started in his defense.

Brown shook his head and waved him off with a flick of his wrist. "Just get out of my office; I don't want to see you. And take this one with you," he said, pointing at Mac.

After they'd left, Brown propped his elbows on his desk and began massaging his temples. "That man," he said, exasperated.

"You're gonna give yourself a stroke you keep this up," Haynes said, a smile in his voice. "All this yelling and screaming you're doing, don't make no sense."

Brown waved his hand from the wrist as if he was brushing away gnats. "I know. It's just that…he gets under my skin. He's always up to something, but things always seem to work out for him somehow. I just don't get it," Brown said, closing his eyes and rubbing them with his palms.

"Who knows," Haynes said from his spot leaning against the doorjamb, "maybe all that praying he's been doing is paying off, huh?"

"What? You're a Jesus freak too? God help me, I can't stand another one around here."

"I don't know. If Nate keeps coming through like he does and you keep making a fool out of yourself the way you do, I just might have to cross over." Haynes began to laugh as Brown looked up, his mouth open and his face slack.

"Get out of here and go home," Haynes said. "You're on dayshift and it's thirty-five minutes past your forty-two. Now get out, you're sitting at my desk."

With a deep sigh and heavy groan, Brown hoisted himself from the chair and headed toward the locker room, mumbling as he went.

Waiting until he was sure Brown had left the building, Haynes walked to the office door and looked over the CID pod. "Richards!" he called over the top of the cubicles. "My office, now! And bring Mac with you." Heads turned to watch the two detectives make their way back into the lieutenant's office for the second time that afternoon.

"What-da-ya got?" Haynes asked as soon as they sat down.

***

"Hey, hey. Wake up," Gracie said softly into Amber's ear while shaking her shoulder. "Amber. Amber, wake up."

Amber jumped at the touch, pulling the blanket up around her neck. She reached to turn on the lamp beside the bed.

"Wait, wait. It's me, Gracie." Seeing her reach for the lamp, she said, "No light, please." She touched the back of Amber's hand.

"Why? What's happened?" Amber asked, sitting up, concern in her voice. She pulled on the small chain and a soft white light blossomed in the room.

Gracie turned away, drawing her hand to her cheek, attempting to cover the deep purple and green bruise growing on the side of her face.

"Oh my God…who did this to you?" Amber said, getting up and caressing the girl's face, careful not to put pressure on the wound. "Did Israel do this? Did he do this to you for talking to me? I'm so sorry. I'm so sorry."

"No, it wasn't Israel, it was Jake. He likes his pleasure with a little pain mixed 'n it, if you get my meanin'," Gracie said, settling on the edge of the bed. She licked at the corner of her lip where it was swollen and cut. Exhaling, and then looking up at Amber, she watched for a reaction. She saw pity. She saw acceptance and love. "Were you really serious about us getting outta here tonight?" Hope filled both her voice and her eyes.

"Oh, yes, will you help me?" Amber sat next to the girl draping an arm around her slender shoulders.

Gracie smiled up at her. "Good. We better hurry. I brought these for you."

Amber turned and looked to where the girl was pointing and saw a stack of clothes on the arm of the sofa.

"I didn't think you'd wanna be running 'round in that miniskirt and tank." She smiled and got up to retrieve the pile of clothing. She handed Amber a pair of sweats and a t-shirt.

Amber couldn't help the smile growing across her face as she slipped on the pants and pulled the thin shirt over her head. She stopped to whisper a prayer as she slipped on the socks and sneakers the girl had brought her.

"C'mon," Gracie said, after turning off the light. She cracked open the door and looked around the loft. "Okay, this way," she whispered.

They slipped along the wall heading to the rear stairway. At the top of the stairs, Gracie put a hand on Amber's chest. "Wait here."

"Why, what's going on?" Amber said, desperation clinging to her words. She tried to peek over Gracie's shoulder through the partially opened door.

Gracie turned slightly and spoke back over her shoulder. "Israel has guards posted. Sometimes he does, sometimes he doesn't. Tonight, he does. Something must be up."

"What are we going to do?" Amber asked, squeezing Gracie's shoulder.

"We're getting outta here." Turning, she looked at Amber. "Stay here, I'll be right back." Taking a deep breath, Gracie loosened her ponytail, shook her hair loose, and walked through the door with a casual stride. "Oh, hi guys," she said in a voice that sounded small and a bit surprised. "Got a square?" She fumbled clumsily with her hair, brushing it forward just enough to make it look like she was trying to cover the rapidly spreading discoloration on her face.

One of the two men walked over, fishing a cigarette from his breast pocket. He offered it to her. Lighting it once, she had it perched between her lips.

"What happened to your face?" the man asked.

His buddy walked over, and without asking, took her chin in his hand and turned her face to the light. They looked at each other and grinned.

Gracie turned away, allowing her shoulders to droop as she walked back toward the door and leaned her forehead against it.

From just on the other side of the door, Amber leaned close, straining to hear. A single streak of cold sweat found its way down the middle of her back as she waited in the darkened hallway. She slowed her breaths, fighting for control, imagining crouched figures hiding in every shadow and Israel coming for her at any minute.

Outside on the landing, the man that offered Gracie the cigarette looked at his partner and tried to hide his smile. He pulled Gracie by her shoulder, turning her back around. "So what you get disciplined for?"

"Does it matter?" Gracie said, managing to pout and sound defiant.

The man rubbed his chin, this time allowing his smile to spread across his face. "No, not really. What happened?" He brushed her hair back and traced the outline of the bruise.

His partner folded his arms across his chest and leaned his broad shoulders against the far wall. Exhaling, he draped his feet one over the other at the ankles, obviously not enjoying the game as much as his friend. "Let 'er be, man. She's had it bad enough already."

Gracie made eye contact with him. "It's all right. It's just the way it is around here. You know Abyss, huh?" She smiled weakly.

Stepping forward, the second man looked at Gracie closely. "Really, I want to know what happened. Please."

Gracie took a deep breath. *I sure hope Amber's Jesus is watching. Here goes nothing.* She brushed the hair back, revealing the entire bruise. "Your boy Big Jake likes getting rough with his girls during sex, okay? He beat me." She turned away again, hiding her face, hoping her ploy was having the desired effect. "So now you know, go ahead and have your laugh, ha ha."

The two men were silent.

Gracie waited, not daring to push too hard. "Hey, Amber's God, if you're watching, please, a little help," she whispered under her breath.

"Jake. Big Jake?" one of the men asked, his voice taking on a tone of agitation.

"The new guy?" asked the other at almost the same time.

"Yeah, Big Jake, the new guy," Gracie said, trying to sound vulnerable and disgusted all at once. She didn't have to try too hard.

For the longest time nobody said anything, then the muscled man started toward the door. "I'm gonna kick his butt. That's no way to treat a woman of Abyss."

Gracie jumped in front of him, blocking the door. "No, wait, I don't want to be the cause of any trouble between the brothers. I'm just a Honey. That's what we're here for, right?" She looked back at the door, hoping Amber was hearing all this and finding somewhere to hide.

"There's rules, little sister, and he just broke one."

The other man came forward, taking Gracie by the shoulders and moving her gently to the side. "Getting disciplined is one thing, but this—this is way outta bounds. Nobody just beats you for no reason." He stopped and licked his lips before continuing. "You're one of us, and we stand by each other."

Hearing their words stirred her feelings and pulled her back to the only family she had really known. For a moment, Gracie weakened and wanted to tell them everything. She knew she could get points with Israel if she made him believe that she'd caught Amber trying to sneak out and had set her up. Maybe she would get to be Israel's girl, for a while anyway.

She swallowed and stepped aside, allowing both men to pass her. Closing her eyes, she waited, hoping Amber had gotten out of sight.

The door swung shut behind them, sealing with a soft click. Gracie dared not move. Holding her breath, she looked up. Her lips moved but no words came out, mouthing a silent prayer. She looked from the door where she stood down the short flight of stairs that led to the outside and freedom.

Gathering her nerve, Gracie tiptoed back to the door and pulled it open. Poking her head into the darkness, Gracie took a shallow breath and began to call out when a hand fastened vice-like over her mouth.

"Shush, they're right down the hall," Amber whispered into her ear. She pushed her back out through the door and pulled her into a vigorous embrace. "I was praying so hard. I thought for sure they weren't buying your story."

Gracie smiled and pushed away, breaking the embrace. "C'mon. Let's get out of here before they come back."

They ran down the final flight of stairs, slammed against the crash bar, and without stopping, burst out the door and into the night. They ran, not daring to speak again until distance had been established between them and the warehouse.

Panting heavily and with an ache growing in her side, Gracie pulled Amber into a darkened alley just off one of the main streets. Hidden in the shadows, they leaned against the wall trying to catch their breath and finally slid down and sat on the trash-covered ground.

"This running thing," Gracie gasped between breaths, "is new for me."

Amber turned to look at her new friend. "You were pretty good back there. Remind me never to cross you." She smiled between gasps of her own.

Gracie dropped her gaze. "For a minute, I almost turned you in back there." Her voice was soft, her words hesitant. "Abyss, you know, they're the only family I've had for the longest time. Now—now I just turned my back on them. Tell me I did the right thing, Amber." She locked her eyes on Amber's face; fear, regret, and hope all warring across her youthful countenance.

Amber leaned over and wrapped an arm around Gracie's shoulder, pulling the girl against her. "I know."

Gracie pulled away, arching her face back so she could look into Amber's eyes.

Amber smiled at the girl's shocked expression. "I heard you stop back there. I won't lie to you, I was praying you would hold true to what you told me, but I won't pretend to believe that it was easy for you." She got to her knees, positioning herself so she could look directly into Gracie's eyes. "I will promise you this, Gracie, I will stick by you. I will never forget what you did for me. No matter what." Amber stood up and reached a hand down. "Now, let's get out of here and find a phone."

Gracie looked at Amber's hand for a long moment and then shifted her gaze to look in the older woman's face. Finally, she accepted the proffered hand and rose to her feet. "Let's go," she said, smiling. "We'd better stay off the main streets on this side of town; Israel might be out cruising."

"Right," Amber agreed. Together they stole down the alley, stepping over pieces of broken furniture and around empty crates and boxes. From above them, the reflection of the full moon rippled on the surface of stagnant puddles as their footfalls disturbed the quiet surface of the shallow pools. At the sound of every approaching car or of voices carried on the warm summer breeze, they froze, plastering themselves deep in the shadows against the walls of the towering buildings.

CHAPTER THIRTY- FOUR

EVEN IN THE EARLY HOURS of the morning, CID thrummed with activity. Various detectives sat typing and reviewing reports from the day's activities. Several different styles of music played softly, floating over the open space. Looking up, Nate could see the red light flashing over the interview door, indicating that an interview was in process.

He looked at the time indicator on the computer monitor; it flashed 2:15 AM. Rubbing bloodshot eyes, he clicked the start icon to turn the computer off. Standing, he pulled his cell phone from his pocket, checking the time against the time on the monitor. The battery indicator flashed, showing less than one bar left. Stopping, Nate plugged it into the desktop charger.

Settling back into his chair behind the desk, Nate again opened the file, trying to discover what it was Sabrina had been onto. Grabbing his face in his hands, Nate groaned in frustration. "Ahhh, God, help me," he said in bitter dejection and slipped from his chair to his knees. Dropping his head against his forearm, Nate sighed. "I know I've been wrong in not seeking You in earnest, trying to do so much on my own, but please, Lord," he spoke in strained tones, barely above a whisper, "I've got to find her…please protect her—"

"Ahemmm…"

At the sound of a throat being cleared, Nate looked up directly into the dour face of Lieutenant Haynes.

"What on earth do you think you're doing? This is not a bloody church. Get up off your knees, man," Haynes said, leaning forward, his hands slightly extended toward Nate.

"Sir, I was just…just—"

"I know what you were doing; it's just that you don't do it here. God is not your partner. MacGilvery—Mac, whatever you call him, is."

The cell phone rang.

Haynes stepped closer to Nate, who had managed to climb back into his chair. He smiled knowingly at Nate and then sat on the corner of the desk. "So I guess you figure that you can just sit in here, and God will go out and find Amber for you, huh?"

The cell phone continued ringing. Nate looked from the incessant phone to Lieutenant Haynes.

Haynes reached out and silenced the cell phone. His voice taking on a fatherly quality, but managing to maintain a questioning air, he said, "Son, I'm going to do you a favor. Instead of writing you up for this, I want you to get up off your knees and do some real police work. We'll just forget this ever happened."

The phone began to ring again.

Nate stood up and looked into Haynes' smiling face. Without speaking, he turned away and reached across the desk, picking up his cell phone. Looking at the caller ID and not recognizing the number, he sighed, silenced the phone, and dropped it into his pocket. He turned back to look at Haynes. "I was hoping it was the lab."

Haynes frowned at him for interrupting him to check the call. He stood, his smile replaced by a look of frustration.

The phone rang again, vibrating against Nate's chest.

"Turn that blasted thing off while I'm talking to you," Haynes said, starting to get upset. "First I catch you—"

On an impulse, Nate raised a hand, effectively pausing the lieutenant, and flipped open his phone. He arched an eyebrow at the lieutenant's expression of unbelief. *I hope this is the lab. God, let this be the lab…* "Richards," he clipped into the phone.

Angry at being blown off, Haynes stood.

Nate jumped to his feet, causing Haynes to step back and raise his hands in a defensive posture. Nate turned toward him, squaring his shoulders. "Where are you?" he asked excitedly and then dropped back into the chair, quickly scribbling notes.

Haynes frowned, but stepped closer in spite of himself.

"Okay, I'll be there in fifteen— no—ten minutes! Stay inside. Stay out of sight." He snapped the phone shut, ending the call.

"Who was that?" Haynes demanded, his earlier anger forgotten.

Nate silenced him by raising a finger. Flipping open the phone again he dialed. After two rings a distracted voice answered the line. "Mac, I've found her!" Nate blurted without preamble. "Be down front in two minutes. I'll pick you up." He snapped the phone closed and turned, grabbing his jacket off the back of the chair.

"Who was that on the phone?" Haynes demanded again.

"That, sir, was God. He's found the girl and is holding her, waiting for me to pick her up. If you don't mind, sir, I don't want to keep my *Partner* waiting." He smiled, saluted, turned, and hurried out the door.

∗∗∗

As the door swung shut, Haynes slammed his fist into the opened palm of the opposite hand. "Yes!" He said, then looked up at the ceiling and added under his breath, "Not that I'm ready to sign up yet." He laughed out loud and spun away, heading back to his office. In his wake, papers scattered and floated to the floor, settling against the half-wall of the pod divider. Overhead, the fluorescent lights flickered and came back on, filling the workstation with an eerie yellow glow. Around the room heads popped up, looking from one to the other with confused expressions. Then without a word spoken, they ducked back down, refocusing on the stacks of paper and reports on their desks.

***

Nate brought the Jeep to a screeching halt in front of the convenience store, Michael W. Smith's "Friends" blaring from the speakers. Both he and Mac jumped out of the car, guns in hand and held discreetly by their sides. The soft echo of screeching tires faded and the smell of burnt rubber thinned on the already acrid odor of the stale air surrounding the late night convenience store.

Several men, who had been standing near the entry to the store, turned and walked toward Nate and Mac when the vehicle came to a stop. One of a few working girls, hammering out the details of a possible deal, dropped her half-smoked cigarette and tugged at the hem of her dirty jean miniskirt, looking seductively at the newcomers. They all backed off as Nate held up his badge and they saw the Glock .40 held down by his side.

For a moment, no one moved. A strained silence settled on the area.

With a cry of delight, Amber ran from the store and melted into Nate's arms. Mac stood back, watching the streets and searching the shadows for furtive movements. He held his gun in the low ready as he watched the backs of the quickly retreating crowd.

"Are you all right?" Nate asked, holding Amber around her shoulders, holding her close to him.

"I'm fine," she said between nervous giggles of relief. "I'm fine," she said again, more to herself than to Nate this time.

"Freeze!" Mac called out. "Show me your hands, now!" Supporting his grip, Mac brought his off-hand up and pointed his gun at a young lady running toward Nate and Amber.

Both Amber and Nate turned to see Mac approaching the girl, his eye focused down the barrel. The girl froze, fear etched in her eyes. She held her hands palms forward above her head. Her mouth was agape, trapped in a silent O.

Nate pushed Amber behind him, trapping her against his back and swung his handgun up, sighting in on the unknown female.

"No!" Amber screamed and forced herself between the men and Gracie. "No, Nate, she's my friend. She's the only reason I managed to get away."

Mac raised the barrel of the gun upward and held his support hand up, palm facing Gracie. Putting his gun back into his holster, he approached Gracie slowly. "Sorry, ma'am, I didn't know who you were. No offense, I hope," he said and extended his now empty gun-hand in goodwill.

"Nahh, I'm used to you cops. You're all the same—either you're pointing your guns at me or cop'n a feel," Gracie said dryly.

Mac looked at his hand, suddenly embarrassed. "I hope you don't think I was gonna—that I was trying to…" He failed to finish his statement.

Gracie began to laugh and squeezed Mac's hand. "He's kinda cute when he's blushing," she said to Amber. Then turning to Nate, she asked, "Is he married?"

"Careful, Mac," Amber said with a lilt in her voice, "she's only sixteen and a little young, even for you."

Still holding Mac's hand, Gracie squeezed it again and smiled coyly at him. "Too bad, you really are cute." She released his hand and walked over to stand by Amber.

Laughing, Nate reached out and pulled Gracie into a hug, "Thank you so much Miss…?"

"Just Gracie. I ain't no 'Miss' nothing," she said, sobering.

"All right then, Miss Nothing, let's get out of here and get you something to eat," Nate finished, looking over her head, scanning the street for possible hostiles in the area.

"Let's get out of here, buddy," he said to Mac.

Settling into the car, Nate handed an unopened CD over his shoulder to Amber in the backseat. "I picked this up for you."

She looked at the Hill Song CD in her hand and began to cry. She hit him on his shoulder playfully. "You still owe me lunch and this doesn't count."

"You got it." He smiled into the rearview mirror at her reflection. "You never looked better," he said softly.

Gracie cut her eyes at Amber and smiled, "Not really, huh? Yeah, right." She giggled.

Amber looked back at the girl and held her gaze. She elbowed her softly in the ribs as they shared a private laugh.

"What are you two laughing about?" Mac asked, looking back.

"Nothing," the ladies said together and began laughing again.

Nate looked up and caught Amber's eye again, smiling at her. "First, we get something quick to eat and then we head into the station. We need statements from both of you, and then we're heading to Mom's for a real breakfast."

Not stopping until he was clear of Old Town, Nate pulled into the drive-thru of a local fast food restaurant and ordered Amber and Gracie a small breakfast meal. "It'll be a couple of hours before you're done at the station," he said, passing the bags to the backseat.

Mac closed his cell phone and turned to look at Nate. "I updated the L.T. on our status. He told me to tell you he's already got a call in to the patrol commander and the briefing is set for 0700 hours in the conference room. He also said, and I quote, 'I almost joined the team.' Whatever that means."

As they pulled back onto the freeway, Nate smiled and opened his cell phone, pressing the shortcut key, calling his parents. "Hey…Mom…no, no, everything's all right… somebody here wants to talk to you." He handed the phone over his shoulder to Amber.

"Hi, Mom, it's me," Amber said.

CHAPTER THIRTY- FIVE

NATE WATCHED ANXIOUSLY through the observation window as Detective Jasper Solvack interviewed first Amber, then Gracie, checking and rechecking the written statements and confirming the identity of Israel Vega, aka Isaac Velasquez. He walked to the far wall in the darkened room and ran his hand nervously through his thick curls. Resting his palm on the ivory-colored wall, Nate sighed and sagged against the supporting coolness of the bulkhead.

Solvack looked up to where he knew Nate would be watching and nodded. Nate hefted himself from the wall, gathered his papers, and headed out of the small room. Mac grunted and stood to follow.

A few minutes later, Nate walked into the interview room followed closely by Mac. "Hey, how you girls doing?" he asked as Gracie came back into the room, escorted by a uniformed officer.

"Tired, really tired," Amber said, walking to him and leaning her head against his chest. "Get me out of here?"

"Sure," he said into her hair. Then turning his attention to a, in spite of her attempt at bravado, nervous Gracie. "How 'bout you, Miss Anything? How you doing?"

"I'm scared. I just ratted out Abyss; they'll kill me for this. I don't know what I'm gonna do." She began shaking her head from side to side, looking at Amber with tear-filled eyes.

"Come here," Nate said and enclosed her in a three-way embrace. "Let's get these ladies out of here, Mac."

"Gotcha covered, boss. Already called Elva. She'll meet us at your folks' house in about an hour."

"Copy that." Then turning, he looked back in through the opened door. "Are you finished with them, Solvack?" At the man's affirming nod, Nate herded the tired ladies toward the exit.

Exiting the glass door at the rear of the building, they squinted against the brilliant sunrise, which blossomed during the four-hour interview session. As they made their way to the parking lot, two white Hondas turned the corner at the far end of the street. The vehicles stopped, taking up both lanes. Like a pair of drag racers, the vehicles revved their engines and suddenly accelerated at the foursome as they attempted to cross the otherwise empty street.

Gracie screamed.

Nate pushed the women to the far curb and dove after them. The front bumper of the far vehicle clipped Mac's foot as he jumped to the curb, sending him in a sprawl. Scrambling to his feet, Nate drew his handgun and took aim at the fleeing cars but didn't chance taking the shot.

An unsuspecting driver in a police vehicle pulled out just as the two vehicles sped by his location and barely missed hitting him. With a lurch, the police car accelerated, crashing through a retaining wall and slamming into a parked vehicle. Nate grunted in frustration and rammed his gun back into his holster.

Turning, he ran to where Mac and the two ladies lay in a heap. "Everybody okay?" he asked.

"Caught my foot on the bumper, but I'm all right," Mac said, getting to his feet.

"I told you! I told you they would kill me! I never should have left them. Israel is never gonna let me live." Gracie sat on the ground being held by Amber muttering to herself.

"You're okay, Gracie. We're all okay," Amber said, attempting to comfort the girl. She looked at Nate for reassurance.

Nate knelt down beside them and stroked the girl's hair back from her face. With a thumb, he pushed away a tear as it fell. "Gracie, look at me," he said softly. "Gracie…look at me. You're all right and I won't let Israel or anybody else hurt you. Okay?"

He reached out and she took his hand. "Come on. Let's get out of here. I've got a safe house already set up for you."

***

Twenty-five minutes later, the foursome pulled into the garage of Reverend and Mrs. Richards. Sherri and the Reverend, still dressed in pajamas and bathrobes, met them at the door. Rushing out to meet them, Sherri first collected Amber in her arms, planting kisses on her cheeks, then offered a welcoming hand to a very reserved Gracie.

"You girls come right on in and let me get you something to eat," Sherri said soothingly.

"Hey, thanks guys," Nate said, forcing an air of lightness into his voice. At his mother's dismissing wave of her hand, he turned to Mac and shrugged. "Well at least we got here without incident."

As the garage door closed smoothly in its track, both men scanned the road for any sign of white cars.

Nate looked at Mac and laughed. "One thing for sure, I know where I stand with the woman folk 'round here."

"Don't feel bad, Son, she's let me know exactly where I stand with her now for almost four decades," Reverend Richards said, slapping Nate on his shoulder. "Well, men, what do you say we get inside and have us a cup of coffee ourselves?"

"I'll take you up on that," Mac said, striding toward the kitchen door without waiting.

Reverend Richards looked at his son and laughed. "I like this new partner, feels like he's one of my own already."

"Yeah," Nate laughed lightly. "Pop, you see Sabrina lately?

His dad sobered and looked hard at him for a few seconds. "Yeah, was down this morning…well, yesterday now," he said, starting again toward the door.

"Dad, I—," Nate began.

His dad stopped and looked back at him. "Look, Son, you don't owe me an explanation, but you might want to at least call Karl and let him know you're still thinking about him."

"I will…this morning," Nate said, chastened.

They reached the door and were greeted with the sound of laughter and loud talking. The fragrance of bacon and eggs coupled with the aroma of fresh ground coffee wafted out through the open door and drew the men inside. Entering the kitchen, they saw the three women and Mac seated around a table piled high with scrambled eggs, a plate of bacon, biscuits, coffee, and a large dish of cheese grits.

"Save us some?" Nate asked, closing the door behind him.

"No bets on that," Gracie said and Mac nodded in agreement, his mouth full. The girl was visibly more relaxed, but not quite at ease yet. Nate worried about her.

Reverend Richards smiled at the girl and placed a loving hand on her shoulder, taking notice of the slight tension at his touch. He withdrew his hand with casual purpose after giving her shoulder a slight squeeze and a fatherly pat.

Pouring himself a cup of coffee, he proffered the pot to Nate, who raised an empty cup as the Reverend filled it. "Oh, Elva called, said she was stuck in the motor pool trying to check out a car. Said it might be awhile, but everything should work out."

Father and son leaned against the counter, saluted each other with upraised cups, and smiled as they watched Amber pour her fifth packet of Splenda into her cup of coffee.

After everyone had eaten their fill, Reverend Richards walked over to his wife, laying his hand on her shoulder. He leaned forward and kissed her upraised cheek. Nate and Amber had an idea what was coming, but Mac and Gracie, unfamiliar with the ritual, kept up their conversations.

Reverend Richards put his fist to his mouth and cleared his throat, "I think it's time we ought to pray and thank God for delivering you girls safely to our home and out of harm's way."

Nate caught Gracie's eye and acknowledged her fear and concerns with a tilt of his chin. "It's not over yet, Dad. Remember that darkness we talked about the last time I was here? Well, we're in the thick of it, and you guys may have brought it to your doorstep by wanting to be involved. We'd better pray for continued protection for our little champion here. She took a big risk helping Amber the way she did."

"Son, your mother and I have been fighting against that darkness in this valley for the last fifteen years. It's nothing new to us. Jesus fights for us," his dad said, taking his mother's hand.

Nate nodded as he watched his mother look into his father's face with total agreement and confidence. But he knew his mother well enough to know that the confidence she exuded came not from her husband but from her faith. He smiled and nodded again with one quick dip of his chin.

Amber reached over and took Gracie's hand in her own and nodded as well.

Nate smiled at the gesture. "We also need to pray for her future. She has no family left."

At this, Sherri got up from her seat and walked around and stood behind Gracie, hugging her around the neck. "Well, she can stay here as long as need be. I need another girl around here anyway since your sister moved back east."

Reverend Richards stretched out his hand, taking Nate's on his left and Amber's on his right. The rest followed suit, joining hands all around until the circle was complete. Reverend Richards bowed his head and began the prayer, his solemn voice carrying over the intimate gathering. "Dear Lord," he began and continued to pray, thanking God for delivering Amber out of danger and for bringing Gracie into their lives. He went on asking the Lord to provide for all their needs, including protection from retribution from Abyss and a positive future for Gracie.

Just as they finished, the doorbell sounded, filling the house with the first few bars of "Shout to the Lord," a contemporary worship song. "I got it," Nate said and broke from the circle. Mac followed, flanking him and drawing his handgun as he went.

Nate looked at Mac and then moved toward the front of the room. The morning sun was already heating the wooden surface, the knob felt warm in his hand. He opened the door.

Re-holstering his handgun, Nate greeted Elva. The short-statured lady stood patiently just outside the glass door and smiled. "Sorry I'm late," she said, fanning herself with a sheaf of papers.

"No, come on in," Nate said, opening the door. "Everybody, this is Elva. Elva, everybody," he said, by way of introduction.

"Don't mind him, Elva, come on in and have some breakfast," Sherri said.

Elva walked over to the kitchen, stopping near the table. "Don't mind if I do," she said, reaching past Mac for a biscuit and making an egg and bacon sandwich.

Gracie looked suspiciously at the little lady, wondering what her role in all this would be.

As Elva settled down, her badge swung out from her chest, identifying her as a CPS social worker.

"Wait—wait," Gracie said, jumping up from the table. "Nobody said anything about no foster home. I knew you were lying. I should have known better." She stared at Amber with hard, tear-filled eyes. "I trusted you."

"I didn't know," Amber started, in her own defense. Then she turned to Nate. "What's going on here?"

After a while, Elva heaved up her huge briefcase and dropped it on the table. "So this is Miss Gracie, huh?" she said, without looking at the girl.

Gracie cursed, turned, and stormed away from the table. "Just like I thought, Gracie gets screwed," she said not so much under her breath.

Amber went after her and stood with her. "Hey, just like I said, I won't leave you hanging. You stood by me, and now I'm going to stand by you. Okay?" When Gracie didn't answer, she asked again, "Okay?"

"Okay," Gracie said, but didn't sound convinced.

Back at the table, Elva opened her briefcase and pulled out a two-and-a-half-inch thick binder. There were papers clipped to it and stapled with each other in a mismatched fashion, which only she seemed to understand. "Ah, here it is," she said, pulling a certain stack of papers from the folder.

She laid the papers on the table and started leafing through the pile. "Yes," she said to no one in particular. "Grace Marie Wallace. Date of birth, June 17th, 1992. No siblings and an orphan. Criminal history…"

Gracie cringed as the little lady began reading out loud.

"Two charges of prostitution, possession of a controlled substance, and numerous alcohol and tobacco violations. No school worth talking about, well, not since seventh grade when she was an A/B student." Elva closed the folder, having stuck the papers back in.

"You forgot to tell them that I picked my nose once too," Gracie said caustically. "You people get on my nerves. Don't you believe in people's privacy?" She waved at Elva with her middle finger extended before allowing Amber to turn her away.

Elva looked at Nate and sighed, "You sure you want to do this to your parents?"

"I don't think you could stop them now," he said and smiled. "But I guess it really depends on Gracie and what she wants."

"What do you mean it depends on me?" Gracie asked, coming back to the table.

"Well," Elva said and looked at the girl with a stern eye. "Reverend and Mrs. Richards are licensed foster parents and have agreed to let you live here with them. Based on your attitude and lack of manners, I'm not so sure it will be a good idea, if they even want you here anymore," Elva said, sounding disinterested.

Gracie rolled her eyes but said nothing. Encouraged by Amber, Nate looked at his parents, who were exchanging glances between themselves.

After a few moments, Nate accepted a form from Elva and filled out the necessary paperwork, declaring Gracie to be in a state of imminent danger and placing her into State's custody. Then to his mom and dad, he said, "Now, you guys won't need to be at the hearing on Monday at the courthouse."

They nodded their heads in unison and smiled at Gracie. "It's not our first ride on this train, Son. Besides, the young lady still hasn't said whether she wants to stay here or not. We won't force her," Reverend Richards said matter-of-factly.

Gracie brightened. "You guys serious? Then absolutely!" she said excitedly. "Will you stay here too?" she turned to ask Amber.

"No, I have my own place, but I'll be around and I'll give you my numbers," she answered.

"I wish you would reconsider that," Nate said.

"But," Sherri interrupted, addressing Gracie, "you'll have to follow house rules and attend church with us. We won't try and force you to believe or anything, but you will have to go along with us. We can work out the other details together later on." Sherri smiled brightly, hoping to soften the declaration.

"Of course," Elva said, "when school begins, and if you're still here, you'll have to register and attend. Emphasis on attend."

"What's to keep me from just running away?" Gracie asked.

Amber stepped around in front of the teen and focused her attention on her. "Just your desire to prove to your stepdad and all those other freaks, like Big Jake, that they were wrong." She smiled. "But mostly because you're worth it."

The girls smiled and embraced. Afterwards, Gracie walked over to Sherri and reached out her hand. Ignoring the gesture, Sherri pulled the girl against her breast and hugged her tight.

Reverend Richards walked over to Gracie and extended his hand, waiting for her to accept or deny the legitimacy of the gesture.

For a quiet moment, she stood squared up in front of the older man and then without speaking, reached out a steady hand and returned his handshake. They shook briefly and, then again, silently released their grip and went to separate parts of the room, Reverend Richards back near the breakfast bar and his son and Gracie next to Amber.

They sat around for a while talking quietly but laughed when they heard a low buzzing sound and found Mac asleep with his face in his palm, elbow resting on the table.

"Speaking of sleep," Nate said to Amber, "since you insist on leaving, I'd better get you home."

"Yes," Elva said, "I've got another stop to make over on the north side. Can one of you guys come along for police presence?"

Startled awake when everyone laughed, Mac volunteered, "I'll do it. I had some sleep last night; you've been up all night, Nate."

"You sure?" Nate asked.

"Yeah, I'll get Elva to drop me off at my car, and I'll follow her over. I'll put you out on the board, forty-two, until, what—fifteen-hundred?"

"Thanks. Fifteen hundred. Good, I'll see you then. Let the L.T. know I'll get my reports done when I come in later."

***

After saying their goodbyes, Nate and Amber found themselves alone on the freeway heading to the west side of the valley. Amber sat with her eyes closed and leaned against the window, her arms folded across her chest. The only sound was the hum of the tires on the road.

"I really don't want to be alone yet. Can I stay at your place?" she asked, her eyes still closed.

"Whoa—sure," Nate started. "I thought you were asleep." Nate looked over at her, but she hadn't moved. "You can have the bed; I can sleep on the sofa."

"Thanks."

Fifteen minutes later, Nate pulled up in front of his apartment building. Taking a moment to scan the area, he turned off the CD player and killed the engine. "Hey, we're here," he said, touching Amber on the corner of her chin.

Her eyelids fluttered open and she smiled. "Mmmm, good. I'm looking forward to a hot shower and lying down."

A few minutes later, standing in the cool darkness of Nate's living room, a welcome relief from the heat, they smiled at each other, remembering the last time they were in his apartment together.

"You first," Nate said, indicating the shower.

"You sure?" she asked, already heading toward the towel cabinet.

"Yeah, I need to check my messages anyway."

After they were both showered, they dressed for bed. Amber wearing a t-shirt and pair of borrowed sweats, while Nate wore a pair of shorts and t-shirt of his own. Nate collected a set of sheets for the sofa and then walked with Amber to his bedroom.

She laid down and got tucked in under the covers, pulling them up to just beneath her chin. "Sit with me for a while?" she asked, her voice timid.

"Sure," Nate said and sat next to her on the side of the bed, draping an arm over her shoulder.

Amber rolled onto her side, tucking into a ball. "Thanks, Nate," she said from behind closed lids, "I mean, for everything."

Nate watched her and brushed a strand of loose hair from her face. She opened her eyes, smiled at him, and then closed them softly with a contented sigh.

Nate scooted up to the head of the bed, resting his back against the wall. Without notice, Amber changed position, resting her head in his lap. Nate smiled and readjusted his arm over her shoulder. She didn't move. Together, they slept.

CHAPTER THIRTY- SIX

ISRAEL SAT ON HIS DAIS LOOKING DOWN at the large man, bloodied, bruised, and sprawled on the floor before him. "Big Jake," he said in a patient, yet patronizing voice. Standing slowly, he walked down to where Jake lay on the floor. Israel nodded to Lo who left silently.

Jake looked up through swollen eyes and groaned, trying to speak through blood-engorged lips. Stretching his hand in a feeble gesture, he attempted to rise to one knee. "Iswill," he slurred, "mmm sawee."

"What was that?" Israel asked, kneeling down next to the man.

"I'mmmm sarree," he managed with greater effort. "I di'n't mean no h'rm."

Israel patted the man's head as if he was a puppy nuzzling his master's hand. Laughing, Israel stood and addressed the assembled group, "He said, he's sorry."

The group echoed Israel's words as well as the mocking tone. And then in quiet voices, they began to chant, ""ABYSS, ABYSS, ABYSS," over and over, growing in intensity until the building reverberated with their call.

Israel nodded at the two men standing like sentinels over Jake. Grabbing him by the upper arms, they pulled him in rough fashion to his feet. Israel turned his back to Jake and looked at the group of women who were looking on with furious expressions. "Do you want him?" he asked the group of females.

Their voices rose with cursing, swearing, and an emphatic chorus of yeses. He stepped aside and swept his arm across his body at waist level as if opening a door. With a vicious roar, the group of ten to fifteen women fell upon the man with savage beatings.

Israel turned his back to the scene and walked with a casual pace back to his throne-like seat. Settling there, he watched the discipline play out before him with minimal interest.

After several minutes, Lo re-entered the room and crossed in quickstep to Israel. Seeing his friend's face, Israel sat up in weary anticipation.

"They're both gone," Lo said, his voice low, "but they were seen with that detective boyfriend and his partner."

Israel screamed a primal roar and instantly the room fell silent. He looked at Jake, now curled into a fetal position surrounded by his female attackers. "Kill him!"

He rose and walked out of the room, followed closely by Lo and his lieutenants. The sound of the attack died down as the large door closed behind him. "How long?" he asked.

"Maybe four hours," Lo said, checking his wristwatch. "The guards reported seeing the girl, Gracie, at about one this morning, and when they went back to let her know they'd dealt with Jake, she was gone."

Israel looked at his second in command who had continued to walk with him, his lieutenants standing a respectful distance away. "Did they leave together?"

"Dunno, but I'm pretty sure they must have. Don't think Amber could have made it out alone." Lo stopped walking, grasping his hands in front of him, fingers interlaced, and waited for Israel's decision.

"Okay," Israel said, coming to a determined line of action. "We have to assume they are still together." He rubbed his chin. "Gracie?" he asked and then answered himself, "The girl that interrupted us when, ah…and told us the delivery had arrived, right?"

Lo dipped his chin, "Yeah, same one."

Israel spun to face his lieutenants. "Break it down. Get everything and everybody out of here. I figure we got, at best, four to five hours."

For a minute, nothing happened. Then Lo took over. "Move!" Instantly the crew burst into action, the men spreading in several directions at once.

Israel stood off at a distance watching his family go to work. With several different scenarios running through his mind at once—chiefly, how would he get Amber back?

"What about Jake?" Lo asked from near his elbow.

Breaking his reverie, Israel focused on his *second*. "Dump him on the south side. They'll call it retribution for the fool I cut there a week or so ago."

"You heard the man," Lo said, turning to his underlings. Then turning to his female, Lo said, "Bring the car around to the alley, I need to get Israel out of here before the cops show."

The woman smirked and turned at a run, disappearing through the crowd. Israel grinned to himself, watching the organized chaos unfolding around him. Grasping his hands behind his back, he walked slowly toward the rear loading dock. Israel smiled. The thought of a cup of coffee and a good book occupying the chief part of his mind warmed him. *Yes,* he thought, *coffee, a good book, and Amber.* He laughed and got into the car as his female driver opened the door, securing him in the back seat hidden behind heavily tinted windows.

CHAPTER THIRTY- SEVEN

NATE GROANED AND MOVED HIS NECK AND SHOULDERS in slow, careful circles, working out the muscles frozen from having slept sitting upright on the bed. Squinting tired eyes, he turned, trying to see the clock on the nearby nightstand. "1330 hours," he moaned. He still had an hour or so before he would be expected at the office.

Nate glanced around his small bedroom before looking down at Amber who was still sleeping, curled tight across his outstretched legs. Careful not to awaken her, he lifted her head and lowered it, replacing his leg with a pillow.

Flexing sleep-stiffened joints, Nate stretched his legs out one at a time and walked with soft steps out of the bedroom and got dressed for work. Pausing before he left, he wrote a note telling Amber where he'd gone, how to contact him, and told her not to attempt to leave the apartment without him.

Just before 1500 hours, Nate walked through the door of CID, greeted first by Mac. "Got the search warrants for the warehouse and Vega's car," he said. "Patrol wants SWAT in on the warrant service. You got a problem with them running with it?"

"Nahh," Nate said, rubbing the back of his neck. "From what Gracie told us, it's probably best that they do. The last thing I want is to walk into a gunfight and be out-gunned." He sat behind his desk, grabbing a stack of files as he did so. "Any coffee around here?" he asked.

"Who daht asking for my coffee?" Lieutenant Haynes asked in a very poor Jamaican accent as he strutted into the pod. "I know I don't hear nobody asking about the lieutenant's coffee."

Nate leaned back putting his feet crossed at the ankles onto the desktop. "The last time we had this conversation, sir, I thought we determined who it was that provided the coffee around here." The men laughed.

"Yeah, but who brought the coffee this morning?" Haynes said, placing a cardboard cup carrier on the desk, steam wafting up from three medium-sized cups of Library coffee.

Nate's jaw fell slack as Mac came forward, claiming one of the cups. Mac tipped the cup toward Haynes in appreciation as he sat on the corner of the desk.

"Oh yeah, who's da' man?" Haynes asked with a cocksure smile on his face. "All kidding aside," he said, straightening up and dropping the attempt at the accent, "you gentlemen did a fine job; just wanted to say thanks."

Nate lifted the final cup of coffee from the carrier and saluted Haynes with the upraised cup. "It wasn't us, sir. We can't take the credit for what God did for us. He practically put her in our laps."

"Just say thanks, you cad," Haynes said, smiling.

"Thanks."

"Looks like we can tie the Fuentes and the Franks shooting to this guy as well," Mac said.

"All we have to do is find him," Nate added.

The door opened and a uniformed patrol officer walked in. "Congratulations on solving the missing person," Officer Johnson said. "I hear you guys are serving a warrant on the warehouse where she was taken. Can I get in on that?" He looked from Nate to Lieutenant Haynes. "I already got it cleared with my duty sergeant." He smiled.

"Was she able to give you any details on this guy or why he took her? Anything weird or unusual come up?" Johnson finished, sounding casual.

Nate glanced at Mac, who was apparently not paying attention, eyes closed and savoring the coffee. "Naaah," Nate said, "if it's okay with the L.T. I don't mind if you tag along, but SWAT's running the service. You'd better hook up with them if you want to be there at entry."

Johnson stepped back toward the door. "Thanks, man, I owe you." He slipped out and the door sealed behind him.

Mac opened his eyes. "I really don't like that guy."

"Kind of weird if you ask me," Haynes said, shaking his head.

Nate stared at the closed door for a moment before speaking. "Sabrina didn't like him either. He's always been square with me, but—"

"That's just it," Mac said, "there's always that *but*; and it's that *but* that weirds me out."

Nate laughed, then stood and looked at his wristwatch. "It's gonna be another hour at least before SWAT's even ready to move. Come run by the hospital with me, I haven't checked on Sabrina in a day or two."

Mac stood with a groan and grabbed his sunglasses off the desk. "Wanna come, L.T.?"

"Somebody's gotta stay and watch the mad house," he said, smiling. "Besides, I've got a stack of papers on my desk I need to get done before Brown comes in."

Nate and Mac headed for the door, and Lieutenant Haynes walked back toward the lieutenant's office. Haynes stopped and looked back over his shoulder. "I told Brown about your little prayer vigil last night. He wasn't too happy."

Nate stopped and looked at his friend. "Yeah, what did he have to say about it?"

"Nothing you could say in church or in the company of a lady," he said.

Nate raised his hands, palms up, "I was out of ideas. It was all I had left."

Haynes smiled and shook his head again. He waved his hand in dismissal, turned, and walked away, his shoulders shaking with laughter.

***

Nate approached the door of the Intensive Care Unit and stopped, his hand paused above the touchpad. Mac looked at him, but did not speak, standing in silence watching his new partner. Nate swallowed and looked over at Mac. "Here goes."

The doors opened with a swoosh, like the room had taken a deep breath; immediately the sights, sounds, and smells of the ICU enveloped them.

Mac tapped Nate on the shoulder, "Go ahead, I'll wait over here." He walked off taking a seat just inside the unit's waiting area.

Nate smiled and dipped his chin, then turned toward the sliding glass door that separated his friend's room from the open bay of the ICU. Brushing the curtain aside, he saw Karl sitting beside the bed, an open Bible on his lap.

"Hey, Bro," Karl said, standing and grabbing Nate in a hug. "Your dad said you'd be coming by."

"I'm really sorry that I haven't—"

"What, and let those guys do God-knows-what to Amber? No, you did the right thing and you know it. If you'd been sitting around here instead of trying to find that girl, Sabrina would have gotten up and kicked your butt." The two men fell into easy laughter.

Karl put his hand on Nate's shoulder and guided him to an extra seat beside the bed. Nate looked at Sabrina for the first time since coming into the room. "How's she doing, any better?"

"Actually, yes." Karl beamed. "She's been awake twice now. Only a few minutes at a time, though. She can't talk yet, but I'd swear she recognizes me." Karl brightened and grabbed Sabrina's hand, stroking it softly across the knuckles.

Nate smiled, watching as Karl rubbed Sabrina's hand and forearm, tenderness and caring evident in every stroke.

"You remember that cute little nurse with the southern accent?"

Nate nodded, but truthfully he didn't remember the woman.

"Well anyway, she says that Sabrina doesn't really see anything yet. That she's just opening her eyes due to internal stimuli, but I know better. My baby looked at me and smiled." Then turning his attention to the unconscious woman, he said, "Didn't you baby? You smiled at me, didn't you?"

Nate laughed out loud at the baby talk this giant of a man was employing to his sleeping wife. He cleared his throat, coughing into his fist. "What does the doctor say?"

"Says we've already beat the odds." He looked Nate in the eyes. "Prayer works." He turned his attention back to Sabrina, but continued talking. "How's Amber? Did the guys hurt her?"

"Looks like she got slapped around a little bit, but it could have been a lot worse. Know what I mean?"

Karl stopped stroking Sabrina's arm and turned back to look at Nate. "Yeah, a lot worse."

Nate fussed with his hands for a moment. "My new partner is working out fine. You've got to meet him."

Karl laughed. "I remember when they first assigned you to Sabrina. Boy, she was not happy about that…'giving me some wet-behind-the-ear pup off the streets'…. Boy, she must have fussed about you for a month of Sundays."

They both laughed again, this time until tears escaped their eyes. Nate recalled how stiff Sabrina had been with him after her last partner retired, and Nate had replaced him. "Well," Nate said, catching his breath, "Mac's a little different, but he's a darn good cop. And he's gonna be a darn good detective before he's done. He has the nose for it."

"'The nose for it', huh? You're even talking like her. Poor sap, does this guy know what he's in for? What'd you say his name was?"

Nate laughed again and realized how much he missed laughing these last few days. "MacGilvery, but we call him Mac. Fits right in. Went out to Mom's with me this morning and beat me to the table."

They were laughing again when someone knocked softly on the glass of the door. Mac stuck his head around the open curtain. "They're calling for us. SWAT's ready to go in."

"The one time they move quickly," Nate grunted and stood.

"Karl, this is Mac," Nate said. "Mac, meet Karl."

The two men shook hands and exchanged pleasantries in brief introductions. "How is she?" Mac asked.

"Like I was telling your partner here, she's doing fine," Karl said. "She's doing fine."

CHAPTER THIRTY- EIGHT

NATE PARKED ABOUT A HALF BLOCK NORTH of the warehouse near the Meridian Road and West Idaho Street intersection. From this location, he had a direct line of sight into the main door of the building.

Like a swarm of insects, the SWAT team burst from their concealed positions and, with military precision, entered the structure accompanied by the rapid-fire burst of small explosions, and the cover of expanding clouds of tear gas. With a thunderous crash, Nate heard the battering ram break through the huge bay door, splintering it and tearing it from its hinges.

At the same time, officers on the south and east sides of the building broke in through windows and poured through the breaches. Once inside, the officers fanned out, leapfrogging to secure the main floor and establish positions of defensive cover.

Gunfire erupted through the clouds as male and female gang members tried to escape, some with damp cloths wrapped around their faces, others coughing and gagging while firing blindly. The officers returned fire.

From the catwalk, fire from automatic weapons erupted, hitting one officer in the leg. The shot propelled him into a vicious spin, slammed him to the floor, and he writhed in pain. Answering fire silenced the sniper and fellow SWAT members egressed, carrying their injured officer between them.

Immediately new team members flooded forward filling the vacated positions.

The lead SWAT officer turned and, making eye contact with the fire-team leader, Corporal Watson, pointed two fingers at his own eyes, and then pointed to the stairs leading to the second floor.

The four-man fire team broke into a trot. The rifleman went first, taking point. Behind him, the automatic rifleman took the cover position at his oblique, preparing to lay down suppression fire. As the rest of the team made slow, steady progress up the stairs, the remainder of the unit secured the bottom floor, fastening the hands of those persons taken into custody with thick plastic zip ties, and seating them on the floor under the watchful eyes of armed officers.

After a few minutes, Nate got the code-four, and after seeing it was all clear, he and Mac approached the building carefully, their guns still at the low ready. Nate made contact with the SWAT team leader, Sergeant Fiender, first. "How's your man?"

Sergeant Fiender wiped dust-laden sweat from his boyish face with a soiled cloth and stuffed it back into his pocket before answering. "EMS got him out of here. Not much more than a flesh wound, really."

Nate looked puzzled.

Noticing his expression, Fiender squinted at the bright sunlight and explained. "High velocity round caught him on his mask pouch and took him for a ride. Good thing. If that round had'a found flesh, he'd lost a leg. As it is, he'll have a pretty good scar there to lie about how he got it later."

Nate whistled through pursed lips. "Wow."

Fiender laughed and then cursed softly. "He'll probably want days off to recuperate," he said, making quotation gestures with his fingers. "I'll buy him a beer and let him skip next Saturday's 10K full-pack run. Maybe."

"You're a kind man, sarge," Nate said, extending a hand to the slightly older officer.

Fiender laughed again, slapped Nate's open palm, and changed the topic. "Well detective, no Vega. He had to know we were coming. I'm just surprised he left so much junk behind for us to find."

As the long minutes passed, Nate turned his attention back to the building, watching the various search teams carrying labeled boxes and bags out of the warehouse. The teams stacked them in a roped-off area to await transportation back to the station to be booked. He shook his head. "This doesn't make sense," he muttered.

Fiender grabbed and squeezed Nate's shoulder. "NHI, man, it doesn't have to make sense." He dipped his chin and slid it side to side in a slow easy movement. "NHI." Then he turned and walked away as if that settled the whole question.

Nate watched him go, unable to accept the 'too simple' answer. "There has to be another reason," Nate muttered to himself.

He looked up to see Mac coming toward him. "Mac, why would this guy kill Fuentes, then Franks, kidnap Amber, and then keep her alive?"

Mac opened his mouth to speak, but Nate interrupted him.

"Remember now, this is supposedly the same guy who hit Big Dawg and his boys two weeks ago."

Mac inhaled again and raised his index finger as if to make a point.

Nate interrupted him. "Then he takes out that wannabe gangbanger down on the Southside. Why? How does it all tie together?" He stopped and stared at Mac.

Mac furrowed his brow and inhaled again, but hesitated before speaking. When he saw that Nate was actually waiting for a response, he shrugged his shoulders and said, "I don't know."

Nate smiled. "You know, for a minute there, I thought you were actually going to say something useful. Like you had this whole mess figured out."

"Naaw, not that, but I did find something you might want to see. I didn't want to move it 'til the CSI guys could get a photo record. Come on." He started back the way he came.

His interest piqued. Nate swung his arm in a low arc and said, "Lead, I'll follow."

A few minutes later, Nate found himself looking up at what appeared to be a throne. The chair, oversized and about three and one half feet above the floor, rested on an elevated platform. "What in the world?" he said softly and walked up the three steps to the dais.

Nate stooped, put on a latex glove, and picked up one of many labeled compact discs. "How many of these did you find?" Nate asked the white-clad CSI team member. The man looked up at the two detectives as he placed a numbered CD marked "Amber-26" into a collection bag for transport.

The small man pushed his black plastic Clark-Kent-styled glasses back up the bridge of his nose. "This is number 26," he said. "No telling what they are. Text, images, heck, there may even be video on 'em."

"When can we find out?" Nate asked, a huge lump forming in his throat as he wondered what Amber hadn't told him.

"We can do a preliminary check out in the van if you want; don't want to use any of the systems in here. Might be rigged to shut down and do a data dump or something," the tech whispered, as if someone might be eavesdropping. "But," he said, regaining his voice, "the only way to really know what's on 'em is to take them back to the lab and put them on playback—one at a time. We're talking about hours just to process the CDs, let alone everything else we took out of here. Now, of course, that's not accounting for the data reclamation from the unallocated spaces and the re-write files."

Nate raised his palm, stopping the man mid-sentence. "Who do I need to talk to get a look at one of those CDs now?"

Standing behind the CSI tech, out of his line of sight, Mac mouthed the smaller man's words, mimicking him and trying his hardest to make Nate laugh.

Nate cleared his throat and cut a hard glance at Mac, who straightened up as the CSI tech turned to follow Nate's gaze. Mac smiled cordially at the man as he stepped past him, but continued his mocking pantomime from a position visible only to Nate.

This time Nate did laugh, but thankfully the CSI tech had not seen or heard the charade performed at his expense.

Arriving at the van, he showed Nate and Mac several more bags of compact discs, all labeled and set in place by their numerical indication: Amber 1-26 "Here you go," he said, pointing to a small standalone computer. "Just take one and put it in there," he said, pointing to the CD tray projecting from the front of the unit.

"Got it," Nate said, selecting one from the pile.

"Just put it in there," the man said.

"All riiiiight."

"We've got it from here," Mac said, patting the shorter man on the shoulder. "But if we get stuck with the machine or something, can I call you for help?"

"Oh, sure," he said, gathering more evidence bags and heading back inside the warehouse. "I'll be back in the throne room. That's what we're calling it because of the chair set up in there." He smiled while pushing his glasses back up, although they didn't appear to have slid down.

"Thanks," Nate said, dropping his chin and shaking his head after the man had left. "I just didn't want him gawking, just in case Amber is, you know."

"Yeah, I got ya'. Look," Mac said, hooking a thumb over his shoulder, "I've got to touch base with the patrol guys on the perimeter, so I'll be back in, what, fifteen?"

"Fifteen should be about right. Thanks, Mac."

"What? Everybody's got a job, right? Mine's to touch base with the uniforms. Besides, Sabrina's not here to keep the press out of your hair. Looks like that job's mine too." He cocked a sideways glance at Nate and trotted over to the yellow tape police line that had been strung around the property. Mac smiled as he neared the area where several news vans and news people milled around, waiting for something to report.

Nate turned his attention back to the disc in his hand and prayed about what he might see. He slipped the disc into the machine, and after a short pause, the screen flickered to life. The "auto play" symbol flashed across the screen.

The "date/time" indicator showed that the disc, number eight, had been recorded two days after the Franks shooting and one day after his discovery of the box with the Abyss symbol at his front door. Snowy static filled the screen, and then the front of the bookstore where Amber worked suddenly appeared.

Bright sunlight lit the image as smiling people entered and exited the bookstore. Then an image appeared of Amber emerging from the side door, crossing the street and heading toward the employee parking lot. The camera followed her.

Whoever was filming Amber had taken the liberty of recording several close-ups, repeatedly focusing on the more intimate parts of her anatomy.

The image flashed and changed to a night scene. The LED indicator showed it was the same day but several hours later and appeared to have been filmed in the park across from Amber's apartment building. This time the image seemed to have been recorded from the inside of a parked car. The view-field dropped and what looked like a pair of a male's white sneakers filled the screen. The camera was moving, swinging and approaching the building.

Suddenly, the forward motion stopped, and the camera appeared to back away at a quick pace, but still tracking on the walkway that led to Amber's apartment. Then from around the corner came an image of Nate and Amber walking together. Nate smiled warmly at the memory, remembering it was the evening before Franks' funeral and he had taken Amber out for ice cream and a movie.

The next image sent a shiver down Nate's spine. A male hand appeared on screen holding a thick triangle bladed knife. With deliberate strokes, the hand then carved a circled 'A' with a slash through the middle on the wall near the corner of the building. The hand then carved the word *pig* in the wall and repeatedly slashed deep angry gashes through it.

CHAPTER THIRTY- NINE

AMBER AWOKE WITH A START, a fist of panic pounding at her heart. Flinging the covers off, she sat up panting and jumped from the bed, trying to remember where she was. She squinted into the creeping darkness. Diffused sunlight leaked in around the corners of the drapes and she pressed her back to the nearest wall. As awareness that she was in Nate's apartment settled over her, she sighed and flopped back on the bed, her knuckle resting against her lower lip.

Pulling the covers to her chin, Amber rolled to her side, knees tucked to her chest. After a while, she rolled to her back and smiled as lighter memories from last night came flooding back. "Nate," she called out while getting up from the bed.

Going out to the living room, she called out again. "Nate, you there?" Finding that she was alone, Amber wandered to the kitchen looking for something to eat. Reaching for the refrigerator door handle, she saw the note Nate had taped there for her to find.

Opening the refrigerator and taking stock of the contents, Amber smiled and rolled her eyes. "A carton of orange juice, half a stick of butter, a loaf of bread, and a half-eaten cinnamon roll. Wow." Removing the note and the orange juice, she settled at the small table to read the message. "Must be grocery shopping day," she muttered softly.

"Men!" Unfolding the note, Amber began to read while playing with a curl of her short hair with an index finger. "'Amber, I hope you slept well. I had to go in for a while. Be back by midnight. There's food in the fridge. Nate.'"

Looking at the carton of OJ and then remembering the loaf of bread, she thought she would have to have a talk with Nate about just what constituted as food. She smiled.

Drawn by the tick-tock from the wall-mounted clock, Amber saw that it was only six p.m. Slapping her thighs with open palms, she rocked up to her feet. "Well, Nathaniel Richards, if you think I'm gonna sit around here and wait the rest of the evening for you—wrong," she said into the air and headed back to the bedroom.

A few minutes later, Amber showered and dressed in fresh clothes borrowed from Nate's closet. She stood at the curb in front of the apartment building and flagged a ride. "The Christian Bookstore on Main," she said, getting into the backseat of the yellow cab.

**

"Detective Richards. Richards!" Butch Jensen, the Channel Six News field reporter called as Nate came out of the CSI van. "Richards, you owe me," Jensen yelled, seeing Nate head back toward the warehouse.

A uniformed officer, holding his hand in front of Jensen's camera lens, waved his arms and directed the reporter back behind the yellow tape he'd ducked under. "All right, Jensen, get back under the tape. You know the rules," the uniformed officer said, in a stern but not unfriendly manner.

"Wait—wait, wait! Richards!?" Jensen said, while being grabbed by the upper arm and escorted backwards by the uniformed officer. "Richards, you lying sac—"

Nate turned and saw Jensen being dragged backwards and laughed out loud. Walking toward the two men, Nate realized he didn't know this particular officer. "Hey, hey, let him—" Nate called out and waved to the officer. "Go ahead, let him in. I got him."

Jensen turned a self-important smile at the officer and adjusted his collar before waving behind him to have the cameraman follow behind.

Nate pointed to the cameraman and dragged a finger across his throat. This time it was the uniformed officer who wore the self-satisfied smile as he stopped the cameraman just as he was about to duck under the yellow tape.

Nate waved Jensen forward. "I owe you, not your camera guy."

"But how am I going to run my story?" Jensen asked with mild frustration.

"The old fashioned way—" Nate said as he turned, "or not." He laughed.

Mac came out of the warehouse, meeting Nate just as he reached the main entrance. "Hey, look what's following you."

"So this is the new guy?" Jensen asked, extending a hand to Mac.

Mac shook Jensen's hand and looked over at Nate. "Never know when I might need a favor. Although it does kind of feel like I'm sleeping with the enemy," he said and laughed.

"Goes both ways," Jensen said. "You guys are always acting like you're above the law, and it's my job to hold your feet to the fire."

This time all three men chuckled and headed back inside the warehouse. Nate looked over at Jensen. "Butch, you guys wouldn't know the truth if it bit you on your lily white butt."

"Ha, ha," Jensen said. "So, what d'ya' got going on here?"

"Okay," Nate said, turning serious. "Some of what I'm going to tell you is not for public information yet." Nate waited until Jensen nodded his agreement before continuing.

Nate acknowledged it with an upward jerk of his chin and said, "Now that we understand each other…our missing person, Ms. Coles, was kidnapped and held in this facility for about fifty-six hours until she managed to escape and contact law enforcement."

"Why? Have you determined a motive for the abduction?"

"No, not yet—" Nate began.

"How's that? Didn't you interview the victim?"

"Slow down there, motor scooter," Mac interjected, making faces behind the man's back.

Jensen turned to face Mac. "I just can't believe you guys didn't interview Ms. Coles. Can you tell me at least if she was molested?" Jensen asked.

Behind them, search teams continued carrying out boxes and bags, all marked and sealed with fragile red barriers of evidence tape stretched across their secured openings. Cameras flashed as photo logs were created and measurements taken. Officers and techs yelled instructions across the cavernous room, checking and rechecking each other, making sure nothing was overlooked or left behind.

"From the looks of things, this was more than the average flophouse," Nate said, indicating the building with a sweep of his hand.

Noting the huge circled "A" painted on the far wall, Jensen said, "Can I take it from the symbol that these are the same guys responsible for the Franks and the Fuentes murders?"

Nate noted that Jensen was careful to list Franks' name first. *Always trying to work an angle, this guy.* "You're free to assume whatever you like," he said. "But our job is to find proof of exactly what did or did not happen here."

Jensen was busy looking around, writing notes and making small drawings on his small pad of what he saw inside. "What's upstairs?" he asked, pointing with the notepad.

"Now that's where it gets interesting," Mac said.

"Oh yeah, why?"

"Come on, I'll show you." Mac started toward the stairs leading to the second floor. "You coming, partner?" He asked, seeing Nate hadn't moved.

"Naaah, you guys go ahead. I've got something to look into down here first. Maybe I'll join you in a minute." He watched them walk off together, Jensen busy plying Mac with questions, and he was sure that Mac was feeding him a line of bull. Nate smiled at the thought.

Nate walked with deliberate purpose to the room behind the throne-like chair and looked on the floor where Amber had been almost raped. Anger swelled inside him thinking about the two men holding her on this very spot and taking liberties with her, touching her. He spun back to the door and punched the wall, barely missing the same CSI technician that had helped them earlier.

The smaller man jumped back in fear and then settled against the wall. "I read the report," he started. "I figured this must be the room where the assault happened, but we found no traces of semen or fluids on the floor at all, maybe what might be sweat is all." His voice was soft, his tone, one of comprehension. "I don't think they raped her," he finished.

"No, no," Nate said, sobering. "She told me they hadn't. It just makes me angry, you know?"

The tech nodded his head in understanding. "I've got a daughter myself. If anything like that ever happened to her, you'd have to lock me up. Of course, you'd have to prove it first, and if there's anything I know, it's how to clean up a crime scene." He laughed at his own joke.

"Yeah, I bet you do," Nate said easing into laughter with him. "About that little... you know, about the discs," Nate began.

The tech winked at Nate conspiratorially and said, "What? I have no idea what you're talking about."

"Thanks," Nate said and walked out of the room. Leaning against the wall just beyond the door, he prayed, "Thank you, Lord. Thank you for not letting those monsters violate her. Thank you." He rubbed dry hands over a rough face and with a deep sigh heaved himself off the wall.

Looking up, he saw Mac and Jensen coming out of the girls' room upstairs. He chose not to go up there; he didn't want to see it.

"All right Jensen, seen enough?" Nate asked the reporter as soon as the man stepped from the stairs.

"This guy," he said, looking down at his notes, "Vega, Israel Vega, so he's responsible for all that's been happening here in the valley of late, huh?"

"Off the record?"

"Come on Nate, I need something I can use."

Nate stared at Jensen without answering.

"Okay then, off the record," Jensen conceded.

"Well, since it's all off the record, Butch, I can tell you, I don't know."

Mac burst into laughter. Jensen looked crestfallen. Nate turned and walked away. "Come Jensen, tour's over," Nate called over his shoulder.

After depositing Jensen back at the media circle, Nate and Mac both laughed as the reporter, now back amongst his own kind, was swarmed by his less privileged peers.

Turning away from the scene and stifling a laugh, Nate said, "I'd better call Amber. She should be awake by now."

The phone in Nate's apartment rang again, and after the seventh ring, the answering machine picked up. "Hi, this is Nate...." He heard his own voice speaking in the receiver. "...please leave a message." The machine beeped. "Amber, pick up. It's me," he said into his cell phone.

***

Below on the street outside the building, as Nate's voice rang out through an empty apartment, Amber sat smiling in the backseat of a taxi. The growing anticipation of seeing her coworkers made her giddy with excitement. She settled feather-light against the backrest, her fingers interlocked and wrapped around one knee and smiled brilliantly at the driver as the woman eased the yellow cab away from the curb and into the flow of traffic.

CHAPTER FORTY

"BINGO," ISRAEL SAID, as he watched Amber climb out of the cab and walk briskly into the bookstore. He turned and looked at Lo. "This time we won't be so nice."

Lo, his eyes hidden behind dark glasses, nodded at his captain. "You want me to grab her as she comes out or go in and get her?"

"Her boyfriend won't be too far behind." He looked at his watch. "Even with what we left 'em, they should be done at the warehouse by now. You'd better go get her."

Lo put his hand on the car's door handle and paused. "Israel, you know I'm down for you, but this girl, is she worth all this?"

Israel narrowed his eyes, his focus distant and cold. "Oh yeah, my friend, she's worth this and more. And this time when we're finished with her….this time, she won't even remember she ever had a boyfriend."

Lo nodded and stealthily stole away from the car. He entered the store from the side door nearest the rear of the building. Taking a moment to look around, he found Amber laughing with an older woman at the far end of the cavernous room near the counter. She had not seen him.

In a slow circular route, Lo made his way toward Amber, approaching her from behind. Once she was alone, he approached her, leaned forward, and whispered a short message in her ear.

Amber stiffened.

Lo stood and walked back toward the door he'd come in and exited. After about fifteen seconds, Amber followed him out, her face ashen and her movements expressionless and wooden.

"Where is she?" Amber demanded once she made it out the door. "Where's Gracie?"

Lo grabbed her in his rough, vice-like grip, one hand around her arm and the other trying to cover her mouth.

"You lied. You don't have her. You lied. Help! Somebody, help me!"

The squeal of tires drew her attention to a white Honda speeding toward them, and without being able to see the driver, she knew Israel was inside. "Please!" she screamed again. "Somebody, somebody please help me!"

***

"Foolish, hard-headed woman," Nate said, jumping back behind the steering wheel of the Jeep.

"What?" Mac asked, pulling the passenger side seat up from the recline position.

Nate dropped his note, with Amber's addition scribbled on the bottom of the page, into Mac's lap.

Mac read the handwritten addition. "'Went to bookstore. Meet me there. Amber.'" He snapped his seatbelt shut just as Nate tore from the curb and into traffic. "What was she thinking?" Mac asked rhetorically.

"She wasn't. If Israel doesn't get her, I'm liable to kill her myself," Nate said through clenched teeth. "I just get her back and before we can even get the paperwork done, she's gone and putting herself in harm's way again." He slapped the steering wheel.

Mac reached down, activated the emergency lights, and grabbed the microphone. "This is David-9-8-0."

"Go ahead 9-8-0," dispatch said.

Mac pressed the microphone key and braced himself as Nate slid the Jeep through a turn. "Send patrol units to the Christian bookstore on Main. Code-three. Possible kidnapping in progress."

"Copy that. Units to respond?"

Immediately voices filled the airway identifying their unit numbers and their ETAs to the bookstore. Nate accelerated.

As the Jeep made the turn onto Main, Nate saw Lo dragging a kicking and screaming Amber toward a white Honda as it slid to a halt near the curb. "Hold on," he said to Mac and the Jeep accelerated again.

Nate held the accelerator to the floor and steered the Jeep directly at the white Honda as it approached the side entrance. Drawing close, he downshifted and jerked the wheel hard, throwing the Jeep into a tailspin and slamming it into the driver's side door of the Honda and knocking it onto the sidewalk.

As the two cars came to a stop, both Mac and Nate jumped from the Jeep, already drawing their weapons. "I'll get the driver," Mac called as Nate ran for Amber.

Running headlong into Lo, Nate slammed his shoulder into the giant man.

Seeing Nate approach, Lo turned toward him, releasing his hold on Amber, and reaching for his waistband.

The two men collided. The blow sent them both rolling into the street. Nate's Glock .40 caliber handgun slipped free from his grip and spun wildly on the sidewalk, stopping just out of his reach. The 9mm Smith & Wesson Lo was drawing fell free and slid back toward the bookstore's side entrance. Both guns lay harmlessly on the sidewalk, each out of their owners reach.

With cat-like agility, Lo was back on his feet. He attacked.

Nate sidestepped the attack. Lo's hammer-like fist landed a glancing blow to the side of Nate's face, staggering him.

Turning, Lo growled and launched himself at Nate again. This time Nate was ready. Reaching out, he caught Lo's right wrist in his right hand. He spun with a violent twisting motion, turning away from Lo. Following the flow of movement, Nate brought his left forearm crashing onto Lo's hyper-extended elbow. He was rewarded with the loud crunch and tearing sound of ligament and muscle being pulled beyond their normal range of motion.

Lo collapsed to the ground. Tucking his injured arm against his chest, he rolled to his feet. Standing with his feet spread and knees bent slightly, he roared and faced Nate. Chest heaving, he prepared to attack again.

The mammoth man screamed a deep, primal snarl, pain and anger propelling him. He started forward, flexing his sore arm and cursing. He screamed again and launched himself at Nate.

"You might want to reconsider your options," Nate said from a few feet away.

Staring at the business end of Nate's recovered .40 caliber handgun pointed directly at his face, Lo stopped. Gingerly, he raised his arms above his head.

Black and white units poured into the small street, and uniformed officers sprang from their cars, leaping to action and securing the scene. Patrol officers grabbed Lo's shoulders and spun him around, dropping him facedown onto the street. Disregarding his injured arm, they pulled both hands behind his back and handcuffed him. He bared his teeth in a pain-induced grimace. Arching his back, he twisted, attempting to bite the arm of the officer holding him down. He roared as he fought against the restraints. A single knee dropped in his back, brought the fight to an end.

Nate looked over to the flashing lights of the paramedic's van just in time to see an unconscious, but handcuffed, Israel being transported away from the scene. Apparently, because of having been knocked out during the vehicle collision, he was being transported to the local ER. Nate waved the paramedic van to a halt. "Where you taking him?"

"St. Al's, why?" The driver asked.

"Take him to Luke's. We got an injured officer in Al's and if he winds up in the ICU they'll be neighbors. Not a good thing." Nate rubbed his shoulder and grimaced.

"Gotcha," the driver said and pulled away from the curb, his overhead lights flashing as they reflected off the darkened windows of stores and businesses closed for the evening. With sirens silent, the van left the downtown business district.

Walking up behind Nate, Amber laid her cheek against his shoulder. "That's gonna hurt in the morning," Amber said, sounding small.

Turning at the contact, Nate didn't answer but only looked at her hard. Anger and fear battled with his relief at her being okay.

Amber looked away first.

With her back turned to him, Amber said, "I know it was stupid. I just didn't think he would come looking for me here. Not so soon anyway. I'm so sorry, Nate." She began to cry.

Nate grabbed her by her shoulders and gently pulled her back against his chest, wrapping his arms around her. Amber fingered his forearms, leaning her face against the bulge of his bicep and rested her face into the fold of his arm.

"You're all right and that's all that really matters. I was so scared I'd lost you again," Nate said, his own voice sounding strained. He loosened his grip on her shoulders and she turned within his embrace to look up at him. "Amber, I—"

She reached up and touched his cheeks with trembling fingers and pulled his face down toward hers. "I know. No more talking," she whispered.

"Hey," Mac said, slapping Nate on the shoulder, coming up behind him. "Cool move with that spinning arm bar. For a minute I thought I was going to have to come over and help you out. But—" Then noticing how they were standing, he said, "Oh dude, sorry. Bad timing, huh?"

Embarrassed, Nate and Amber stepped back from each other. Amber, brushing non-existent hairs from her face, used her hand to try and hide the flush of heat crawling up her neck while Nate rubbed his shoulder and grimaced with very real pain.

Nate looked first at Amber and then at Mac. "Let me get her situated, and then we can get down to the hospital to make sure our boy is properly taken care of, and give him a chance to talk before he lawyers up."

"Yeah, the sooner we question him, the better," Mac said. "Wouldn't want him to all of a sudden get amnesia." He turned to face Amber. "I'm glad you're okay, but the next time you go and get yourself kidnapped, I ain't coming after you. Two's your quota, young lady, and yours is filled."

"Oh, don't you worry about that! I'm done with this cops and robbers, damsel in distress stuff." She smiled up at Nate. "I just want to finish school and get a nice quiet job in an office somewhere far away from bullets and freaks."

Mac leaned forward and kissed her cheek. "See ya' later." And with that, he turned and walked toward Nate's wrecked Jeep.

An uncomfortable silence settled between Amber and Nate as they stood trying to figure out what to say next. Nate cleared his throat. "Ah, even though Israel and Lo are in custody, I would feel a lot better if you weren't alone…I mean, by yourself tonight."

Amber stared up at him.

Nate arched his brows. "I wasn't suggesting you stay at my place. That wouldn't look right, but I could call my folks. They've got the room, and that way you could see Gracie again."

Amber smiled at his discomfiture. She reached out and took his arm. "Come on, my knight in shining armor, and take me home." Then noticing the looks from the other officers standing nearby, she added, "To your parents' house." And then they both smiled.

CHAPTER FORTY- ONE

Senior Patrol Officer Marion S. Johnson watched as a uniformed officer lowered Lo into the rear seat of the patrol car and panic seized his heart. Ice cold tendrils of fear drilled into his spine. Johnson bit his knuckle and rivulets of sweat broke free and ran down his face. He knew just one word from Lo and everything he'd been working for would come down around him. *How had things gotten so out of control?*

It was all supposed to be so easy. A few extra guns sold here and there, a little extra cash. The guns were all slotted for destruction and he'd fixed the records. There was no way of tracing them back to him. He cursed and slammed a fist into his open palm.

He wiped sweat from his face. "I got do something. Gotta keep that fool from talking."

He knew Lo would sell him out to save his own hide. Gangbangers did that kind of thing all the time, like whores trading goods for services rendered, he reasoned. Johnson continued to wipe sweat from his face, which had nothing to do with the heat. His hands trembled. He knew he only had one chance at fixing this.

Discreetly, Johnson walked over to the car where Lo was secured. That the windows had been left partially open for ventilation would make this easier. He stood with his back against the rear door and spoke in hushed tones. "You haven't said anything, have you?"

Lo stared at him with hooded, angry eyes. "I was wondering how long it would be before you came crawling over here trying to save your worthless skin."

"Shut up and listen. Maybe I can help us both." Johnson looked around to see if anyone was watching him.

From inside the police cruiser, Lo laughed. "Ha! So I'm supposed to believe you care about me, huh? You are a worthless piece of—"

Johnson turned and looked down at him, all pretenses gone. "Look, there's no love lost between us, but right now I've got to help you. So shut up and listen for once."

Lo leaned back against his cuffed hands and smiled smugly up at Johnson, knowing that even though he was the one handcuffed and locked in the rear seat of the patrol car, he had the control.

Johnson glowered, reading the truth in Lo's expression. "I'm going to drop you a key and a way out of here." He paused and looked around again. "What you do with it is up to you."

Checking again to see if anyone was watching, Johnson dropped a black metal handcuff key and a small .22 caliber two shot pistol through the window. He walked away with casual strides, trying to hide his agitation.

He joined a group of officers standing near the two vehicles that were at rest on the sidewalk. Soon he joined in the familiar pattern of bravado, talking and joking about the evening's events. The officers laughed easily together as they recounted other scenarios of which the night's events had reminded them.

Johnson watched Nate as he headed toward another of the small clutches of patrolmen gathered in the street near the bookstore. Johnson curiously watched as Nate tapped one of the female officers on the shoulder, leaned forward and said something to her. The officer nodded and walked away, followed by the Coles woman. Then turning to a newer officer,

Nate pointed to the unit where Lo was locked away. He waited a moment and spoke again.

Officer Daly, the rookie in the group, turned and smiled while fanning at the crowd of laughing officers like a mother shooing her errant children out of the kitchen. Apparently, he'd drawn transport duty. Reaching the patrol car, Daly looked through the rear widow, checking on his prisoner. Confident that Lo was secured, Daly entered the vehicle and drove away, preparing to deliver his ward back at the station for questioning.

A single line of perspiration made its way beneath the weight of the bulletproof vest and down the valley of Johnson's spine as he watched the vehicle drive away. Once again, control had been wrenched away from him and placed in the hands of someone else.

***

About three blocks from the bookstore, with a muffled click, Lo quietly released the final catch on the cuffs allowing them to fall free of his hands. Pulling the gun from his waistband where he'd hidden it, he checked the chamber and saw he only had two shots. Deciding against a simple execution, he opted for a hijacking instead, thinking he would get a car as well as an extra weapon.

In the front seat, the patrolman hummed along with a familiar tune playing on the FM station. As he brought the vehicle to a stop at a stop sign, Lo sat forward in a rapid motion, pressing the barrel of the gun between the wire mesh that separated the front and rear seats. "Stop the car or I'll blow your brains all over the dashboard," he said with a menacing growl.

Lo was pleased to see sudden fear gripping the young officer's face. *He couldn't be more than 22 or 23 years old,* Lo thought. His being a rookie played directly into Lo's hands. "If you so much as breathe without my telling you to, you're a dead man. You hear me?"

The young officer nodded his head, but did not take his eyes off the image in the mirror of the enraged man with the barrel of the small gun pressed behind his head.

"Now let this window down as far as it'll go." Lo tilted his head toward the window of the door beside him.

The motor buzzed and the window slid down, stopping about one third of the way inside the door frame.

"Put both your hands back on the steering wheel."

"Good."

"Keep your left hand on the steering wheel and turn the engine off using your right hand," Lo said. "You doing good," he said again, once the officer complied.

"Now pass that key through the window mesh, back here to me."

The officer hesitated.

"Don't make me kill you, fool," Lo said, slamming a hand against the wire meshing.

"Okay, okay." The officer said and passed the single key through the meshing, then returned his right hand back on the steering wheel alongside the other.

Using his elbow, Lo slammed it into the window, shattering the glass. Reaching through the enlarged opening, he let himself out of the rear seat. *I guess that fool Johnson was good for something after all.*

Lo chuckled. "I'm glad I didn't kill 'im earlier." Then with a growing rumble like the crashing of heavy stones, he guffawed.

The confused and scared young officer sat in silence, watching the strange drama unfold and wondering how it would end for him.

Opening the driver's door, Lo reached in and dragged Daly out by his collar. Forcing the officer to his knees, he grabbed the man's duty weapon, which was still snapped securely in the holster on his belt.

That's a good little man, Lo thought and smiled at the back of Daly's head.

"Freeze!" a commanding voice boomed from behind them.

Lo chanced a look over his shoulder to see Officer Johnson sighting down on him. "You dirty, double-crossing—"

"I said, freeze!" Johnson repeated. For a moment, everything at the intersection seemed to stand still. Johnson lowered his handgun and smiled.

With a growl, Lo dropped to his left and rolled to his side, coming up firing, emptying both shots at Johnson.

Two small explosions erupted in the hot summer air, echoing along buildings and through the tree-lined street. Officer Johnson hadn't moved. Locking eyes with Lo, he glowered dark and knowing. A scowl crept across his features like a flame consuming a branch; his brows knit together, his eyes full of malice and odium.

Awareness washed across Lo's face as he reached for the service weapon he'd stored in his waistband.

Johnson fired the single shot that ended Lo's life. As the final darkness claimed him, Lo knew he'd been had; that Johnson had won.

Holstering his gun, Johnson keyed his shoulder microphone, "TV916, ten-seven, officer down! Shots fired. I repeat, officer down. Roll EMS my location."

Dispatch confirmed Johnson's location and repeated the traffic on air. "Prisoner escape. Officer down, all available units respond. Prisoner escape. Officer down, shots fired. All available units respond."

Johnson ran over to Lo's body and handcuffed him, rolling him to his side for appearance's sake. Then he went to Officer Daly who was just starting to realize that he had not been shot. "You all right?" Johnson asked the young officer.

Daly nodded his head, his expression blank.

"You sure?" Johnson demanded. "We better have EMS check you out to be safe. Come on. Sit over here," he said, escorting Daly to the front of the now empty police unit, facing away from where Lo's body lay in the street.

Settling Daly at the hood of the car, Johnson retrieved the dropped .22 from where it had fallen. Opening the cylinder, he then replaced the two blank cartridges with two already expended .22 caliber casings, placing the gun back near Lo's body.

He returned to the front of the car and sat next to Daly, as several patrol cars slid into the intersection, lights and sirens blaring. Officers poured out of their units with guns drawn, fanning out to establish a protective barrier.

Johnson lifted a weary arm in a gesture of exhaustion, waving off the arriving officers. Holding up four fingers, he informed them that the crisis had passed and that everything was now code-four. Everything was under control.

He heaved a deep and weary sigh and stood draping a hand over Daly's shoulder. "Come on, kid. Let's go deal with this mess."

Daly looked up, shaken. "If you hadn't come along, he'd 'a killed me. You saved my life. I owe you, man," he said, just as other officers joined them at the front of the car.

"But he didn't and that's what matters," Johnson said, offering the young officer a hand up. "You don't owe me nothing."

One of the newly arrived officers saw the twenty-two lying next to Lo and took control of it. Though he had been careful to avoid blood contamination, Johnson noted that the officer handled the gun roughly, already sure of the shooter's ID. He was not being chary about preserving prints.

Johnson smiled. Everything was working out just fine. He was back in control. He looked at Daly. *The kid will tell everyone that Lo got the jump on him, and I happened along just in time to assist, shooting only after being fired at twice.* Johnson looked down at Lo's lifeless eyes and rubbed a hand over his own.

He sobered. *How many now?* He thought to himself. The Fuentes kid, Franks, and he did not even want to think about the other one.

He groaned.

One of the uniformed officers beside him turned. "You all right? Maybe paramedics should check you out just to be safe."

Johnson waved him off. "Naww, I'm okay. Just hot." He pulled at his collar and fanned at his neck for emphasis.

The officer slapped Johnson on the shoulder as he began to walk away. "Good job here tonight. It's about time one of them got it, huh?"

Johnson smiled weakly, "Yeah, one of them." He looked down at Lo's lifeless body sprawled on the hot asphalt and muttered, "Yeah, NHI."

CHAPTER FORTY- TWO

JOHNSON SAT IN THE DRIVER'S SEAT of his patrol unit and stared at the scene playing out in front of him. The coroner was busy placing Lo's body in the dark canvas bag used for transport. With a soft thud and a groan, he dropped his forehead to the backs of his hands resting on the steering wheel. The air conditioning did little to cool him off. He pulled at his collar, seeking relief from the heat but to no avail.

Putting the car into gear, Johnson rolled slowly forward, cleared the intersection, and then headed toward the designated hotel for debriefing. If his ruse was going to work, he had paperwork that needed to be completed.

***

Israel woke up to find himself in the back of a moving vehicle. A uniformed officer leaned over him to pass a pouch of some sort from a paramedic to someone else in the driver's compartment. He saw the paramedic turn to look down at him, touching and wiping at his face, pulling on the straps, which were lying slack over his chest. Moving slowly, he found that he had been uncuffed. When he felt the vehicle slow, he knew what he had to do.

Israel watched while the police officer, still looking forward, laughed and joked with the driver. When the paramedic riding in the rear tending to him looked up at his partner, Israel exploded upward.

He burst up from the cot in an explosion of sheets and blankets. Wrapping the sheets around the officer's neck, he choked him out while planting a solid kick into the face of the paramedic. Pulling the officer's baton from his duty belt, Israel jammed the handle into the paramedic's temple.

"What's going on back there?" the driver called over his shoulder. The van swerved in the street. Equipment fell from their positions on the walls. Shattering glass exploded as kicking feet and crashing bodies fell into them.

"Dispatch, emergency! Emergency! Loose prisoner on transport…police officer down!" the driver said in a desperate rush into his microphone. "We're stopped near Front and Capitol. Repeat…Front and Capitol. Request assistance." The driver slammed the vehicle in park and the two combatants fell forward, crashing into the crawlspace that separated the cab from the back of the rig.

Israel kicked free from the last of his restraints and pushed against the paramedic as the medical officer turned back in an attempt to get a hold of him. Grabbing the latch on the rear door, Israel jumped free of the vehicle and disappeared into the night.

Tending cuts and bruises on his partner, the two paramedics turned to render aid to the unconscious officer. They remained in the open bay of the rear compartment and waited for assistance to arrive.

The police units screeched to a stop, jamming into the intersection. Again, officers jumped out, guns at the ready.

"He's gone. Ran…that way," the paramedic said in short gasps of breath. The driver leaned back against the doorframe and relieved himself from his command position and from the officer's care to other arriving EMS workers.

One of the senior officers took over. "Dispatch, TV9001."

"Dispatch. Go ahead for 9001," the disembodied voice responded.

"Cancel units responding to this location. Direct all incoming units to begin an area search near Capitol and Front south of Front heading toward the river."

For the third time that night, Treasure Valley Police cars blocked off a city intersection and established a perimeter.

***

Israel slid down the rocky bank into the cold water of the Boise River. The cold water flowed fresh from Lucky Peak Reservoir, revitalizing and waking him after the heat and strain of battle. He swam with the current, allowing it to carry him downstream and away from the police search party. He fingered a large bump on his head and grimaced.

After floating and crawling along the bank for some time, Israel got out of the water a few miles downstream. He decided to get away from the river, knowing it was the first area to be searched.

Dragging himself up the bank, Israel saw a bicycle leaning unchained against a picnic table. Within minutes, he rode off on the stolen bike.

***

Officer Johnson jumped up from the hotel bed. He was frustrated at his having to be sequestered for questioning following the shooting. Snapping his head around, he focused his attention on the police radio sitting on the table. "All available units respond to the area of Front and Capitol. Subject, Israel Vega, last seen fleeing on foot southbound on Capitol from Front. All available units respond."

Johnson ran for the door, grabbing his duty belt as he fled. "Where you going?" Conley, the escort officer asked. "You're supposed to stay here until questioned. You know you can't leave. Johnson! Johnson!" Conley screamed after the fleeing officer.

The door burst open into the hallway and half a dozen stunned officers jumped in surprise as Johnson sped by them. "Hey, where's he going?" several officers called out, but no one moved to intercept him.

Conley ran after Johnson. "Somebody stop him! He hasn't been questioned yet!"

Johnson fled through the glass door leading to the rear parking lot and disappeared around the line of patrol cars just outside the door.

"I need your car," Johnson said to an officer just pulling into the parking lot.

"What?"

Johnson yanked open the door of the patrol car and grabbed the startled officer by his collar and duty belt. He then jerked the man from behind the wheel of the car. With a clatter of equipment and leather, the officer rolled out from the car and onto the still sun-warmed pavement. "Hey! What the...?!?" the officer screamed as he collided with the asphalt.

Johnson settled himself behind the steering wheel and with overhead lights activated, accelerated out of the parking lot. The uniformed officer jumped to his feet and hurriedly covered his face just as rocks and other small debris peppered him with explosive force projected from the patrol vehicle's tires.

***

Satisfied that Amber was tucked away safely, Nate checked the door of the Jeep, wincing as the twisted metal protested at being moved. "You ready to take a crack at this Lo character?" Nate asked Mac. The two men settled into the car as they discussed the interview strategy.

Mac leaned back against the headrest and looked out at the scene being swept over by the crime scene crew. "How you gonna do it?" Mac asked without turning from the window.

Dropping the gearshift into drive, Nate drove the Jeep off the curb and back into the flow of Main Street. He focused on the backs of his hands curled tightly around the steering wheel.

Mac turned and looked at Nate. "You all right? You want me to handle the interview? You can observe and direct from the desk."

Nate didn't answer, but continued driving, unknowingly following the route Daly had taken back to the station. Hearing the emergency call come over the vehicle's police radio, Nate locked eyes with Mac. He pressed the accelerator to the floor.

Mac reached over, flipped on the emergency lights, and latched his seatbelt.

Nate parked the Jeep north of the intersection at Main and Carlton. Mac got out first and walked toward the crime scene. Investigators grouped near the edge of the roadway. Nate pushed open the door and cringed again as the bent and twisted metal protested. He heaved a sigh, swung his legs out in defiance of his stiffening muscles, and groaned. Sitting in the open doorway, he rested an elbow on the door and leaned a weary forehead into the bend of his arm. Peeking up to the dark heavens, Nate sent thoughts heavenward. *Thank you, Lord. I'm so glad to have this over and behind us. Thank you again for getting Amber away from those*—His thoughts were interrupted when one of the techs called him.

"Detective Richards?" a CSI team member called out. "Looks like one of your bad guys bought it here. Johnson dropped him just as he was about to shoot Daly."

Nate nodded and shook the man's extended hand. "Yeah, looks like," he said, looking around. "Anybody know how this happened?"

"Daly said the guy somehow freed his hands and had a gun with him."

Nate arched a brow and dropped his chin, tilting his head slightly to the side. "A gun?"

"Yeah," the man pulled up his folder and checked his papers. He pulled out a form and handed it to Nate for inspection. "Ahhh, yep, a twenty-two, two shot. Small enough to hide and good enough for a close up down and dirty," he said, reaching for the form.

Nate nodded again. He closed his eyes and tried to remember who searched Lo before securing him in the rear seat of the car. "Smith," he said, snapping his chin up. "No way Smith missed a gun, small or not."

"Somebody missed it," the tech said and closed his file, tucking it in his armpit.

Off to the side, Nate noticed Mac nosing around with his flashlight, bending over, kicking rocks with the toe of his shoe and checking the roadway. "Excuse me," he said, dismissing the tech and turning toward Mac.

"What you got, partner?"

Mac was kneeling down and poking at something with his finger. He picked up something and held it up to Nate. "Look at this."

Nate opened his hand and Mac dropped the item into his palm. "Is this what I—?" He sniffed the object, interrupting himself. "It is, and relatively fresh."

Mac stood up. "Now you tell me, what is fresh blank wadding doing in the middle of a shootout?"

"Looks like somebody's been shooting blanks," Nate said, looking around as if the person would still be standing there.

"Blanks," Mac echoed.

"Blanks," Nate repeated. He dropped the wad back into Mac's outstretched hand. "Why is there a blank wad in the middle of a shooting?" Nate asked rhetorically. Without speaking, he turned and headed for the Jeep, aching muscles all but forgotten. Settling himself behind the steering wheel, Nate looked up again and said, "So much for being over, huh? What're You trying to tell me, Lord? I know this wad being here means something. But what?"

"Hey guys," Mac called. "Looks like you missed something." He pointed to the area where the small wad of paper had been found. There lying near the spot, was a second wadding. Once the crime scene techs responded, Mac turned and jogged over to catch up with Nate.

As they drove away, Nate looked at Mac. "You thinking what I'm thinking?"

"Yeah, like did anybody check the gun that Lo fired? And why would he take a gun loaded with blanks into combat?"

"Not to mention where he got it from in the first place," Nate said. "No way Smith missed a gun on a search."

"Where to? The station?" Mac rubbed a hand across his face. "The more I think about it, the more it doesn't make any sense."

Nate nodded at him to keep talking.

"There's no way a soldier like Lo takes an unloaded gun into battle. If it was a bluff, it was a bad bluff, one that could'a got him dead real quick." Mac leaned back into the seat and closed his eyes.

Nate nodded and returned his attention to the road. They rode in silence for a while. "We've got to check that gun and then review Daly's audio, if he made one." A few minutes later, Nate pulled the Jeep into the parking lot at the Treasure Valley Police Department. The men sat together for a while then as if on cue, both got out.

Standing in the wingspan of the open doors, Nate and Mac turned to face each other, leaning against the Jeep. Mac opened his mouth to speak, but was interrupted by an anxious voice on the police radio.

"All available units respond to the area of Front and Capitol. Fleeing felon: Subject, Israel Vega, last seen fleeing on foot southbound on Capitol from Front. All available units respond," the dispatcher's voice spoke into the night. "Subject, Vega, considered armed and dangerous. All units respond."

Nate slammed the palm of his hand on the top of the Jeep and jumped back in behind the wheel of the car. "Let's go."

"He's got to be gone by now, no need running downtown," Mac said, snapping his seatbelt shut.

"No, not downtown," Nate said, "he knows where Amber lives. He'll be looking for her."

"Not again," Mac said. "She should be gone by now," he said, hopeful.

Nate lifted a brow at his partner, not sharing his optimism. "You talking about the same Amber I know?"

Mac smiled a nervous smile. "That girl. She's enough to drive a man crazy."

"Welcome to my world," Nate said and smiled sardonically at his friend.

After a few minutes of hard driving, they were soon approaching the apartment complex where Amber lived. "Here we go. Her apartment building's the next one over," Nate said and slowed the Jeep, turning off the headlights. They sat motionless, allowing their eyes to adjust to the dark.

They moved their eyes from side to side, not looking for specific shapes but for the movements in the shadows that suggested a person or a furtive movement. Nate pointed to Amber's patio window, noting the lights and the silhouettes playing between the vertical blinds. He mouthed to Mac. "That woman." He exhaled softly through flared nostrils.

Turning the dome light off so that it would not illuminate them, they eased out of the Jeep, cringing as the battered metal groaned in the night's stillness and trotted toward the lighted window.

CHAPTER FORTY- THREE

INSIDE THE APARTMENT, AMBER LAUGHED with the female officer as she went through her closet, pulling out several different articles of clothing. She turned to the escort officer. "Leslie, did Nate say how long he wanted me to be at his parents?"

"He's a guy, what do you think?" They laughed. Leslie turned her face toward Amber and smiled. Her blue-gray eyes sparkled as she shook out a blouse and folded it. "So, Amber, what's the story with you and Nate, anyway?" Her voice had taken on a soft conspiratorial tone.

Amber stopped and turned away from Leslie. She could feel her neck growing warm. "We're just friends. Why?"

"Well," she said in a teasing singsong voice, "I wish I had a friend like that."

Catching a blur of motion out of the corner of her eye, Leslie turned, reaching for her gun as she did. "Ahh!" she cried out and then was silent. A large, smooth stone slammed with a sickening thud into the side of her head. Leslie collapsed to the floor moaning but clearly unconscious. Her gun fell harmlessly from her hand, jamming itself beneath the edge of the sofa.

Amber turned toward the movement and screamed. Dropping to her knees, she looked first to Leslie's crumpled form sprawled on the floor; a trickle of blood streaked from the corner of her hairline and stained her spiky blond hair. Amber's eyes rose against her will and came to rest on the disheveled, wild-eyed figure of Israel Vega standing in the patio doorway. He was barefooted, muddy, and wet from head to toe. He breathed deep ragged breaths, and his chest rose and fell in syncopated rhythm to the staccato sound of his respiration. He stepped toward her, flexing and un-flexing his claw-like fingers, while staring at her with unblinking eyes.

The next scream froze in her throat.

Amber turned and started to run, panic seized her heart, making it hard to breathe.

Israel leaped after her with feral speed, covering the short distance that separated them in a single bound.

Before she knew it, he was on top of her, grabbing at her roughly, possessively, violently. They collided with the wall near the bedroom door. Wrapping his hands in her hair, Israel slammed her head and back into the wall.

Her breath rushed from her chest.

Amber opened her mouth to scream, and he slapped her hard across the face.

"Shut up," he hissed. His eyes were hard, cold, lifeless orbs. "I told you…" His breathing was hard and shallow. His clothes and hair stank. His breath was foul. "I want you," he said, forcing dry, cracked lips against hers.

Her cry was muffled by his rough lips, and she tried to turn away.

"No one tells Israel Vega no. No one denies Abyss what is his." He pushed her toward the bedroom like a lamb being herded by a dog nipping at its heels.

She veered from side to side, trying to resist him.

He slapped at her face again. "You're gonna give me what's mine."

Amber looked around, looking for something, for anything she could use as a weapon. "Israel, don't," she tried.

He pushed her from behind. "I told you," he said, his voice growing more tense, more frantic, as he spoke, "don't tell me what to do." He shoved her toward the bed.

Amber stumbled the last few steps into the room and tumbled onto the bed face first, knocking her suitcase and overnight bag to the floor. Various articles of makeup scattered across the thinning carpet and rolled beneath the edge of the bed.

With a crushing weight, Israel fell on top of her and immediately began kissing the sides of her face and neck and grabbing at her body.

She fought.

Together they rolled from the bed falling in a heap on the floor.

Amber scratched and clawed, trying to inflict even the slightest measure of pain, but no matter what she did, he stayed after her. In desperation, she reached out and closed her fist around a small tube. Figuring it to be a tube of mascara, Amber summoned all her strength and rammed the cylinder into the side of his face.

With a screeching howl of pain, Israel reared backward, cursing. "You're gonna pay for that," he said and cursed again.

Amber looked into his soulless eyes and saw the huge fist start its downward arc and steeled herself against the blow she knew was coming.

"I thought I'd find you here," a male voice broke in through the chaos.

Still expecting the blow to land, Amber covered her face with her arms. When nothing happened, she chanced opening her eyes and saw Israel's face and body diminish in size like it had been sucked backward.

Confused, she tried to focus on the incongruity between what she saw and what she had heard. The voice had been male, but Leslie was the only other person in her apartment.

Forcing herself to her knees, Amber saw the back of a uniformed officer, too large to be Leslie, grab Israel, and throw him bodily from the bedroom out into the living-dining area. She followed them and found Leslie still lying unconscious on the floor, a small pool of blood collecting beneath her ashen face. Propping herself up, Amber used the doorframe as support.

The two men collided with mammoth force as patrol officer Johnson grabbed Israel by the collar and slammed one fist after another into the Hispanic man's bloodied face.

Seemingly oblivious to the pain, Israel fought back like a man possessed, landing several blows of his own. As the men traded blows, blood spatter dotted the carpet and walls.

Amber ran over to Leslie, grabbed the woman beneath her armpits, lifted her, and began dragging her toward the front door. She was desperate to leave, but unwilling to abandon her friend.

A loud crash sounded and drew her attention back to the combatants. She turned just as Officer Johnson grabbed the limp body of Israel Vega, lifted him by his collar, and slammed one last resounding fist into his face. The head jerked backward and bounced with the impact. Then Johnson dropped him and Israel lay in an unmoving heap between the officer's feet.

Johnson stepped over Israel and charged toward Amber. At the look in Johnson's eyes, Amber dropped Leslie and turned to run, but she realized she had waited too long to act. Johnson grabbed her, pulling her back into the apartment and closed the door behind them.

He grabbed Amber around the neck, fastening his bloodied fingers like cogs in a wheel and began to squeeze slowly. "I'm sorry, Amber, but I can't take the chance that he told you anything about me."

Amber pulled at the claw-like fingers as they clenched tightly around her neck. "He didn't tell me anything," she managed through a restricted airway. "I promise…he didn't."

Johnson's face relaxed into a faraway smile and he loosened his grip. He looked into Amber eyes and then drew her face up close to his. "I never intended for any of this to happen, you know."

Amber pulled at his hands, managing a little more freedom for her airway.

Johnson's face had gone slack, his expression dull and distracted as if he were focusing on a scene from somewhere in his distant past. He looked at her again and loosened his grip even more but did not release her. "I didn't mean to kill the Fuentes kid, he was a mistake...the gun just went off. He wasn't even supposed to be there. You understand? A mistake. Stupid kid should'a been home...not running the streets." He squeezed.

Amber nodded, not understanding at all what he was rambling on about but wanting him to remain relaxed.

Johnson kept talking. "You see, I had been showing the gun to one of Israel's so-called soldiers." He laughed. "I didn't know the gun was loaded, it was marked for destruction. Fuentes, I thought he was one of them. He was in their neighborhood. It was late at night, so I pointed the gun at him just to scare him to show the rest of 'em that I was *The Man*." He tightened his grip slightly, his voice still soft and distant.

Amber fought against the tightening fingers. "I see—I see. I know it wasn't your fault. I'll tell them it wasn't your fault. I'll help you," she squeaked.

Johnson refocused on her. "Help me? You? You can't help me."

Amber nodded her head, still locked in the vice-like grip. "I can get Nate to help you. We'll tell everyone it was a mistake."

"I'm really sorry, Amber, but I can't. I've got to be sure. I have to control all the angles. But I want you to know, I won't do it no more. I'll make it all better."

In that moment, Amber realized two things: One, for whatever reason, Officer Johnson had gone mad; and two, she knew he was going to kill her.

"You see, Franks stumbled onto one of my sales. I had just finished the deal with Lo and Israel when he drove into the alley all blacked out, even the internal lights were dark. I'd told him a hundred times don't come into Old-Town snooping, that I had it all covered. He was always sneaking into alleys and behind buildings trying to catch people. You know, making out in their cars."

Amber nodded again, trying to buy herself some time. He'd loosened his grip while he was talking and fresh air poured into her lungs. She had to keep him talking.

"Franks' death..." he began as his eyes lost some of their focus. "It wasn't as bad as it looked though. All that stuff, that extra stuff, they did that after he was already dead. I made sure he didn't suffer. One easy shot in the temple."

Amber focused on his eyes as the realization of what he was saying, that he had killed Officer Franks, settled over her. Again, she knew he would kill her. He had to kill her now.

He looked at Amber, imploring her to believe, to understand. "He was dead well before they did all that other shooting and setting fire to his car and all."

Johnson looked at Leslie on the floor and then he released his grip on Amber's neck. She stepped back, creating a small barrier of distance between them.

She realized that while he had been talking, he had walked her into the kitchen, trapping her between the wall and the cabinets and blocking her only possible route of escape. Although he had let go of her, she was still trapped.

He laughed a sick, tormented laugh. "That's why I carved that symbol in his chest. You see, I went back after they had all gone." He waved a hand in the air. "You know that circle "A" thing they claim as their icon, or whatever. I couldn't let them get away with shooting Franks up like that and setting him on fire. They were wrong. They're not real people, none of 'em."

"But you had already killed Franks; he was already dead." She knew it was a mistake as soon as she'd said it.

Johnson refocused on her. "I'm sorry, Amber, but you do see that this is how it has to be, don't you? The way I see it, Israel got the drop on Leslie, and then he killed you. But just like with Daly, I get to be the hero again. I killed him."

Amber looked into Johnson's crazed eyes and wondered who Daly was. She also wondered whom it was that Johnson had killed.

He was still talking. "And then Amber, my secret will be safe. No one will know. No one will be able to expose me and then everything will go back to normal."

Johnson stepped toward Amber, his huge hands reaching for her. "I really am sorry," he said as he closed the distance between them.

Amber bumped into the wall behind her and gasped with a quick intake of breath.

"That's far enough Johnson," Nate said, coming in through the open patio door, the red beam of his Glock's targeting lamp centered on the back of Johnson's head. "That's far enough," he repeated. "Mac's at the car calling for backup. It's over. I found the wadding you left in the intersection."

Nate pulled the piece of gunpowder-stained cloth out of his breast pocket with his left hand while still covering Johnson with his Glock. "Give it up, Johnson. You can't get away. You can't win. Let it go."

Johnson turned to face Nate, Israel's blood still on his hands, the overhead light in the kitchen reflecting on his badge. Johnson took a palsied step backward and sat with a heavy thud into one of the chairs at the small table. Dropping his head to the table, he began to cry. "It wasn't supposed to be like this. I'm not like them. I'm not like them. They're not human. I'm the good guy. I'm a good guy. They're the animals, not me. Not me."

Nate waved to Amber with short quick flicks of his wrist. She ran past Johnson and into Nate's outstretched arm. Nate wrapped his arm around her protectively while still holding the Glock .40 caliber targeting beam squarely on Johnson's forehead.

He studied Johnson again as he sat weeping in his soiled uniform, bloodstained from his tussle with Israel, his holster empty. Then Nate remembered that Johnson's gun would have been collected after the shooting earlier that night. Nate shook his head from side to side, as a complete understanding began to sink in about just how far this fellow officer had fallen.

With gentle pressure, Nate pulled Amber with him and began backing toward the open patio door, hoping to get Amber out of the apartment before having to deal with Johnson.

"I'm not like them. I'm one of the good guys," Johnson said again, his head still down.

Nate turned his face slightly from Johnson to help Amber through the door and at that moment, a primal roar sounded.

Johnson launched himself from the table toward Nate, his exposed duty knife in his hand. Before Nate could react, a shadow passed between him and Johnson, intercepting the charging man's bulk.

Amber tried to scream, but her throat was starting to swell shut and it came out as little more than a squeal.

Israel and Johnson crashed to the floor, and after a moment, they lay still with Johnson straddling the man beneath him. After a strained moment, Johnson stood and turned, pulling the bloodied knife from Israel's chest. With feral eyes, he screamed and charged at Nate, Amber still tucked in the crook of his arm.

Nate fired.

Sirens sounded in the near distance.

Johnson looked down at his shoulder where the round had slammed into him, shattering the joint. He roared in pain.

"Don't do it," Nate said, his voice flat. He locked eyes with Johnson and shook his head slowly from side to side.

Johnson stepped forward.

Nate dropped his chin, sighting down the length of the barrel and shifted the targeting beam from Johnson's shoulder to his forehead.

Johnson staggered, holding the knife out in front of him with his uninjured arm. He looked at Leslie, still unconscious on the floor and then at Israel. His breathing became labored; his shoulders and chest heaving.

He locked eyes with Nate and screamed in agony and despair. He charged, raising the knife above his head.

Nate fired a single shot.

Johnson's head snapped backwards as his body collapsed to the floor. Dead.

From across the room, Israel groaned and moved. Nate put a protective arm around Amber again, holding his gun at the low ready.

Israel moaned again. "Amber."

Nate shook his head. "No," he said, looking at her.

"But he's dying, Nate," she whimpered, pulling Nate toward the mortally wounded man.

Mac rushed into the room and swept across it, sighting down the barrel of his handgun. Realizing that Nate and Amber were all right, he lowered his own weapon to the low ready. "What the heck happened here?" he asked, seeing Johnson sprawled on the floor. Turning, he saw Leslie and crossed over to her, tending to her wound.

Amber knelt beside Israel and pressed a folded dishtowel against the gash near his neckline. He was groaning and his breathing had a hollow, airy quality. She lifted his head into her lap.

He struggled to speak. "S-s-ssaved you from Johnson. Sorry. I'm sorry for what I did to you." He paused and coughed, a spattering of blood coming up with the effort. "Not bad for an animal, huh?" he smiled weakly.

"No, no Israel, it wasn't bad at all," Amber forced through her bruised throat. "Israel, I forgive you."

"Forgive me?" he asked weakly. He struggled for a breath, wheezing with each intake and growing visibly weaker, a scarlet pool spreading beneath them. "T-too late for that."

She took his face in her hands. "Israel, remember when I told you about Jesus? He will forgive you too. Just ask Him to forgive you," she said through her tears.

Israel Vega focused on Amber's face one last time, his eyes suddenly clear. "So beautiful," he whispered in a strangely clear voice, and then he exhaled deep and long, slumping into her knees.

"Just ask Him," her voice barely a whisper.

Amber reached out a trembling hand to Israel's face and pushed his lids closed over sightless hazel eyes. Lowering his head back to the floor, Amber folded Israel's arms across his chest.

"Come on," Nate said softly and offered her his hand.

She took hold of him, accepting his strength while getting up from the floor, her pants sticking to her, wet with Israel's blood. She leaned her head against Nate's chest as he wrapped strong arms around her and held her tight.

Sirens sounded loudly from just outside the apartment. The sound of officers approaching could be heard. Mac met them on the patio, signaling with his flashlight to indicate which apartment to enter.

"How's Leslie?" Nate asked, looking over Amber's head, stroking her hair with long soft strokes.

"I'm no doctor, but I think she'll be fine," Mac answered. He looked around the apartment, taking it all in. He ran his hand through his hair and inhaled deeply. "Is it always like this working with you?"

Nate smiled wearily. "Ask me again tomorrow."

The paramedic team rolled a gurney into the apartment and went to where Leslie lay in a thin pool of her blood. Lifting her onto the cart and securing her to the gurney, they treated the gash on the side of her head. Reading the unasked question on the detectives' faces, he said, "Head wounds always look worse than they are." He smiled reassuringly. "She'll be fine. 'Course she'll have one heck of a headache and a cute little scar to brag about."

CHAPTER FORTY- FOUR

SABRINA SAT UP IN THE HOSPITAL BED; her head still wrapped in bandages, and her eyes shadowed by a raccoon-like mask. She offered a feeble hand to her husband and held his with stiff but steady fingers.

Karl smiled and bent from the waist, kissing his bride's cracked, dry lips. Their two children, fifteen-year-old Cynthia and their college freshman Karl Junior, looked at their mother with open expressions of love and gratitude. Around the room, not-so-silent prayers of thanksgiving lifted from happy lips in murmured chorus.

Karl stepped aside, allowing Nate to approach the bed.

"Hey you," Nate said, a smile in his voice.

"Hey yourself," Sabrina answered weakly.

"So you ready to come back to work and stop your goofing off, laying up here at Club Med?" Nate gestured with his hand, indicating the hospital at large.

Sabrina was surrounded by her friends and family, a swell of laughter spreading around the room. Karl and their two children, Nate, Mac, Amber, and the Reverend and Mrs. Richards were all there.

Nate held Sabrina's hand and smiled warmly, tilting his head toward Mac. "Sabrina, this is Mac…er, ahh, Chris MacGilvery. He's been your replacement since you started this vacation."

Karl cleared his throat and met his wife's eyes, having spoken to Sabrina earlier about her wanting to have a minute alone with Nate. "We're gonna step outside for a sec and let you guys catch up," Karl said, leading his children out of the room, albeit reluctantly. Reverend and Mrs. Richards came forward and placed gentle kisses on Sabrina's forehead before they, too, left the room.

Cynthia, the youngest child, turned away from her father, still holding his hand and said, "I'll be right outside, Mom, okay? I'll be back before long. All right?" Her voice broke.

Sabrina smiled up at her daughter and gently touched her face. "I'll be right here, sweetie. Just give me a few minutes with Mr. Richards." She squeezed her daughter's hand.

Sabrina turned her head with apparent difficulty and looked at Mac. "So, you're the scrub I saw hanging around CID for the last few weeks, huh?"

Mac smiled and dipped his chin. "Yours are pretty big shoes to fill, Miss Lady." He squeezed her toes.

"You're a friendly one, aren't you?" she said, looking at his hand on her foot.

"Nahhh, I just know you can't catch me if I was to take off running." He laughed and saw the light of acceptance growing in her eyes.

Sabrina grew serious and motioned for Nate to come closer. "I know who shot me," she said.

Nate looked across the bed to where Mac had repositioned himself. "Tell me," Nate said, his stomach suddenly filling with dread.

"Give me a drink of that water; my throat feels like sandpaper." She pointed at the white Styrofoam cup sitting on the bed tray near her waist.

Mac reached for the cup and found that it was empty and refilled it from the pitcher beside it. He passed the cup to Nate; who held the straw up to Sabrina's lips.

Leaning forward, Sabrina drank long, using a series of short, breathy draws on the straw. Fatigued, she lowered her head back to the pillow, closed her eyes and sighed. For a long moment no one spoke.

Sabrina fluttered her eyes open, but looked as if she was seeing a dream from a distance.

Nate and Mac exchanged glances.

When she spoke again, her voice had softened just above a hoarse whisper. "The night of the jewelry store robbery," she began, "I heard the two-eleven silent in progress at Reid's and the call for units to respond."

"I knew guys would be pouring in from everywhere, but I was the closest." She saw the look of guilt flash across Nate's face and grabbed his hand. "What? You feeling guilty that you wasn't there?"

Nate looked away.

"If you're wishing it was you in this bed with a bullet in your head instead of me, well I'd trade places with you in a New York minute." She laughed and Nate and Mac chuckled along with her.

"Nate, God knows what He's doing. If it was better that you were here and I was out there working the Franks' case, don't you know He could have made that happen?"

"I just—"

"I just nothing. Let God be God, boy, and you just do the detective thing, okay?"

This time the smile reached Nate's eyes. "Okay."

She motioned for the cup again, and Nate brought it up to her lips. After she drank her fill, she continued. "Patrol cars came in from every direction. I advised dispatch I would be running silent code. I didn't want to spook the bad guys into taking a hostage or anything like that. After letting dispatch know I was on the ground, I told them that I was taking position on the south side of the building and to let approaching units know that I was a plainclothes officer and then gave my physical including clothing description. What I'm saying is there was no reason that there should have been any confusion."

Again, Nate and Mac looked at each other as the idea of what she was saying began to settle on them.

She spoke through closed eyes. "I made my way around the corner of the building," she continued, "and could see uniformed officers positioning themselves around and behind where I'd left my car and some of the others coming in at tactical angles." She waved her hands in the air as if directing the action she was describing for them, pointing first this direction and then the other as she spoke.

"I had just taken cover when the rear door burst open, and two figures ran out with masks on and I thought to myself, this might be a clue." She laughed at her joke.

"I gave the warning, you know, 'Stop, Police!' I ordered them to drop the bags and put their hands up. You know, I really thought they were going to do it at first, but then one decided he didn't want to go to jail and pulled a gun. The next thing I know, bullets were flying every which way, but I thought I hit him."

She smiled at Nate's worried expression. "What you frowning for? The shooting's over now. Anyway, I knew I needed to move so I shuffled off to my side, and when I did, the second guy grabbed his piece and got in on the fun. For the most part it was just move and shoot, move and shoot."

Sabrina looked from Nate to Mac and then back to Nate making sure she had their undivided attention. "Guys, I saw the dirt-bag drop, and then a uniform came around the corner. I made eye contact with him. I saw him raise his gun and I saw the muzzle flash. The next thing I remembered was waking up in here."

She closed her eyes and laid her head back against the pillow. "I never believed I'd live to see the day when one of Treasure Valley's own would turn a gun against one of the family. Nate, it was Johnson. Johnson shot me."

Nate took her hand in his and held it. He watched as silent tears trekked from the corners of her eyes and disappeared into the bandages behind her ears.

Silence filled the room, and again, the only sound heard was that of the monitors and other machines that made up the everyday background noises of the hospital.

Finally, Sabrina brushed away her tears. She turned to look at Mac. "Remember those files I had you pull?"

Mac nodded. "I gave them to Nate back before Brown assigned me to help on the investigation."

"Did that have anything to do with what you were talking about that day on the range?" Nate asked.

"It was nothing more than a hunch, really," she said. "But I found it odd that with all the rounds fired at the Franks' shooting there was only one fatal. Close contact forty-cal to the temple. The rest was just overkill. I checked the coroner's report, and he said the rest of the shots were post mortem."

"Franks was already dead when the other shots were fired," both Nate and Mac said together, drawing on her conclusion.

"The odd part is that the recovered round from the Fuentes kid had a peculiar marking on it. It stood out because we had found that same marking on the round recovered at the stop-n-rob shooting last year. I just happened to have worked that case, so I remembered the strange groove markings. When the recovered round showed the same markings, I checked the file to see what happened to the gun from that case. It had been marked for destruction. Guess who was in charge of destroying the weapons?"

"Johnson," Nate said in a low voice.

"Johnson," Sabrina confirmed. "But before I had a chance to go over any of this with you, the robbery happened and, well, you know the rest."

Nate rubbed his face with the palm of his hand and exhaled loudly. "The only question is, how did Johnson know you were on to him?"

"Wellllll," Mac said, drawing out the word for emphasis. "That may be my fault. I had just been assigned to CID and wasn't real sure about how things worked. Johnson was hanging around CID a lot back then, remember? Well, anyway, I told him what I was looking for and asked how I could find it. I told him I was getting some files for Detective Jackson, and he must have put two and two together."

"That son of a," Sabrina began, but didn't finish. "I've decided to work on my cursing," she said and chuckled.

"Apparently he was selling guns marked as destroyed back to the streets. As long as he controlled the books, no one was the wiser," Nate said.

He grabbed Sabrina's hand again and waited until she looked at him. "Johnson's dead."

"What happened?" she asked while trying to sit up again. "How did he die?" She stared into Nate's face looking for an explanation.

"It's a long story," he said with a shallow sigh. He looked back over to Mac, and after taking a breath said, "I shot him."

Sabrina looked from Nate to Mac, not sure if she wanted to believe what she was hearing. Finally accepting it as real, she asked again, "What happened?"

"I'll get you the details later, when you're feeling better." He brushed her forehead with his knuckle. "Johnson was also responsible for the Fuentes shooting."

Sabrina closed her eyes and her throat bobbed as she swallowed.

"I've already met with and apologized to the kid's mother. I felt it was necessary after the way Johnson treated the crime scene."

She nodded, remembering Johnson's NHI comments overheard by Mrs. Fuentes and the uproar it caused at the station. "Sounds like a lot's happened in the time I've been away. So what else has happened since I've been gone?" She waved her hand. "No, don't tell me. But what did Brown have to say about you solving the case and all? I bet that put a snag in his craw."

"Well, let's just say he hasn't been chewing my butt as much these last few days. He's not ready to come to church with me yet, but he's at least stopped yelling for the time being." He laughed an easy laugh.

A knock sounded at the door.

Turning, Nate saw the door swing slowly inward and Lieutenants Brown and Haynes stuck their heads through. "You decent in there?" Haynes asked, stepping in.

Nate caught Brown's eye before going to Haynes and extending his hand.

Sabrina tried to push herself up. "Well, speak of the devil. Larry, we were just talking about you." She began to laugh and took Lieutenant Brown's extended hand.

"I bet you were," he said and looked at Nate.

Haynes sat on the bed next to Sabrina, pushing her legs to one side. "Ain't nothing wrong with your legs. The bullet hit your head, if I remember correctly," he said in his familiar drawl. Friendly laughter floated around the room.

"Well," Brown said, his voice sounding formal in the newly settled quiet. "How long before you get out of this place and back to work? That partner of yours," he tilted his chin toward Nate, "needs you."

Sabrina looked at Mac and then at Nate. "Oh, I don't know, looks like his new partner's doing just fine."

Nate took note of the words *new partner* and caught the look in Sabrina's eye.

Mac swallowed and moved away from the wall where he had been leaning. He smiled.

"Besides," Sabrina was saying, "I've decided that it's way past time for me to retire."

Brown exchanged looks with Haynes. He stepped forward, coming again within arm's reach of the bed. "The captain thought you might say that. He authorized me to offer you these, if you'll stay." He held out his hand showing her a pair of silver lieutenant bars. "Any division, you can have it, even CID if you stay."

Sabrina took the bars and held them in her hands. She looked at her reflection and saw the contrast of the white bandages against her dark face and smiled. After a minute, she dropped the set of bars back into Brown's hand. "I figure when one of your own men tries to blow your face off and you live through it, well, that might be a clue that your grace card is just about up. And as much as I'd like to take the captain's offer, I can't. I'm done. I'm gonna go home and be a mom and a wife and drive both my husband and children absolutely crazy."

"Told you," Haynes said and slapped his thigh laughing.

"Well, I had to at least try," Brown answered him. He turned his attention back to Sabrina and extended his hand. "I'll have Admin draw up the papers. I'll have them sent out to you in the next week or so." He looked around the room, taking in everyone, dipped his chin, turned, and left without speaking.

Sabrina laughed and clasped Haynes' hand as he reached out to her. "Nicest bedside manner, that man," she said, looking at the slowly closing door.

Haynes grabbed her knees, giving them a slight shake. "Well, I'd better catch up to him. He's my ride, after all." He leaned forward and kissed Sabrina on the cheek.

After the two men had gone, the room fell into an awkward silence. "When exactly were you gonna tell me?" Nate asked, speaking into the quiet.

"Today," Sabrina said in a sober, motherly voice. "Nate, I'm getting too old for this stuff. It's time to let you young bloods run the streets and create your own stories. Besides…" She rubbed the bandage, leaving the statement unfinished.

"Yeah," Nate said and gave her a hug. "But like this? So sudden? I'm not ready."

Mac walked over next to the bed and laid a hand on her shoulder. "When Brown put me with Nate I never thought I'd be replacing you. I fully expected you to come back."

"What? You don't like working with Nate?" Mac looked from Sabrina to Nate and back again, his jaw slack.

Sabrina laughed. "Gotcha."

The small group sobered again, and after a few minutes, the family began to trickle back in. Nate and Mac excused themselves, trying their best to sneak out unnoticed.

CHAPTER FORTY- FIVE

NATE AND MAC MADE THEIR WAY with slow, careless steps out to the upstairs lobby overlooking the north parking lot. Nate stuffed his hands into his trouser pockets and leaned heavily against the wall behind him, allowing his shoulders to catch his weight.

Mac walked around in front of him and waited for him to look up. "You all right?"

Nate didn't answer, but lowered his head and looked at his shoes. "There's just so much that's happened. The shootings, Amber, and now Sabrina dropping this on me—"

"Thanks," Mac said with a laugh, trying to lighten the mood.

"You know that's not what I mean. It's been good working with you." He reached out, tapping Mac on the shoulder with the side of his fist.

"Lookie," Mac said, tilting his head toward the elevators.

Nate looked up and saw Amber standing by the elevator and wondered how long she'd been there. Amber shifted her weight from foot to foot as if she wasn't sure if she wanted to come in or leave. She started when she saw him moving toward her.

"Hey girl," Nate said, remembering the almost kiss outside the bookstore. Excited, he pulled her into his embrace.

She went limp in his arms and looked up at him with soft, serious eyes.

Seeing the heaviness in Amber's face, Mac cleared his throat and excused himself, stepping inside the elevator, which had just opened to deposit its riders. "I'll meet you downstairs," he said as the doors slid closed, separating him from them.

Nate pulled Amber tight against him, the warmth of her nearness exploding through him, awakening his senses. His mind filled with the joy of coming to this place where he was finally ready to tell her how he felt about her. He buried his face in her hair and enjoyed the fresh shampooed fragrance.

After almost losing her twice, Nate promised himself he would not let another opportunity slip through his fingers without his explaining exactly how he felt.

She smiled weakly, but it failed to reach her eyes.

"Amber," he began, "there's something I need to say to you. Something I should have said a long time ago…but, Amber…well," he stammered.

She stepped away from him, turning her back to him.

He walked behind her grabbing her with gentle fingers around her shoulders and pulled her back against him. She didn't resist.

She lowered her chin, touching his knuckles. They stood that way in silence for a moment.

Finally, she turned and looked at him with understanding eyes. And just like at the bookstore, she took his face in her hands and, leaning forward, kissed his cheek. "Nate, I— I have to go."

He smiled into her sad face, willing her to feel his joy. "Go?" he said, not allowing himself to hear what it was she was saying.

She lowered her chin and began to shake her head from side to side, tears brimming in her eyes and falling freely down the olive-toned skin of her cheeks. "I just—I just can't stay here. Too much has happened."

He looked at her lips, heard her voice, but still his mind and his heart refused to understand her words.

She looked up at him, her face wet with tears, her lip quivering slightly. She focused on his eyes, studying his face.

"But Amber, I love you." Nate said in a soft voice.

She pulled away from him and went to stare out the window. She looked down toward the parking lot where Mac was sitting on the crumpled bumper of the Jeep two floors below.

Nate came to stand beside her and watched as gray clouds rolled in over the Boise Foothills, red shadows stretching out long and lean as the evening sun set. "Looks like it's going to rain," Nate said in a neutral tone.

Amber leaned her forehead against the glass of the window. Tears fell from her chin and splashed on the windowsill.

He turned to face her. "Amber, I need you." His own heart began to fill with the pain he saw in her eyes. "I—I love you."

She still didn't look at him, but kept her forehead against the glass. She reached up and brushed tears from her cheeks and wiped her nose with a crumpled tissue. "It's like the tree, huh?"

Nate raked his memory, attempting to grasp what she could mean.

"It's like your dad says; the tree falls in death, but the seed brings new life." She tried to smile and rolled her shoulders along the glass until her back was against the window, and she looked down the length of the corridor.

"I feel like I'm dead inside. All the time I was in that warehouse and I was so sure that Israel was going to rape me, I hated him. I wanted him dead."

Nate touched her arm. "That was only normal; you were afraid."

She turned her face toward him with a jerk. "What would your dad say about that, huh?" she asked and the tears fell again. "All this time, I thought I was encouraging you, helping you to find God." She dropped her chin. "But it was me, Nate, I needed Him. When my time of testing came, I was no better than Israel. Jesus came and gave himself for us all, even Israel. All I could think of was myself. Saving myself."

Nate stepped toward her. She backed away.

"I hated him, and he gave his life trying to save me. What does that make me, Nate?" She looked up, her eyes red and swollen, her face flushed as her hands stretched toward him, palms up. She shook her head again. "I can't do this, Nate. I can't. I—"

"But Amber, God forgives us if we ask. That's what you told Israel and you know it's true. Or are you the one that's forgetting what you believe?" He tried to laugh, but it sounded hollow, forced.

"I know. I don't know. I don't think— I need some time. I need to find some peace in myself. Please."

She looked up at him with pleading eyes. Although he knew she would stay with him if he asked her to, a greater part of him knew that if he wanted to share a future with her, he had to let her go. But how long would he have to wait? "Where will you go?" he asked.

Her shoulders drooped and she relaxed. She brushed tears from her face and then stood up as tall as her five foot four inches would allow. "Maybe to my mom's down in Florida or maybe my brother's. He's been asking me to come for a visit at the mission. His kids are getting so big now." She chuckled weakly.

Nate extended a tender hand, and using his thumb, brushed a tear that hung from her lashes. "Amber, I will always be here."

"Will…will you wait for me?"

"Forever."

"Thank you." She leaned forward and touched her lips against his tenderly, and inhaled sharply as a tingle of excitement raced along the surface of her skin.

Nate wrapped his arms around her; his fingers spread wide across her upper back and kissed her long and hard, pouring into her all his need and desire. Finally, they separated and Nate cupped her chin in his hand. "I'll be here."

Then he released her and stepped away. He fastened his eyes on her as if burning the image of her face into his soul. He pushed the elevator call button and waited in silence.

The ding of the elevator door rang and the doors slid noisily aside. Amber wrapped her fingers in Nate's and backed into the waiting car. The doors began to slide closed and she released her grip as she disappeared behind them.

Moving to the window, Nate watched as she made her way through the maze of cars, finding her own and eventually driving away. Only then did he call for the elevator car to take him on his way to locate Mac.

As Nate opened the door to the Jeep, Mac met his expression with an anxious look on his face. "Call just came out. Dead body over on Waterbury."

Nate pulled his eyes from the parking lot and looked at Mac. "Suspicious?" he asked.

"Nah, not unless you call the fact that his hands are tied behind him and he appears to have shot himself in the back of the head twice. Do you consider that to be suspicious?"

Nate rubbed his face roughly with the palms of his hands, exhaled, and leaned his head against the backrest. "Well, one thing's for sure, he ain't going anywhere. Let's get a coffee and go check it out. It's your turn to buy."

Mac looked at his partner. "You okay?"

Nate smiled weakly then directed the Jeep out of the parking lot and eased it into traffic north onto Eagle Road.

"Hey," Mac said, throwing up his hands in exasperation, "I bought last time."

"That was last case," Nate said. "New case, new count. Rookies first. You buy."

Nate fastened the seatbelt, laughed at the puzzled frustration that colored Mac's face. "So this is how Sabrina felt. I could get used to this," Nate said and smiled. "Let's go, partner."

THE END... BOOK ONE

A NOTE FROM THE AUTHOR

Thank you for reading *Notorious*, the first installment of the Nate Richards Mystery series. Now that you've finished this book, I would love to hear from you. You can email me with your thoughts on the book or become my friend on Facebook. You can even sign up for my newsletter, which will give you updates on upcoming releases and all the other craziness going on in my corner of the world.

If you would like to help this story succeed, please tell others about it. You can loan your copy to a friend, and ask your local libraries and bookstores to order it.

In addition, if you could please post a review on amazon.com, or goodreads.com, it would be very helpful.

My email address is:
rayellisauthor@gmail.com
You can download discussion questions or follow my blog entries at:
http://authorray.blogspot.com
Please visit my web site at:
http://www.nccpublishing.com/rayellis.html
Follow me on Twitter at:
Twitter@RayEllisWriter

ACKNOWLEDGMENTS

As with any project of significance, it is never completed alone or without help. This is no less true of *Notorious*. First, I'd like to thank God for His grace and the gift of His wonderful Son, Jesus. Without Him, none of this would have been possible or necessary.

Secondly, I'd like to thank the ladies of the Tully's Critique group: Angela, Cheryl, and Ruth. Without you three ladies, I would still be stuck on "rain fell in sheets and chilled him to the core…" It's an inside joke, but I know my ladies will get it.

Next I would like to say thank you to the many talented people who gave me their time and talent to help bring this project to launch: Judy Marker Simmons, Debbie Sloane, and of course, my wife and children who have lived with Nate and Amber as guests in our home for these last few years.

Thanks to my wife, especially, for believing in me when I began to doubt myself. And finally, thanks to my church family at Nampa Christian Center for its prayerful support. And thank you to my readers.

ABOUT THE AUTHOR

Ray Ellis is a veteran law enforcement officer, former United States Marine, and ordained Christian pastor. Ray began his career in law enforcement with the Orange County Sheriff's Department in the city of Orange, California in 1989. After working for a number of years in the maximum security facility, he transferred to patrol, working along Orange County's coast as well as the inner canyons and barrios.

After eight years in Orange County, Ray moved to Idaho and continued his law enforcement career where he has served as a patrol officer, detective, and officer instructor for the Idaho POST Council. In 1999 Ray was appointed as a primary instructor for the Idaho POST Academy Police Training Institution for Idaho, instructing on subjects of arrest control, cultural diversity, and instructor development. From 2007-2011 Ray served as the lead sex crimes investigator for the agency where he works.

Ray is active in the writer's community in Idaho and has recently served as the president of the Idahope Writer's Group. In 2011, Ray was selected as one of the Top Fifty Authors in the state of Idaho. Ray's recognition continued in 2012, when he was selected as one of Idaho's Top Ten Authors.

Ray was first ordained into the ministry while living in Orange County and now serves as the Associate Pastor at his home church in Nampa, Idaho. Ray has been happily married to his wife, Sharon, since 1983 and has three grown children: two sons and one daughter. Ray currently lives with his family in Idaho.

MORE BY RAY ELLIS

Dead List (A Nate Richards Mystery - Book Two)
    Previously released as *D.R.T.* *(Dead Right There)*

Insidious (A Nate Richards Mystery - Book Three)

"I" – A Short Story

Note: The novel *Notorious* was previously released as *N.H.I.* *(No Humans Involved)*.

PREVIEW: DEAD LIST

By Ray Ellis
A Nate Richards Mystery – Book Two

Registered sex offenders in the Treasure Valley have started showing up dead, killed with apparent violence and forethought; and Detective Nate Richards finds himself pitted against a psychotic killer set on ridding the valley of the unclean.

When Chrystal Johansson, the only female on the killer's list, barely escapes the attempt on her life, Richards takes her into protective custody. Driven by a voice he calls *God* and a group of men he calls *the Uncles*, the killer sets a deadline of two weeks to complete the valley's cleansing.

Around him, the community divides about the actions of the vigilante. Some hail the killer as a modern day knight, only doing what they wish they could; while others curse him as being part of the sickness he claims to fight.

In the midst of the chaos, Nate finds his faith tested when he discovers a sympathetic link in his own heart for the killer's ideas, if not his actions. Will he find the strength to keep his own path from falling into darkness and bring the killer in, or will he succumb to the powerful sway of street justice?

With the deadline quickly approaching, and the city threatening to tear itself apart, will the killer fulfill his calling, or will Nate stop the killings before another victim turns up on the **DEAD LIST?**

DEAD LIST - CHAPTER ONE

WET SNOW LOOKED LIKE A SPILLED CHERRY SNOW CONE spreading from beneath the man's downturned face. Detective Nate Richards, of the Treasure Valley Metro Police, looked down at the body stretched out on the ground at his feet. A quick glance suggested a single blow to the side of the man's head had ended his life. Nate shook his head, dislodging snow from his loose curls, the white flakes contrasting against the coffee-colored tone of his skin. He shivered. I hate winter. Nate looked up momentarily, drawn by the halo that encircled the streetlight as its russet glow illuminated the night sky.

His partner, Detective Chris MacGilvery, worked a short distance away, talking to the on-scene patrol officer. The unbroken surface of the snow, pristine in its whiteness, made the whole scene eerily bright. MacGilvery cupped his hands and blew into them, attempting to thaw them out, his gray-blue eyes reflecting the light from the snow. He had been assigned as Nate's partner when Nate's previous partner, twenty-year veteran Sabrina Jackson, retired after being shot in the line of duty by a rogue cop.

Looking up with the memory, Nate flexed tight muscles in his jaw and stooped to better examine the body. Remembering his scripture reading from that morning, Hebrews 9:27, "And it is appointed unto men once to die, but after this the judgment." Nate wondered where this man's soul was now.

He looked over the crime scene trying to decipher its secrets. Shaking his head from side to side, he considered the snow. It was not helping, no footprints led to or away from the body. The snow will have to be collected and sifted for possible evidence. He rubbed gloved fingers across his chin.

"Mac," Nate called out, "witnesses?"

"None. A man walking his dog found the body and called it in."

Nate made his way over to Chet Baraza, the patrol officer in charge, and looked in the direction of the sirens sounding in the near distance. "I guess we can tell the paramedics to downgrade," Nate said, extending a hand to Baraza.

The group of patrol officers laughed. Baraza chuckled and shook Nate's hand. "He's DRT. Dead right there, man, this one's not going anywhere on his own. He must'a dropped like a sack of potatoes. Farrumph!" the officer said and gestured as if dropping a heavy load.

Wheels crunched in the snow as the paramedic van pulled up and rolled to a stop just outside the crime scene. The overhead lights flashed brilliantly against the snow perforating the velvet drape of the night sky. The already too bright landscape sparkled like an oversized diorama as the red and white lights of the van played against it. The driver, a middle age balding man, stepped from the van. "What'd'ya got?" he asked nobody in particular.

Nate dipped his chin toward the body. He looked back at the driver and shook his head from side to side in a slow sweep.

Pulling on rubber examination gloves, the paramedic bent over and examined the four-inch gash in the temple of the victim, paying particular attention to the jagged edge. He stood and whistled, blowing air through pursed lips. "Wow, that's...," he began. "That's—that's bad." He looked over his shoulder at his partner who was quickly pulling gear from the van. "Bag it, Jeff, this one's DRT. Better call the coroner, Nate."

***

Mac finished talking to the witness and, after getting his contact information, released him to leave. Turning to face the group of officers, he jogged-skidded his way back across the thin sheet of ice on the street to join Nate and the others near the body.

Nate locked eyes with Mac before they both turned to face Baraza. The veteran street cop pulled his note pad from his breast pocket and frowned as he prepared to check his information against what the detectives already had.

"The old guy," he said, indicating the RP (reporting party) "called in a medical-assist-man-down at about 2015 hours…just after the first call came into dispatch about what sounded like a single gunshot being fired."

Nate looked back at the body of the unidentified man lying face down in the snow. "Anybody pull I.D. yet?"

"Naaa, it was obvious he was dead. Thought we'd wait for five-one to call it, and of course, you guys."

"So you're a doctor now, Baraza," Mac chided.

Baraza frowned, feigning injury. "You don't need a M.D. in front of your name to know you can't live with a hole like that in the side of your head. I'm thinking long gun, .22 caliber, maybe."

"That much damage from a twenty-two?" Mac asked, arching a brow.

"Heavy load, low velocity at close range," Baraza finished. "Maybe a tumbler. Of course, it's just my guess. But I'm only a lowly street cop, not like you bright boys up there in Criminal Investigation Division." He smiled sarcastically and, with a tap of his fingers, tucked his pad back into his jacket pocket.

Nate cupped Baraza on his shoulder and pushed him, causing him to slide on the ice, barely managing to keep his balance. "I'll see you in the morning, wise guy."

Baraza laughed. "Heck, we'll be back for morning briefing before you even finish your paperwork."

The men laughed, and Nate turned his attention back to the dead man belly down in the snow. Looking up, Nate saw the coroner's van pulling into the intersection. The deputy coroner, a tall dark haired man in his mid to late twenties, got out and prepared to bag the body.

"Hold on there, cowboy," Mac called to the deputy coroner.

Nate waved a hand to get the coroner's attention. "We haven't finished here yet; crime scene's still mine."

"Works for me, I'll wait in my wagon. Too cold out here for me anyway," he said and hefted his bulk back into the van.

Flipping open his cell phone, Nate called the on-call crime scene tech. Rosie answered on the second ring. "Hey, sorry to bother you this early…"

She cut him off. "I'm already en route. Got in late and heard the call go out. I should be on scene in about…now." She honked her horn as she parked her van across the street from the crime scene. Rosie, a fifty-something Hispanic woman, was almost as tall as she was round, with a personality just as big. She was a no-nonsense, fresh-off-the-streets type girl.

Bumping the van door closed with her hip, Rosie opened her bag and began to set up her camera. "What do you want?" She asked over her shoulder.

Nate and Mac smiled knowingly as Rosie sorted the varied baggies and evidence containers. "Better get everything. We don't know what we have yet," Nate answered.

"You can get me the heck out of here," MacGilvery added sarcastically and glanced over at Rosie.

As Rosie began to create a photo log of the crime scene, recording the location and placement of items of interest, Nate and Mac stepped back to consider what they had discovered. A half hour passed, and Rosie signaled that she had finished with the preliminary photos and was all set to begin evidence collection.

"Ready?" Nate asked.

"Nope," Mac said joking.

"Oh, shut up," Rosie cut in. "We're ready."

"Okay," Nate began, "I'll walk the route. You watch Mac and Rosie you—"

"I'll stand by for collection and tagging. It's not my first ride on this train you know"

Nate smiled.

Standing near the head of the body, he looked at the scene again. Studying the body's position, Nate moved around it trying to determine the victim's direction of travel at the time of attack. Beginning at the corpse's feet, taking slow steps moving in a spiral search pattern, he progressed outward from the body. Nearing the head again, he stopped, feeling something hard beneath the toe of his shoe. "Mac…I think I got something."

Nate knelt down and retrieved a small rectangle shaped piece of plastic from beneath his right foot. Reading the writing on the side of the object, he recognized it to be a 16-gigabyte thumb-drive.

Holding the thumb-drive between his index finger and thumb, Nate dropped it into a small evidence bag held by Rosie. She cut her eyes at him. "Next time use rubber gloves, Sherlock."

He exchanged glances with Mac. "What'd'ya think?"

"I think you should wear gloves." He cleared his throat and chuckled. "I don't believe in coincidences," he answered. "Let's get it back to the lab and see what the boys in cyber tech can do with it."

Rosie didn't smile. "Let's just get it dried out and see if there's anything on it."

Nate nodded and continued the swirl pattern outward to about ten to twelve feet from the body. Mac tracked his progress from the side, looking for anything that Nate may have missed.

Nate positioned himself near the shoulders of the body, directing Mac to the opposite side near its knees. "Okay, let's roll this fellow over and see who we have here."

Aided by the cold and rigor mortis, the body rolled easily and rocked onto its back like a saucer settling into place. Its hands and arms splayed, frozen above his head. Blue eyes stared unseeing through ice crystals into the night sky.

"Whoa," Nate said, "you know who this is?" He reached into the dead man's pocket and retrieved his wallet. Opening it, he passed the ID to Mac.

Mac forced air through pursed lips. "So justice finally caught up to old Bobby."

"When did he get out of prison, anyway? I thought he got fifteen to life on his last jaunt to State."

"Yeah, fifteen, but only two fixed. He must have made parole."

"Only two years for child rape." Nate shook his head. "Maybe he should'a stayed in prison."

***

Dead List, by Ray Ellis is available for purchase at your favorite book seller.

NCC Publishing
Where The Light Shines

www.ingramcontent.com/pod-product-compliance
Lightning Source LLC
Chambersburg PA
CBHW052018240626
47153CB00006B/1866